Hard As Nails

Hard As Nails

HelenKay Dimon

KENSINGTON PUBLISHING CORP.
http://www.kensingtonbooks.com

BRAVA BOOKS are published by

Kensington Publishing Corp.
850 Third Avenue
New York, NY 10022

All Kensington titles, imprints and distributed lines are available at special quantity discounts for bulk purchases for sales promotion, premiums, fund-raising, educational or institutional use.

Special book excerpts or customized printings can also be created to fit specific needs. For details, write or phone the office of the Kensington Special Sales Manager: Kensington Publishing Corp., 850 Third Avenue, New York, NY 10022. Attn. Special Sales Department. Phone: 1-800-221-2647.

ISBN-13: 978-0-7582-1583-3
ISBN-10: 0-7582-1583-5

First Kensington Trade Paperback Printing: July 2008
10 9 8 7 6 5 4 3 2 1

Printed in the United States of America

To Brooke Marshall for being one of the first to know and for showering me with such amazing support at every turn. Congratulations to you and Tarik for finding each other. You deserve the romance novel happy ending you've found.

ACKNOWLEDGMENTS

This book follows up on my first published novella, *Hardhats and Silk Stockings* in the *When Good Things Happen to Bad Boys* anthology. Thank you to all the readers who wrote and asked for happy endings for former secondary characters Adam and Cole. I hope I did those fine men justice with their stories . . . and that you love my third hero, Ray, as much as I do.

Thanks also to Kate Duffy, an extraordinary editor who understands authors, the business and my quirky (i.e., needy) personality. Your willingness to explain and share your knowledge is something special. And Kate is not the only amazing one at Kensington. Thanks to all of those folks who make these books happen and especially to Kristine Mills-Noble for the best covers ever.

Some other folks made this book happen: my agent, Ethan Ellenberg, who handles the business end so I don't have to, and my friend Wendy, who reads every first draft without complaint and provides comments that improve every sentence. The remaining mistakes are mine and likely due to my failure to listen.

As always, the biggest "thank you" goes to my husband, James. I could not write any of these without your support and understanding.

Contents

THIS OLD HOUSE

Chapter One

Never tick off a woman holding a sledgehammer.

Cole Carruthers added that piece of wisdom to his mental checklist for dealing with the opposite sex the second he stepped into the entry of the three-story Victorian house in the pricey Dupont Circle area of Washington, D.C.

One glance at the woman standing in the living room off to his right and he questioned the wisdom of being there at all. He'd come to see an elderly woman about a house. Actually, he'd come to get an elderly woman *out* of the house.

As his gaze wandered over his unknown companion's khaki short-shorts, down her mile-long legs, then back up to her rounded ass . . . well, he knew one thing for certain: right house, wrong woman.

He expected a greeting from someone bent over a walker. The same friendly, white-haired someone who a month ago sold this historically-protected property to his partners, Adam and Whit Thomas. Looking at the peeling wallpaper and exposed floorboards, Cole wondered if his usually astute friends had jumped on the deal too fast. The place could crumble and fall on top of them before the construction permits came through.

And the smell. Reminded Cole of damp shirts left in a dryer too long. He doubted the windows had been opened during the last decade.

But that wasn't the problem of the hour. No, convincing the former owner of the house to get out held the number one spot on that list.

Two weeks ago Gilda Armstrong had nearly set the kitchen on fire making her special cheese biscuits. Now she refused to move to her reserved room at a nearby assisted-living facility.

The refusal made Gilda Cole's problem. Not that he volunteered. No, he just didn't refuse as fast as his business partners at yesterday's weekly meeting. Next time he'd take a swallow of coffee *after* a vote instead of during.

Despite being shanghaied an hour ago, Cole assumed the job would be simple enough. He thought he'd have no problem making his standing Thursday racquetball game with Adam. Cole glanced over at the sledgehammer-wielding mystery woman again. He had not counted on finding her.

"Looks like racquetball is out today," he mumbled under his breath.

Facing away from him, the non-grandmother stood in front of the dark, hand-carved fireplace staring at the ornate mirror towering above it. With the tool balanced in both hands, she concentrated on a spot on the wall.

He didn't see whatever she saw. Probably had something to do with focusing on the way her slim white T-shirt skimmed the top of those shorts.

On the outline of her tan arms and lean legs.

On the wavy black hair falling over her shoulders and down her back.

Yeah, this lady was no grandma. He'd guess she was somewhere in her twenties. Which meant she was not the woman he came hunting. Which was a damn shame.

"Uh, ma'am?" His voice echoed back at him, so he stepped into the cluttered room and tried again. "Hello?"

She ignored the slam of the front door and continued to ignore him now. A lecture on safety and self-protection seemed in order. He'd get to that right after he explained the concept of trespassing.

The warped wood floors creaked under his weight. "Ma'am, I need you to—"

She finally turned around. Her dark eyes widened and a tiny "o" formed on her full mouth. Then she yelped. Actually made one of those sounds heard best on dog frequencies.

"I'm here to—"

"Get out of here right now, or I'll call the police!" She managed to demand and yelp that time.

Through all the screeching, Cole saw the culprit. Earphones connected to an MP3 player. She never heard him coming. "Sorry to scare you. I didn't mean—"

"Last chance," she warned.

"For what?"

But she was already moving. With a fierce battle cry, she jerked the sledgehammer over her head. The move nearly wiped out the antique chandelier above her. Crystals clanged together from the hit.

On instinct, Cole put his hands up to his chest to ward off an attack. "Whoa, lady, I'm—"

The sledgehammer wobbled forward, then sideways, and then the heavy end fell behind her. Slammed right into the wall. Not against the wall. Through the wall in exactly the move Cole had tried to prevent with his approach.

Any interest in figuring out the who, what, and why of this mystery woman evaporated in an instant. "Damn it, lady. Watch what you're doing."

For the moment more concerned about protecting the house than with having a sledgehammer lodged in his forehead, Cole dodged around a high-back chair to get to her.

She moved just as fast in the opposite direction. Spinning back to face the wall, she tugged and pulled on the visible end of the hammer. Metal crunched against wood. Chunks of drywall fell to the floor. The hole increased to twice the original size before the sledgehammer popped free.

She whipped back around, her cheeks puffing in and out. "I will scream this place down before I let you hurt me."

"Hurt you? Lady, you got this all wrong."

With a bit of a grunt, she hoisted the sledgehammer high above her head. "Or rob me."

That explained the self-defense moves. She thought he had come to steal something. Never mind that his company owned the damn house. He could take the lightbulbs if he wanted to without running afoul of any laws.

"I'm not a burglar."

"Sure you aren't."

He pointed at her. "Put that thing down and listen to me."

She lowered the weapon until the heavy end aimed at the dead center of his chest. "Until I know who you are and what you want, the sledgehammer stays where it is. Talk fast, or I clock you and call the police."

For a petite woman, she sure was fast. Strong, too. That mean look behind those bottomless dark eyes didn't strike him as good either.

Pretty and furious. From his experience, not the best combination in a woman. More like the kind of thing that defined trouble. He wasn't in the mood for trouble. Wasn't much in favor of broken bones either. Not when those bones belonged to him.

"Have you calmed down?" he asked.

"Depends. Are you leaving?"

With her hands settled at one end of the handle she couldn't distribute the weight and hold on. Her stiff arms began to shake as the heavy end started dipping toward the floor.

"You already busted up the wall. I'd prefer if you didn't wreck the floor, too," he said.

"That was your fault for walking into my house."

Either the lady was confused or his hearing was going. "You're trying to tell me that you own this place?"

"Yes."

Nope. His hearing worked just fine. Her lying seemed to be the problem. "Do you have a deed to prove that?"

"Not on me."

Her comment sent his gaze slipping down her curvy, compact body. When he finally met her stare again, he noticed red blotches staining the olive skin of her cheeks.

Angry and swinging a sledgehammer. Yeah, this day just kept getting better. If she had PMS, Cole figured he'd be leaving the property in a body bag. Maybe more than one.

"I know why I'm here. Why are you?" she asked.

"I'm still stuck on the part where you think you own this place." And how she refused to put down the sledgehammer.

"You came here to discuss my ownership rights?"

"Something like that." Nothing like that, really, but she had finally stopped screeching, so he decided to encourage her.

"Well, then, rest assured. The property is mine." She nodded as if that somehow made her words true. "Now, get out."

A dark-haired, black-eyed beauty claiming to be the seventy-eight-year-old owner of the ramshackle house. In addition to being a one-woman wrecking crew, it looked as if the pretty lady was insane. Great. He had managed to stumble on the one thing worse than an angry female. A crazy one.

"Not to upset you or anything since, you know, you have the big weapon and I'm unarmed and all, but, lady, you don't own this house."

"Oh, really?" The sharp edge returned to her voice.

"Gilda Armstrong owned this house. Past tense. She sold it. Now it's mine. Mine and my partners'." Cole lowered his hands to his pockets. The same place he kept the cell phone in case he needed reinforcements, like an ambulance.

He smiled in what he hoped was a nonthreatening way

since the woman hadn't actually dropped the sledgehammer yet. "So, one more time. Who are you?"

She hesitated before giving up the information. "Aubrey."

"Do you have a last name, Aubrey?"

"Matheson."

He released a subtle string of profanity under his breath. "Not exactly handing out the information, are you?"

"You asked. I answered."

The pretty lady had a point. "Help me out here. Aubrey Matheson is who in relation to this house?"

"I'm Gilda's great-niece."

Worse than insane. A blood relative.

Cole vowed never to lose an office vote again. "Where is Gilda right now?"

Aubrey eased up on her grip and lowered the weapon until the tip rested against the floor. "Why do you want to know?"

"You have the tendency not to answer questions. In case no one ever told you, it's annoying as hell."

The sledgehammer started moving back up.

"Stop right there," he ordered. "We're not doing the smash-through-the-wall act again. My head's off-limits, too, in case you were wondering."

He waited until her attention centered on him, then he reached down and grabbed the metal end of the sledgehammer. With both hands on one end and her on the other, he tugged.

The quick strike caught her off balance. She stumbled forward and tripped over her toolbox. Her sneaker smacked against the metal with a loud clunk. She swore but kept her grip on the wood.

With her lips clenched together and all of her attention focused on the bar between them, she leaned back and pulled. Huffed. Then puffed. With every tug, a tiny squeak escaped her closed mouth.

All that effort and he never moved. Even thought about

yawning but figured his boredom would only make her more determined. Last thing he needed was for her to strain an internal organ.

If they were wrestling over sheets or a television remote, hell, he'd understand the waste of energy. Probably even keep going and enjoy the view all that exercise gave him. As it was, at six-foot-one and 180 pounds, he probably outweighed her by a solid 50 pounds. If he let go, she'd land on her ass. Tempting, but she didn't strike him as a woman who handled losing all that well.

Then there was the problem of her potential insanity.

"Let go of the deadly weapon, Aubrey."

"It's a tool, not a weapon." The muscles on her arms jumped and tightened. "And, you can just forget about my letting go."

"But I asked so nicely."

She gave one final hard yank.

"Impressive." He waited until her burst of adrenaline passed. As he expected, for a fraction of a second her hold eased. He pounced on the weakness by snatching the sledgehammer right out of her hands. "But not impressive enough."

She stood there, mouth open and hands wide to her sides. When she finally spoke, shock replaced the heat in her voice. "How did you—"

"I used my advanced powers of reasoning and physics." He dropped the sledgehammer on the floor behind him, well out of reach of his beautiful adversary. "And pulled really, really hard."

Her angry gaze moved from his face to his feet.

"Don't even think about it. You'd have to go through me first." He regretted his words as soon as he spoke. Right as that spark of hope moved into her dark eyes.

"I like a challenge."

"Let's stay focused on your aunt. Is Gilda here?"

"In the house?"

"No, in the fireplace." He shot Aubrey his best "are you kidding me" scowl. "Yes, the house."

Aubrey nibbled on her bottom lip. "Why do you want to know?"

"I need to talk with her." He figured that much was obvious, but he said it anyway.

"Aunt Gilda's not here."

He shrugged out of his blazer and threw it over a faded red chair. The black suit worked fine for the office. Not so great for a scuffle in an unair-conditioned old house in the middle of a balmy Washington, D.C., summer. Might as well get comfortable, since he appeared to be stranded with Aubrey until she said something helpful, and that was looking like a long shot.

"What are you doing?" she asked, ignoring the obvious.

"Trying to keep from sweating my ass off." He rolled up the sleeves of his light blue dress shirt. "Look, this isn't hard. I need Gilda—"

"Stop undressing."

"—and I need you to leave this house."

"I'm not moving."

"You are. Once you tell me where to find your aunt, you can be on your way to wherever it is you go when you're not trespassing on other people's property."

"I'm not telling you anything."

He shook his head in mock disappointment. "Aubrey, Aubrey, Aubrey. You're not being a good hostess."

"Aunt Gilda still owns this house. As her closest relative, it is my job—no, duty—to protect her." With every word, Aubrey's nose inched higher into the air.

"Is someone after her?"

"You are."

News to him. "What the hell did I do?"

"You tried to steal this house from her."

Funny how his foreman Ray forgot to mention Aubrey's accusations when he mentioned a problem on the project. That and the fact the woman refusing to leave the house was no one's grandmother. "I paid money for the house and signed some papers. Can't say I recall the stealing part."

"Wait a second." Her dark eyes narrowed. "You're not Whit Thomas."

"No, but I do plan to kill him later if that counts for anything."

"Are you the brother . . . uh, what's his name? Adam?"

"Not him either." Adam was a dead man too as far as Cole was concerned. "I guess you could say I'm the forgettable business partner."

"I don't remember another Thomas brother or partner."

"This conversation is doing wonders for my ego."

Not that she cared. She was too busy narrowing her eyes to squint at him. "I met one of your workers."

"That would be our job foreman, Ray Hammond."

"So, who are you?"

"Not a brother. Frankly, two Thomas brothers are enough. Not related to Ray either, just in case you wondered. I'm a third partner in this real estate venture."

Not that being blood-related mattered in Cole's world. Except for his cousin Hannah, he couldn't think of a single relative he'd trust enough to wash his car. But he trusted Whit and Adam with his life, and Ray almost as much.

"Interesting," she mumbled.

"Aren't I just?"

"Yeah, I can barely contain myself in your presence."

Cole added sarcasm to Aubrey's list of skills. "I can tell by the dramatic eye roll."

"I have other gestures."

"You were less scary when you had the sledgehammer."

"You can go to—"

"Maybe you'll stop making faces if you know my name."

"Doubt it."

"Me too, but it's worth a shot." He extended his hand in greeting. "I'm Cole Carruthers."

She ignored the gesture and glared instead. "Don't bother with the sweet talk. I'm not going anywhere until this house issue gets settled."

If a handshake counted as sweet talk, then this woman needed to date a better class of men. "Remind me what the 'this house issue' is again."

"You guys conned my aunt." She waved a hand in his general direction. "Whatever your company is called."

"T.C. Limited," he mumbled as he tried to remember the last time someone questioned his integrity.

"I don't care about the sign over the door. The point is, the deal isn't valid."

"Actually, it is."

"Until a court says otherwise, I'm staying right here." She plopped down in the red chair. Sat right on his coat. Right next to the sledgehammer.

"Here I am being neighborly, and you're using threats."

"The house's ownership will be in litigation, and you'll be out."

"Sounds as if you've thought this through." He reached down and snagged the handle of the sledgehammer. Better to move it out of her reach than to start a new game of tug-of-war.

"That's right." She shot him a smug smile.

"That should make bathing interesting. Once we shut off the water, I mean."

"You don't scare me."

That, he believed. "And I guess you plan to gnaw on the walls to stay alive, since, you know, leaving the house to get food would result in us changing the locks to keep you out."

She did the eye-roll thing again. "Tell your foreman and your partners and everyone else in your crooked company to find another house and leave this one alone."

"Actually, alone is the one thing you won't be."

Her smile took a little tumble. "Meaning?"

"I'm not going anywhere." Cole sat down on the small sofa across from her and ignored the puff of dust that escaped the cushions under his weight.

Her smile disappeared this time. "What?"

"I have a business interest to protect. Guess that means we're stuck with each other."

With one arm across the top of the sofa and both feet planted on the floor on either side of the sledgehammer, he lounged back against pillows that felt as if they were filled with Gilda's famous burnt cheese biscuits.

All traces of satisfaction left Aubrey's face. "Now who's the one issuing threats?"

"Think of it as a challenge." He crossed an ankle over his opposite knee.

"More like a nightmare."

Cole nodded. "I see you're getting the idea."

Chapter Two

Aubrey stayed put in the big red chair and started counting to ten. She abandoned the project somewhere around number two. Being on the receiving end of Cole's stare made it difficult to concentrate on anything other than glaring back.

His presence threw a monkey wrench into her plans. Cole, with his short, almost spiky blond hair, wide shoulders, and trim, athletic body. Sure, he qualified as an attractive monkey wrench, but still a monkey wrench. An annoying one, too.

"No witty comeback, Aubrey? No arguments about how I shouldn't sit down and get comfortable in *your* supposed living room?"

"There's nothing funny about this situation."

"I bet Adam and Whit will find all of this hysterical."

If so, she wondered about their sense of humor. "Then they should have come in your place."

"Tried that. Believe me." Cole continued his lazy sprawl across her aunt's sofa.

Seeing a lace doily peeking out from under his elbow and another under his thigh made her swallow a smile. His solid body overwhelmed the delicate piece of furniture. The wood frame rocked under his fit form.

Not that she noticed his fit form.

Damn, why was she noticing his fit form?

She tapped her fingernails against the threadbare arms of the chair. She didn't have time for this. Couldn't afford to be distracted. Not now and not by some guy named Cole. She had enough trouble with the males in her life. She didn't need to seek out one more challenge. Cole had to go, and take those striking, crystal blue eyes along with him.

She settled on the practical approach. "You should call your attorney. We can set up a time to go over—"

He barked out a laugh, then covered his mouth. Even did one of those fake cough things. "Sorry. Couldn't help myself."

The guy was growing more annoying by the second. "What's so funny now?"

And why did the rich sound of his voice appeal to her? She chalked up the feeling to having inhaled too much construction dust. In her experience, severe allergic reactions and physical attraction often felt the same—they went away after you spent some time flat on your back.

"Adam is both my business partner and my attorney. I can guarantee he wants me to stay here and watch over you to make sure you don't further damage the house."

Adam, right. She kept forgetting about the slick lawyer. After her experience with lawyers, she didn't want to meet up with that one.

Aunt Gilda talked mostly about the other one, Whit, and his upcoming wedding. So much so, Aubrey started to wonder if her aunt planned on attending the ceremony.

That was one of the confusing parts of Gilda's disease. She remembered bits and pieces, but couldn't fit them together in any comprehensible way. But she did provide some correct information now and then, so when she talked about Whit's leaving for his honeymoon, Aubrey thought she'd have a few extra days to search the house before the construction started.

Then Ray stopped by. Followed by a phone call from Adam. Now Cole showed up. Whit, Ray, Adam, Cole. Hell, everyone at this company except the janitorial staff had come by to ruin her simple search plans.

"There's no reason for you to stay," she said.

"If I left who would protect the house from you?"

"I'll have you know that I'm trying to save the house for my aunt."

Not really. Actually, not at all. Aunt Gilda needed to move out before she hurt herself. Aubrey understood that fact even though she hated the thought of Aunt Gilda's losing her independence.

Cole didn't need to know any of that. Aubrey needed him to believe what she wanted him to believe.

He hitched his chin in the direction of the fireplace. "Looked as if you were trying to knock the living room down one swing at a time. The mantel and mirror are antiques, not practice targets for your sledgehammer skills."

"It was an accident."

"Yeah, yours."

"You snuck up on me."

"Not to point out the obvious, but all I said was hello." Cole wrapped a hand around his ankle.

She noticed his long, elegant fingers. The nails were trimmed and his skin smooth. Not what she expected of a guy who worked on house rehab projects and wore a two-day scruff of blond hair around his chin and mouth.

The rough and sexy unshaven look did not go with the designer suit. Now she knew why. He did not work with his hands. Probably just forgot to shave.

"That can't be the first mishap you've had on a construction site," she said.

"It's the first one that will require hours of investigation and some serious cash to fix. The wallpaper is—or should I say, was—original to the house. It's not a reproduction."

That sounded like more than a drywall patch issue. "So?"

"The taste might be your aunt's, but it was also the taste of the Shipman family when they built the house in 1887. They installed the paper. Until a few minutes ago, it had withstood bad weather, all sorts of disasters, decay, and the passing of time."

She was pretty sure Cole had just compared her to a hurricane and given the edge to the violent storm in terms of preference. "The paper didn't seem all that sturdy to me."

"To be fair, the original craftsman only made it to withstand natural disasters. Not you."

"It's ugly," she said, even though she guessed that really wasn't the point.

"A trellis with big red roses growing on it isn't a pattern I'd choose either." His foot bounced up and down. "But it's historically protected."

"Enough with the lecture. I've seen the plaque by the door. My aunt lives here, remember?"

"Lived. Past tense. You keep stumbling over that little fact."

"I'm ignoring you."

"How charming."

"Look, I know the house was built by someone who did something impressive at some point in history. Blah, blah, blah."

His eyebrow lifted in question. "Did you just say 'blah'?"

"I actually said it three times."

"I see. Well, I'm sure you also know that this house is subject to a special funding grant that requires the owners to make every effort to protect all of the original architectural details."

Uh, no. She had bigger problems than worrying about a few feet of ugly wallpaper. "Of course."

"When my company agreed to rehab the residence under

the National Trust grant, we guaranteed we'd retain all authentic details and replace those we could. That includes colors and, yes, the wallpaper."

"Sounds like a problem."

"Exactly."

"As in your problem, not mine." And boring. Should she mention the boring part?

Then there was the other damage. The stuff he had yet to find. Sure the hole looked bad, but it did not compare to the problem in the back upstairs bedroom. In her frantic search through the old house, Aubrey had ripped the built-in bookcase from the wall with a crowbar.

Yeah, this Cole guy was not going to like that impromptu home improvement one bit. She would have admitted causing the damage, but why invite another lecture now. Not when the current one didn't appear to be over yet.

"Do you happen to have an extra roll or two of antique wallpaper lying around or a reproduction that will match?" He gazed around the large room as if one of those rolls might appear out of nowhere.

"I left my wallpaper in my other pants."

"Then this is a major mess without an easy cleanup solution. We'll have to—"

"Hold it a second. Did you say 'we'?"

"You're the one claiming to own the place."

Well, he had her there. "To be technically correct, Aunt Gilda does."

"Actually, I do. We'll ignore that pesky detail for a second and pretend this is a *we* situation as you claim."

"That's gentlemanly of you."

"I thought so." He had the nerve to flash a sexy grin with that remark. "How much money do you have on you?"

Trying to follow the zigzag in the conversation after that smile seemed impossible. "Money?"

"What else would I be referring to?"

She refused to comment on that. “Uh, not much.”

A tsk-tsking sound matched the shaking of his head. “That’s going to be a problem.”

“Not for me.” She settled back into the chair, grinding his expensive suit jacket into the dusty cushions beneath her butt.

“Looks like you’ll have to work off your debt.”

Damn if he didn’t sound serious with that sentence. “I don’t have any debts.”

“Sure you do.” He whipped out a cell phone and started pushing buttons.

“Are you calling for a cab? I’ll pay.”

“Yes, you will. I’m getting to that now. First, we have rent. Since you don’t have a lease here, I’ll have to charge you the more expensive month-to-month rate. You haven’t been here a full month yet, so that helps.” He grinned over at her. “Well, a little.”

“My aunt owns this house.”

“Not anymore.” This time he didn’t even raise his head. “Then there’s your share of the utilities.”

“I think I’ve flushed the toilet twice.”

His finger hesitated over the buttons for a second. “I’m going to pretend you didn’t say that, but I’m now adding in the cost of a new toilet. Sounds as if cleaning the old one might be a problem.”

“I didn’t mean—”

“Next comes the damage estimate.”

She had no idea what he was babbling about. “What is it you’re doing?”

He showed her the front of his phone. “Adding up how much you owe using the calculator function.”

She was too far away to get a clear look at the screen. “How enterprising of you.”

“Just part of my business savvy. Consider it the secret of my success.”

She rolled her eyes. He never looked up so he missed the exasperated gesture, which was a shame since she did a good eye roll that time.

"You must have been a Boy Scout. Always prepared and all that," she said in her snarkiest voice.

"Nope."

His curt response ruined her even snarkier comeback. "I thought all young boys were the scouting type."

Amusement danced in those light blue eyes when he looked up. "Some of us were more of the in-trouble type."

"A bad little boy? Say it isn't so."

He shrugged. "Not a fan of Boy Scout camp. Too many rules, and the badge thing bored me."

"What did you do?"

"Set fire to tents. Sank the canoes. Spiked the dining hall food and much worse."

She could almost see a younger, blonder version of Cole playing tricks on his fellow campers. She guessed his age to be somewhere in the mid-thirties. The prankster might have grown up, but he lingered under the carefree demeanor somewhere. She could sense it.

Cole wasn't the typical professional type she saw every day at her job as a corporate headhunter. No tie. No boring business suit. No grown-up haircut. No clean shave. No desperation.

She wondered if his look amounted to a carefully crafted image, or if he really tackled life with this level of irreverence. Either way, she'd have a hell of a time finding a company to take him in if he were a client.

Which he wasn't.

Which was a good thing.

"Sounds like typical schoolboy stuff to me," she said.

"I'm guessing posting the fake FBI 'Wanted' posters all over town using the scout leader's photo probably rose above the prank level."

She tried to fight off a smile, but the smile won. "You're kidding."

"Did I mention the scout leader was also the assistant headmaster at my school? That I exchanged a real FBI poster with my fake one at all the post offices in the neighborhood?"

Headmaster. Sounded private and wealthy, exactly as she expected. Only, his appearance didn't quite fit. It was a little . . . off. Too rough and very, very sexy.

"What did you claim the assistant headmaster was wanted for?"

"Armed robbery of a strip joint. The guy deserved it. He hated kids, and we hated him right back." Cole finished whatever he was doing. "I have your total."

Another zag, but this time she followed along. "Lucky me."

"The way I figure it, so far you owe T.C. Limited thirteen thousand, seven hundred, thirty-nine dollars, and eight cents."

Clearly he misspoke. "What?"

He handed her a pen from his breast pocket. "You can make the check out to T.C. Limited."

"Did you not hear me when I said 'what' with the shock in my voice?"

"You'd rather pay in cash?"

"You're still not getting my confusion."

"You don't have that much cash on you, I guess. Well, that's fine." His gaze wandered over her legs. "Really, I'm not sure where you'd stick it in that outfit."

The heated look sent her stomach tumbling. His satisfied smile suggested he'd like to conduct a pat down to check for himself.

That made two of them.

"You expect me to give you thirteen thousand dollars?" she asked.

"Thirteen thousand, seven hundred, thirty-nine dollars, and eight cents to be exact."

"I rounded down."

He shook his head and tsk-tsked her again. "Sorry. I already gave you a small discount to come up with the total. Can't give another one. I'll need the full amount."

"I have three dollars." With her luck, he'd insist she give it to him.

"As I said, a check is fine."

Good thing he'd grabbed the sledgehammer before she did or she'd be swinging it at his fat head about now.

"But I'll need collateral," he said.

"Of course. It would be silly not to."

He treated her to a wide grin. "Exactly."

The doorbell chimed.

Just what she needed—more guests. "Maybe that's the money fairy now."

"Probably just Ray." Cole pushed off the sofa and stood up.

"Why would your foreman be here?"

"For the same reason I'm here. To start construction." Cole looked at his watch. "And he's deadly punctual as usual."

She jumped up and stepped in front of Cole, hoping to block his path. "He can't. Start, that is."

"Try telling Ray that." Cole walked around her and opened the door to greet their visitor. "You're not the Avon lady."

Aubrey peeked around Cole's solid frame and saw Ray. Took in the way his shoulders filled the doorway. Biceps bulged under his T-shirt and dirt covered his faded blue jeans. From the long brown hair hanging in boyish wisps over his forehead and down to the tips of his eyebrows, to the tool belt around his trim waist, Ray was every bit the tall, dark, and handsome construction worker type.

"I don't look good in makeup either," Ray said.

Yesterday Ray had opened the door, seen her, introduced himself, and then turned right around and left. Even promised he would be back later. She had hoped the delay would give her the time she needed to hunt down the jewels and get out of there. Instead, Ray called in reinforcements of the tall, blond, dimpled smile, and all-American boy type. One Cole Carruthers.

"It's about time you showed up," Cole grumbled.

"I can tell by your disposition that you've met Ms. Matheson," Ray said with a chuckle.

When did they start insulting her? "Hey!"

Ray sent her an apologetic smile.

"You could have warned me about what was happening here," Cole said.

"You act as if I could tell," Ray shot back.

Just what she needed, two overgrown boys talking about her as if she were invisible. "Uh, gentlemen?"

Cole continued the conversation with Ray. "You might have mentioned the age of our unwanted guest. Maybe clued me in that she wasn't Gilda Armstrong."

Were they still talking about her? "Wait a second. You thought I was Aunt Gilda?"

Cole didn't bother to look at her when he delivered a caveman grunt.

"She's in her seventies!" Aubrey ran her fingers through her hair to try to shake loose any plaster that might have landed there. "Just how bad do I look?"

Cole shot her a wicked grin. "The exact opposite of bad."

The compliment delivered in that honey-smooth voice shot through her with a little sizzle. She almost felt sorry about threatening his life with the sledgehammer. But, in another second or two he'd say something to tick her off, and the remorse would pass. She'd bet on it.

"I figured you'd realize you had the wrong woman sooner or later. You're slow, but not that slow." Ray ended the male banter and treated her to a welcome nod. "Ms. Matheson."

Cole ushered them both farther inside. "Call her Aubrey."

"I'd prefer if you both called me from another city," she said.

"Not going to happen," Cole said.

She could handle one of them. Two? One younger, maybe mid-to-late twenties and dark. The other one with a few more miles on him, handsome as sin, and light.

Objectively, both men were attractive in a head-turning way. Firm butts, wide shoulders, and athletic builds. All good. But Cole possessed something extra. Something that knocked the air out of her lungs and turned her knees all gooey.

"Why are you holding a sledgehammer?" Ray stood, hands on his hips, and stared at Cole.

"For protection."

Ray's gaze skipped back to the hole in the wall. "From the living room?"

"From Aubrey."

"Very funny." She walked over and dropped back into the red chair with a sigh.

"She broke the wall?" Ray's tone suggested doubt that she could even lift the sledgehammer.

So far only Adam and Whit hadn't shown up to annoy her. They probably were waiting in the car for their turn. "Look, fellas—"

"It's good you're here. I'm going to need some supplies for the next few days." Cole talked right over her. Again.

"Name it." Ray walked around the room picking stray drywall pieces off the floor.

"A change of clothes. Some food. Batteries. Flashlight. The usual."

This time she did the interrupting. "You better need that

for a camping trip. Preferably one somewhere far, far away."

"Depends. Do they let you pitch tents at the Ritz nowadays?" Ray asked.

She watched Cole lounge against the doorjamb, one hand balanced against the wood and the other holding the sledgehammer. The blank look on his face suggested a mixture of boredom and disinterest.

She didn't buy that for a second. Despite the relaxed pose, Cole was engaged in the conversation. If she guessed right, he was preparing for an argument, which was good, since she planned to give him one.

"You are not staying here, Cole."

"Until this issue gets worked out, consider me your roommate," Cole said.

She'd never be able to track down the missing jewelry and save her brother's neck with Cole all over her ass. No matter how intriguing the idea of being alone with Cole in this big house with nothing much to do was, the scenario couldn't happen.

"I'd rather have a dog," she said.

This time Cole winked at her. "You and me both, honey."

Ray cleared his throat. "Anything else you two need for this sleepover?"

Sleepover? "How about insect repellant?"

"Not the two of us. The supplies are for one." Cole stared at her, daring her to disagree. "I warned you about the water and food issues if you tried to stay. You replied with something about my not scaring you."

"Did I also use the word *jerk*? Because it fits."

This time Ray laughed. He didn't stop until Cole and Aubrey both scowled at him.

"Allergies." Ray cleared his throat. "Anything else?"

"Yeah. Copies of the house sale paperwork. Aubrey thinks we stole the property from her aunt. The sooner we show her otherwise, the sooner she'll leave, and you can get started with this job."

All amusement disappeared from around Ray's eyes. His gaze traveled back and forth between her and Cole before settling on her. "You accused the Thomas brothers and Cole, here, of stealing?"

"She did exactly that. I walk in here to escort her aunt out—"

"Leave my aunt alone."

"—and Aubrey starts using nasty words, like 'con job' and 'stole'." Cole balanced the sledgehammer against the wall. "Not nice language at all. Very unattractive, if you ask me."

She hadn't even gotten started on nasty. "I have some other words you might like even better."

"Your charming disposition is company enough. Thanks."

"You are going to regret this," she warned.

"I won't bet against you on that. What about you, Ray?"

"I'm more worried you'll kill each other before I get back with the supplies."

Cole smiled. "Anything's possible."

Chapter Three

Three hours later, Cole had an overnight bag, two boxes of groceries, and enough battery-operated camping supplies for a small army.

Aubrey conducted a mental inventory of the backpack she had stashed earlier in the upstairs back bedroom. Two protein bars, a half bottle of water, and a toothbrush. No toothpaste, just the brush.

Life sucked.

In unspoken agreement not to kill each other, they had decamped to different parts of the house as soon as Ray dropped off Cole's booty. The killing would come later.

As the minutes passed, the general pattern and locations changed, but they stayed apart in the house. First he was in the kitchen, and she was in the library. A half hour later, he was upstairs, and she was in the library. Within the hour, he was in the living room, and she was in the library. At one point, he was outside, and she was in the library watching from the window.

Apparently he planned to have full run of the house and trap her in one dusty room. Not that he forced her to stay there. At first searching through the piles of books and old magazines kept her attention, then hunting through the shelves. Neither activity led to success, except that she now knew her aunt had a passion for sixty cent nurse romances from the 1960s.

For a diversion, one time Aubrey peeked out into the hallway, made sure Cole wasn't lurking around a corner, and crept into the living room to find the sledgehammer. The damn thing was gone. Cole had either hidden it or was carrying it around under his arm. Both choices sounded odd to her, but then, so did this entire situation.

Hours had passed, and she hadn't seen him since the outside spying incident. But she heard him. The man never stopped moving. If he wasn't on the phone or walking around, he was banging cabinets and doing something that sounded suspiciously like stacking and unstacking boxes.

For the first time she wondered if she was the only one searching the house. Cole did quite a bit of snooping of his own. Cole couldn't know where her brother had hidden the stash . . . could he?

As soon as the possibility popped into her head, it jumped right back out. Cole did not have a reason to steal expensive heirloom sapphires and diamonds. No, only Kirk saw that as a good way to escape money troubles. And if she didn't step in and fix her baby brother's mess, well, she couldn't bear to think about what could happen to him.

She'd been too involved with work and business school and the move into her condo to see Kirk spiral out of control this time. If she could get around Cole, she might be able to save Kirk. But she had to keep from strangling Cole first. Every time he whistled, hummed, or sang—and he did one of those at almost all times—she envisioned wrapping her fingers around his throat.

Her MP3 player had gone missing along with the sledgehammer. Now, on top of the jewelry search, she needed to conduct a little recon and grab back her property.

She paced the library until one thought filled her head and wouldn't get out—bacon. She smelled bacon.

Since she had planned for a short day trip just like yesterday, she hadn't brought bacon or any other food. Furniture, knickknacks, and other items still filled the house, but all of the perishables and toiletries and anything practical had been removed.

If she had known she'd be staying overnight, she'd have brought something with her. Something processed and out of a box, sure, since that was the extent of her cooking ability, but something edible.

Then Cole arrived and messed up everything. Smelled good. Looked good. Had food. . . . Well, that last one might turn out to be a good thing.

She inhaled again. Definitely bacon.

Following the intoxicating scent, she found her way to the kitchen in record time. Might even have hurdled a sofa, but she wasn't sure. The promise of crisp bacon held her in its grip and blocked out everything else.

Almost everything. The sight that greeted her made her forget all about food. All about eating. All about Kirk and his stupid problems. Even replaced bacon as her number one concern.

Cole leaned against the ceramic tile counter in old, almost white jeans that sat low on his waist. A gray T-shirt pulling tight across his broad chest before falling loose at the top of his belt.

Everything about him, from his tanned bare feet to the way he dried her aunt's delicate floral teapot, screamed sex. Hot, unthinking sex. If he took such care with china, she wondered how he'd handle a woman.

That did it. All thoughts of him sitting like a proper businessman behind a desk flew right out of her head. If the chiseled muscles filling out those short sleeves were any indication, the only thing he did with a desk was bench press it.

Between the rough scruff under his nose and on his chin,

those pale blue eyes, and that dimpled grin, no right-thinking woman stood a chance. She wasn't even semi-right-thinking at the moment, so her chances, no doubt about it, were bad.

Aubrey knew the truth now. By day Cole played the role of bad boy in an expensive suit. When he took the big boy clothes off, stripped out of the proper workday attire, he oozed danger. Steam practically poured off of him. That look suckered her in every single time.

Kirk who?

Cole finished the drying and threw the yellow dishtowel in the sink. "Need something?"

What she needed and what she *needed* were two very different things. She tried to remember the last time she'd slept with a man. Inhaled a musky, masculine scent. Trailed her tongue across the heated skin of a flat stomach. Wrapped her legs around a trim waist. Enjoyed the rough feel of a hard body against hers.

Spring? No.

Winter or fall? Negative to those.

When she reached back into her mental calendar from last summer and couldn't dredge up a memory of anything but a dry spell, she stopped trying. Too damn depressing. Maybe she had turned into a seventy-eight–year-old woman and no one had told her. Her inactive sex life qualified her.

"You don't strike me as a tea drinker," she said.

"Just cleaning up the items left in the sink."

"That was Aunt Gilda. She loves high tea. Always drinks it while eating these biscuits she makes."

"I heard she prefers those biscuits well-done these days."

Aubrey sat down at the round kitchen table and smoothed her hand over the nicked top. A kick of longing slammed into her stomach. "I remember eating here as a kid. Aunt Gilda would cook these elaborate meals and insist we all dress up."

Wood scraped against the old floor as Cole pulled out the chair across from her and dropped into it. "How much time did you spend here growing up?"

"Hours. Days. Months. Who knows?" Aubrey rolled the edges of the centerpiece doily beneath her fingers, seeking comfort in the feel of a familiar piece of her childhood. There was a time when white lace doilies covered every inch of furniture in the house.

"Did you live here?"

"No. My grandmother raised us."

"No parents?"

She ignored the question and answered one of her own instead. "Grams and Aunt Gilda were sisters. Gramps died while we still were in elementary school, leaving Grams with two young kids to raise and far less patience than she needed. Aunt Gilda stepped in to help."

"She never married?"

"No."

"Impressive she welcomed you in."

The comment struck her as odd. "Why? That's just typical family stuff."

"Not in every family."

"Well, it was in mine." Aubrey shrugged her shoulders, hoping to ease some of the heaviness that had settled in on her chest. "Aunt Gilda never blinked at getting stuck with us."

"Us?"

"Me and my brother."

"This brother have a name?"

"Kirk." Aubrey's chest actually hurt at the mention of her brother's name. The only thing Grams ever asked was for Aubrey to take care of Kirk. Aubrey knew she had failed on that score.

"Where were your parents during all of this?" Cole asked.

Time for a change of topic. Nothing seemed safe, so she stuck with her most immediate interest. Food. "Did I smell bacon?"

The corner of Cole's mouth kicked up in a smile. "Has the time for sharing personal information officially come to an end?"

"Pretty much."

"But it was just getting interesting."

"Unless it's your turn to talk." Part of her wanted to know more about him.

Who was she kidding? All of her wanted to know more about all of him.

His smile grew wider, bringing those cute dimples next to his mouth into view. "The bacon's for my dinner."

"Good to know I'm not the only one around here with an anti-sharing policy." She swallowed down a lump of disappointment.

"Just one of the many things we have in common, I guess."

That was a road Aubrey refused to travel. They were nothing alike. Their paths crossed now only by accident. By felony, really. By Kirk's felony.

"It's almost six o'clock," she said.

Cole leaned back in the chair and slipped his fingers through the lace on the opposite side of the doily. "I'm sure you're making a point."

"Bacon is breakfast food." The food in question sizzled in a pan behind him. The decadent aroma mixed with the scent of fried onions and toast.

"That's more of a suggestion than a rule. Scrambled eggs, toast, and bacon work together at all times of the day."

The meal sounded so good. She hadn't eaten, unless she counted the super-sized amaretto latte she had nursed throughout the morning. Plenty of sugar and caffeine. No nutrition.

"Is this the extent of your cooking talents?" she asked.

"Honey, my talents are endless." His smoky voice carried a promise.

One she wanted to test. "I meant in the kitchen."

"Uh-huh." He wiggled his eyebrows.

Okay, not enough clarification. "The cooking."

"We still might be talking about the same thing, you know."

"Food."

"Oh, that." His slim blond eyebrows fell. "Well, a bachelor can't afford to ignore the kitchen unless he wants to weigh four hundred pounds from eating out all the time."

"That's certainly not a problem for you." The phrase slipped out before she could censor it.

Sure, his significant hotness wasn't exactly a secret. Not if the guy owned a mirror or any other shiny surface. But being mysterious and being obvious were two very different things.

He faked a bow without getting up. "Thank you for noticing."

She'd never be able to wrestle his ego back under control if she didn't put a stop to that line of thinking now. Hottie or not. "Are you going to share your bacon?"

"Depends. You gonna leave the house?"

"Eventually."

"When you do, I'll make you bacon as a going-away present. Until then, it's mine."

She smiled. When Cole didn't so much as chuckle or bother to say anything else, her hunger took over. "Wait just a damn minute."

He tsk-tsked her again. "Temper, temper. Warned you about the food thing and what would happen if you insisted on staying."

"I thought you were kidding."

"Who told you I had a sense of humor?"

"B-but . . . I . . . but, but . . ." Good grief, the man actually had her stuttering. She ran expensive classes on speaking and interviewing skills. After only a short time with Cole, she couldn't force out a sentence.

He leaned in with his hand behind his ear. "I didn't quite catch that."

This time the words exploded out of her mouth. "You're actually going to sit there and eat."

"That's the plan. Yeah."

"In front of me."

"I can turn around if you want."

Her temper heated. "You'd let me starve?"

"There are about twenty restaurants within a mile of this house. You're free to visit any of them."

"I can't."

"I'll give you some money. Won't even add it to your tab."

"You'll barricade the doors if I leave."

"Okay, yeah. That's true." He walked back to the stove and hovered over the skillet. "The choice is still yours."

"Fine. I'll sit here and watch you eat."

He grabbed a plate from the shelves and started loading up with eggs, bacon, and toast. A slab of butter came next. He balanced a jar of jam on top of it all.

With a click he turned off the burner and returned to the table. Side dishes weighed down his arms. A food mountain sat on his plate, enough food for a family of four.

"Forgot my coffee." His plates clanked against the table as he set them down.

When he got back up, she eyed those noisy plates. Eyed him, lingering a bit too long on the way his jeans hugged his butt. Then eyed his plate again.

Steam rolled off the food, sending the comforting smell of breakfast right in her undernourished direction. Her fingers itched to steal a piece of bacon. She could slip it off the side and then—

"You're staring." His spicy, clean smell battled with the aroma of food as he sat back down.

She wanted a bite of both dishes.

His eyes narrowed as he pointed a finger at the corner of her mouth. "You have some drool right on the—"

"I do not." She fought off the urge to wipe a finger across her mouth or at least press her lips together.

"Suit yourself." He scooped up a pile of eggs and balanced them on the edge of his fork. The utensil stopped halfway to his mouth. "Problem?"

"Nothing other than an unwanted houseguest."

"Don't be so hard on yourself. I wouldn't call you unwanted. Not exactly."

"I meant you."

"Oh." The fork moved a fraction. "You hungry?"

More like starving. "Nope."

The eggs hovered in the air, out of reach but not out of sight. Ten more seconds of this food torture, and she'd body slam him against the floor.

"Thirsty?" he asked, as if he really cared.

"Nope."

"That's a shame." The fork and all the good food on it disappeared deep into his mouth. He even made one of those "ummm" sounds as he rolled his eyes in exaggerated ecstasy.

For almost a minute she sat there and watched him shovel food. The only sounds filling the room were the ticking of the clock above the sink and the sighs of appreciation coming from Cole.

She finally broke. "Okay, I give. What's a shame?"

He swallowed then held up a finger as he finished chewing. Then he took a sip of coffee. Then another.

Maybe he could take longer with his answer, but she didn't see how. "An answer this year would be nice."

"I just thought . . ." He wiped his mouth with his napkin.

"Uh-huh."

"You know, if you were hungry or something—" He stopped the sentence to take another bite of his toast.

Her insides churned. "Yeah?"

"I could feed you."

"It's about time you came around. . . ." Cole's words sunk into Aubrey's brain. "Did you say feed?"

This time he picked up a slice of bacon. The smell tickled her senses. Her breath punched out in small pants when he dangled the piece just inches from her waiting mouth. Who knew bacon could be so erotic, so intoxicating.

At least, that's what she wanted to believe. Having a base physical reaction to Cole was out of the question.

"Are you trying to seduce me, Cole?"

Say yes. Say yes. She almost screamed the words out loud.

"Only if it's working," he said in a voice as smooth as glass.

Her gaze moved from the food to his mouth. When a jolt of need bounced through her, she knew whatever game he'd chosen to play was weaving a spell around her.

She blamed the bacon.

Chapter Four

Cole knew he played a dangerous game. Teasing Aubrey. Testing her. Wanting her with a sudden flash of white-hot desire that burned him from the inside out, torching his lungs and every other organ in its path.

That last part sounded like a good thing. At the moment, he wasn't so sure.

Only a masochist fantasized about having roll-across-the-kitchen-floor sweaty sex with a woman who accused him of stealing. Worse, he'd settle for rolling-across-any-surface sex. Hell, they didn't even have to roll so long as they had the sex part. Kitchen, bathroom, porch. Any location worked.

An idiot with a raging hard-on and the common sense of a gnat. Yeah, that was him.

"I'm still waiting for that answer." Using the edge of the bacon, he traced the outline of her lips with a light and careful touch.

Aubrey's dark eyes turned smoky black. "This isn't a good idea."

"Right."

She closed her eyes and exhaled. "So we're agreed."

"Yeah, not a good idea. How 'bout it being a fucking great idea."

Her eyes popped back open. For a change her mouth stayed shut.

"What's wrong?" he asked with feigned confusion.

"Cole, we . . ."

He guided his finger over her soft lips. "Yes?"

"Can't," she whispered as her tongue flicked out to lick against his finger.

"I'm betting we can. At least twice."

They could actually go five times, since Ray, being a good friend, had shoved that many condoms into the gym bag he had dropped off earlier. Actually, if she kept up the tongue action, five would be a huge underestimate compared to what they really needed.

"You're tempted." Cole knew he was. "I can tell from the look on your face."

"It's indigestion." She broke off eye contact for the briefest instant.

Very telling in his book. "Come on, Aubrey. Walk on the wild side."

With a shake of her head, she clamped her mouth shut and inched back in her seat. "Nuh-uh."

The loss of vocabulary had to be a good sign. Since blood had stopped flowing to his brain the hour he met Aubrey, it only seemed fair that she had regressed to talking like a third grader.

The way her black curls fell over her shoulders and across the tops of her breasts sent a shot of lust spiraling into his gut. She possessed a raw sexuality. A woman comfortable with her body yet secure enough not to flash and wiggle to score hollow compliments.

"It's stupid even to think about it, you know." The doily crumpled as she folded the end into an accordion pattern in her fist.

Oh, he knew plenty. He'd also bet "stupid," in this instance, stood as code for "want to jump on top of you and peel your jeans off with my teeth." That was his interpretation anyway. Worked for him. She could use whatever body part she wanted to undress him.

He decided to follow her lead. "But so much fun."

"I'm not into danger."

He lowered the bacon to his plate. "How about temptation?"

"We don't even like each other," she said as her gaze swept across his shoulders like a soft caress.

Didn't like him, his ass. The woman liked something about him just fine. Something other than his gift for witty conversation and impressive cooking skills. Maybe she would *not* like him even better without his shirt on.

Better yet, without *her* shirt on.

"Liking someone isn't a prerequisite for what I had in mind. We're talking simple release, not emotion."

"That's very male of you."

He glanced down at the bulge in the front of his jeans. "I could make an obvious comeback."

"About your lap?" Laughter bubbled out of her. "Is that your subtle way of saying you're aroused?"

"I'd use the word horny, but that's probably another male thing."

Her body slumped in relaxation. The move put her shoulders out of easy reach. Not quite the position he wanted. He preferred her on edge and a bit restless. Being calm and smiling meant she had conquered whatever horniness threatened to overtake her. Damn woman.

"Don't be upset. I'm sure you're very impressive once you get going." Aubrey topped off the condescending tone by reaching out and patting his hand.

"Maybe you'd like a list of references."

She wrinkled up her nose. "I'll take your word for it."

Cole brought her palm to his lips for a slow kiss aimed at making her skin tingle. "Aw, come on. Make me prove it."

"You're regressing back to those childhood prankster days."

If she thought this constituted his idea of a joke, she wasn't nearly as smart as he assumed. Either that or his bedroom charm needed some tinkering. He thought he telegraphed his intentions pretty damn well, but if she needed him to decode, he'd decode.

"We need to do something to pass the time," he said more as a suggestion than a statement.

"It's good to know sex ranks as nothing more than a time-filler for you."

There's the word he kept waiting to hear from her. The comment confirmed what he hoped. They were on the same wavelength. One that started with touching and ended with him inside of her.

"Who mentioned sex?" he asked with as much false sincerity as possible in his voice.

Those dark eyes grew wide enough to swallow her face. "Y-you . . . Yeah, it was you."

"You're stuttering again." And, damn, that was cute.

Everything about her was cute. Stunning, actually. Her dark features hinted at Hispanic heritage. He had no clue where the Matheson name came from, probably her dad, but her olive-toned skin and dark features intrigued him. He burned to see her long dark hair fall across his bare chest. To see the mix of light and dark when they came together.

And they would. Only a matter of time now.

She finally regained the power of speech. Even sat up a little, which put her back within touching range. "You're trying to tell me you weren't suggesting we sleep together?"

"Well," he snorted, "if you want to, I guess we can."

"You guess?" Her jaw tightened.

"I can probably work up some interest."

Good thing the table hid his lower half, or she'd know

they were well past the interest stage and were inching toward the throw-her-across-the-table stage. One look at that button nose, those high cheekbones, and that compact body, and his blood raced.

He had known women. Plenty of women. Being the only son in a wealthy and connected family had its privileges. Having a family he could count on was not one of them, but no-strings sex had always been plentiful. Cole wondered if that would still be the case now that he had been disinherited.

Maybe that's why an instant craving tore through his gut upon meeting Aubrey. Well, once she put the sledgehammer down. As soon as her uncertainty abated, arousal flared in her eyes.

Without knowing his financial situation or his name, she had focused on him. Not his wallet. Him. He found the honesty of the reaction more intoxicating than the most expensive bottle in his parents' wine cellar.

The only part that didn't sit right with him involved her aunt. Aubrey thought he screwed over Gilda. Yet, Aubrey still wanted to screw him. A satisfying idea on a personal level but questionable on a loyalty level.

Not that he was interviewing for a serious girlfriend or anything, especially one who accused him of tricking older women out of their property. Still, despite everything he'd been through with his family, all the fights and turmoil over siding with his cousin Hannah when she broke away to start her own business—without the benefit of family money or the burden of family ties. Despite standing up to his grandfather on his buddy Whit's behalf when Whit asked for Hannah's hand and later swept her off to Las Vegas to get married. Despite being fired and blocked from his trust. Yeah, despite all that, they were family.

If someone needed him, he'd figure out a way to be there. Problem was no one needed him. His parents and the rest of the extended family chose money over him. He didn't have siblings. And, well, Hannah had Whit now.

Aubrey's throaty laugh broke through his mental wandering. When he blinked back to reality he saw her lifting a forkful of his eggs to her inviting mouth.

"What are you doing?" Cole asked despite the evidence.

"Eating," Aubrey answered while chewing on the stolen food. "You didn't seem to notice or care."

Suspicious brown bacon flecks clung to her bottom lip. When her pink tongue swept out and cleaned off the crumbs, his cock jumped in envy. Pushed right up against his blue jeans, begging to get out and meet her.

"You make good eggs regardless of the time of day." She reached over, and this time used the edge of the toast as a makeshift fork to shovel for more eggs.

His toast. His eggs. Damn, nothing was sacred with this woman. He would have given in and offered her a plate of her own . . . eventually. Wanted to push her a bit first.

She never gave him a chance. Jumped right in and took over. If she took that kind of initiative in bed, he'd be needing all of those condoms and sending poor Ray out for more.

Aubrey pulled the plate closer to her side of the table. No pretense or hesitation. Nope, she dug right in.

"Help yourself," Cole said in a dry tone.

"Happy to."

She needed to stop concentrating on food and get back to him. The woman had a one-track mind, and right now it raced on the wrong speedway. "I can tell."

"That's what you get for stealing an old woman's house."

The theft accusations grated against his nerves. He guessed that's why Aubrey kept making them. She would be just the type to enjoy seeing a man squirm.

"You stole my food. Guess that makes us square."

"Not even close." She picked up his cup and drained his coffee. "Do you have any more of this?"

He stared down at what used to be a full plate and now looked clean enough to go back on a shelf without a stop in the sink. "You weigh something like a hundred pounds and are all of five feet tall."

"One twenty-one and five-foot-five." She shook the empty mug in his face. "Coffee?"

In his experience women guarded their weight behind the security of a steel-reinforced vault. Having one come out and volunteer a number without a corresponding silent request for a compliment was new. Refreshing. Renewed his desire to get her naked.

Aubrey did not strike him as the type who would eat a piece of cake then spend the next half hour in a restaurant bathroom trying to purge it from her stomach through her mouth. She wouldn't step on the scale after drinking a glass of water to make sure the liquid didn't throw her over the edge into the next pound.

Been there. Done that. The stick figure, no eating, I-gained-an-ounce-and-want-to-die type made his temples pound. He grew up with one of those. How his mother ever tolerated gaining an ounce while carrying him was a mystery. Probably explained why he was an only child and why she blamed him for being born.

"Bet the other women just love you." He would also bet Aubrey qualified as a wildcat in the sack.

"The ones that matter do."

The strong self-esteem turned him on even more. If she kept this up, the lower half of his body would lift the kitchen table off the floor without any assistance from his hands.

"I don't know where you put it." But he wouldn't mind stripping her down and investigating the question.

"Right here." She sat up straight and patted her stomach. The move pushed up her T-shirt, exposing a sliver of firm belly.

The sight of the smooth skin made him itch to free her breasts and the rest of her body to the warm air. The heat inside him roared to life at the idea. Forget air conditioning; he needed an iceberg.

A new plan flashed in his mind. Get naked, have some fun, usher her out the door, and check with Adam about her allegations. Baseless allegations. Yeah, he'd do all of that. Right now, all he wanted was the naked part.

"You ever figure out how you were going to pay that debt we talked about?" He scooped up the plates before she could insist on seconds.

Food time was over.

Seduction time had begun.

"You mean the phantom debt? The one I don't actually owe?"

Figuring the quicker he dropped the load, the quicker he could get his hands on her, he dumped everything. And misjudged the distance from his arms to the sink.

China tumbled, dishes clanked and banged. He dove to catch the jelly jar rolling across the counter. Spending the evening picking glass out of his feet wasn't on his schedule anywhere.

"I can hardly wait to see the encore to that smooth move." Her deep, throaty laugh filled the quiet room.

So much for being debonair and cool.

Time to stop juggling and start focusing on her. "The debt's real. Even worse, it increases by the minute."

The hysterics stopped, but her wide grin didn't. "You sound more like a loan shark than a businessman. Maybe you spent some time in the Mafia or something?"

"What gave it away, the Nordic blonde hair or the blue eyes?"

"The math."

"I believe I mentioned something about collateral." Cole leaned back against the counter and folded his arms across his stomach in one of those relaxed, in-control stances that hid the inner need driving him. "You'll find my terms reasonable."

"I see we've arrived at the blackmail portion of our program." She crossed one long leg over the other. The move pushed those short-shorts right to the top of her thighs.

And distracted him. Sent mental images of her naked and groaning coursing through his brain. He could see it now: white sheets, dark hair, tanned skin. Nothing separating their bodies as he plunged inside her, lifting her hips off the bed, and driving her shoulders deep into the pillows. She'd come, scream, and yell his name.

Reciting football scores in his head wasn't going to stop this burn. Blood thundered and thumped in his dick until his vision blurred.

His lower half took charge. In two strides he stood over her. Tugging, he lifted her to her feet and into his arms.

"What are you doing?" she asked with a surprised yelp.

"Showing you."

With his palm pressed against her lower back and her hands trapped between their bodies, he bowed his head. Lips brushed over her eyes, across her nose, and then down each cheek. His mouth glided over fine bones and heated skin.

"Cole." She said his name with so little breath, he almost didn't hear her.

This close, with her high round breasts snuggled against his chest, her thighs drew tight against his jeans and her hands smoothed down his shirt to settle on his stomach. The air around them crackled. He wanted her, long and hard, but needed her to take the lead. Sex and the house had to remain separate. That meant the next move belonged to her.

Sooner rather than later would be good.

"Kiss me," he said in a harsh voice, as want pounded through his muscles and down his limbs. Every inch of him tensed.

Her dark-eyed gaze searched his face. When she focused on his mouth, the other sights and sounds of the kitchen ceased. He could feel her reeling him in, breaking down his defenses.

"Kiss me," he repeated. This time the words came out soft and gentle, even though his erection screamed for release.

She whispered his name against his mouth. A small puff of air parted his lips. Teasing with light, gentle kisses, she pressed her mouth against his. A low "mmmm" rumbled up from inside her as she touched her tongue to his lips, nipping and licking. Driving him to temporary madness.

Not enough. "God, Aubrey. Harder."

"Like this?" She nibbled on his bottom lip until he groaned.

"Maybe this?" She gave him a quick kiss with little heat. "Did that satisfy you?"

His erection twitched where it pressed high and firm against her stomach. He gathered her even closer, letting his body tell her about his growing dissatisfaction.

"Hmmm." She wound her arms around his neck. "Let's see if this is any better."

She dragged his mouth down and scorched him with a deep, drugging kiss. A kiss that wiped out good intentions and common sense. One that overpowered him, causing every nerve ending to flare to life.

Gone was the gentle assault. Restless energy radiated off of her. Her lower body cuddled and inflamed him. Fingers tunneled into his hair as her hot tongue rubbed against his. Hot and wet, body against body and mouth against mouth.

"Damn, Aubrey. Yes."

Air caught in his lungs, making breathing impossible. Every inhale hitched, every exhale caught and stuttered. When he finally broke off the kiss, he balanced his forehead against hers to hold on to the warm contact a few minutes longer.

"Better?" Her finger traced the outline of his jaw.

Damn, did she have to ask? "Magnificent."

"You do know your way around a kitchen."

"I'm pretty knowledgeable about every room of the house. Wait until you see what I can do with a shower stall."

Her laugh vibrated against his cheek. "I guess we can consider the kiss a down payment on my bill."

Her words hit him like a big bucket of icy water. If she wanted to kill the mood, she had succeeded.

He blew out a long, painful breath. "Aubrey, about that—"

"Maybe making these payments won't be so hard after all."

No way would he have her rolling over in bed tomorrow morning, looking up at him with those dark eyes, and accusing him of a new sin. Stealing was bad enough.

"Think of it more as a taste of things to come." He forced his hands to drop to his sides. The rest of his body shouted to stay right where he was.

"What are you doing?" A cloudy haze hovered over her eyes, and those sleek arms stayed around his shoulders.

"Stopping." He reached up and loosened her hold around his neck. Otherwise, she might choke him.

"Why in the hell are you doing that?"

Yep, haze gone. Anger firmly in place. He'd buried her desire all right. Scooped up the dirt and piled it on top.

Despite the strong pull he felt for this woman, the situation didn't feel right. Sex for a house. Sex to get out of trouble. Neither of those worked for him. Not on those terms. Sex for sex. Wanting him for him—not for the name or his finances—was the deal. For some reason, accepting less no longer sat right with him.

This being mature thing sure was a bitch.

"We need to call a halt," Cole said as he separated their bodies the rest of the way.

"Are you a complete idiot?"

No mystery there. Yeah, he was. A master idiot. "I'm trying to be sensible."

"You're about to be killed." She shoved hard against his chest with both palms.

"That's not quite the reaction I was going for." Where was the gratitude for treating her like a woman and not just a body? For giving her the benefit of the doubt despite all of her accusations?

"What game are you playing? Clue me in, so I know the rules."

"No game, Aubrey. That's the point. When we have sex—"

"You blew your chance on that one, stud."

She didn't have to sound so sure. "When we have sex—and we will, so stop shaking your head—it will be because we both want it. Not because you need something from me."

She pulled back as if he'd slapped her. "What do you think I need?"

"Money. The house."

Somehow those black eyes darkened even further. "That's the kind of male nonsense guaranteed to get a plate smashed over your head."

"It is?"

"You make it sound as if I proposed we trade sex for money."

Uh-oh. Somewhere along the line he had lost the upper hand in the conversation. "Well, I thought . . ."

"You better deny it before you end up wearing those dishes," she warned.

Red face and puffing cheeks. A damned angry expression for a woman supposedly seeking a quid pro quo.

Cole tried to regain lost ground. "Look, let's back up a step."

"You can back right out the door for all I care." Her chest rose and fell in rapid counts.

"You mean you weren't saying . . . ?"

"I was kissing, you idiot." The words shot out of her and into him like tiny knife wounds. "And you were what, Cole, dissecting my intentions?"

"I didn't mean to—"

"Deciding I had a motive other than putting my tongue in your mouth?"

He knew enough to keep his mouth shut this time. Didn't help though. Her rage kept spiraling.

"I admit I'm new at the one-night stand thing, Cole, but I thought kissing meant kissing, not that cash needed to be exchanged."

Something that tasted like regret boiled up from his stomach. He'd been so sure a second ago that she wanted something from him. At least that's what he thought right up to the minute he started thinking something else.

He mentally composed a convincing apology. He refused to beg, but he could admit some responsibility for their misunderstanding. Cooking her something to eat would play a role. He'd need all of his skills for this one.

Before he could get any of that out, she stomped toward the door with her fists clenched at her sides. How someone so little made all that noise, he'd never know.

"Where are you going?" The real question was whether or not she planned to use a sledgehammer once she got there. After the last few minutes, he might even give her a free shot.

"Wherever you aren't," she called out over her slim shoulder.

"Look, I know you're mad."

"Gee, 'ya think?"

"This is a misunderstanding. Nothing more."

"We were understanding each other fine ten minutes ago." Aubrey turned around and faced him, those cheeks flaming scarlet.

"I screwed up." There. He admitted guilt. Now they could—

"You did."

Seemed as though Aubrey wasn't quite ready to move on. "Let me explain."

"No thanks. If you really want games, then fine, Cole. Get ready to play."

As soon as he figured out how to kick his own ass, he'd get right on the game thing.

Chapter Five

Someone banged on the front door before nine the next morning. At the sound, Aubrey dropped her flashlight and smacked her head on the white marble-inlaid mantel of the fireplace in Cole's bedroom.

First, Cole was up and clunking around before six. Now visitors and a headache. With her luck, tour buses and the stomach flu would start arriving around noon.

"Doesn't anyone sleep in this town?" she asked to the silent room as she rubbed her forehead.

The same room that looked to be almost twice the size of the one she'd slept in last night. When she had gotten to the house, she'd been too lazy to climb one more set of stairs up to the third floor before dropping off her backpack. Apparently Cole had scanned the house for the largest, most inviting bed before settling in.

She stared at his crumpled sheets and the hollows in the pillows from where he slept. A red bedspread sat bunched at the bottom of the bed and half on the floor. Cole might have enjoyed the king-sized mattress, but the lack of air-conditioning had him kicking off the covers.

Hot, sweaty, rolling around naked . . .

Great. That was just the mental picture she needed.

His spicy scent lingered in the room, pricking nerves that

were already rubbed raw from lack of sleep. The memory of the kitchen kiss had replayed in her mind throughout the night. Lying under a thin cotton sheet, shifting and turning, she remembered the feel of his firm body against hers. The sensation of his weight pressing against her thigh with increasing insistence.

Those were the good memories. His calling a halt to their lovemaking. His cutting off her chance of finding satisfaction. His shutting down her attempts to investigate the treasures he hid under that tailored suit. Those memories weren't quite as good.

Even without him standing right there, talking about some topic sure to make her head explode, she felt his presence. The sensation didn't unnerve her. Didn't shake her confidence or fill her with dread. Instead, calm settled over her.

And she didn't like it one bit.

Or her strange actions over the last few minutes. Minutes she had set aside for hunting down jewelry and saving her brother's ass, not for running her fingertips over the clothes of a man she barely knew. Being alone, tempted, and sexually on edge made her a bit nutty. She blamed Cole.

The damp towel hanging on the bathroom doorknob carried the fresh scents of soap and shampoo. All very male. She knew because she sniffed those towels when she snuck into his room. She also helped herself to one of his T-shirts. The soft navy pocket tee was now knotted at her waist.

She even yanked on a pair of his clean underwear. The boxer briefs bunched and bagged, but having the cotton next to her skin sent a tingling thrill shooting through her belly and down her thighs. She could almost picture him wearing them, stripping them off. . . .

What in the hell was she doing?

Back. To. Work.

She needed to focus her energies on Kirk and his troubles.

Not on the softness of Cole's hair or hardness of his erection. Kirk not Cole.

Kirk was the one who deserved a break. After a lifetime of rescuing him, she could use a diversion, too. He had every rough spot a person could have—no mother, father in jail, a drug problem, and money issues. You name it, Kirk either had to deal with it or fell into it.

As the big sister and only constant in his life, digging Kirk out of jams qualified as her life's work. This time he risked serious jail time. This time she might be too late to save him.

She had called in a favor from a former client, more like twenty favors, and gotten Kirk a job with a catering firm. Simple, honest work. Set up parties, serve, and clean. Kirk brought home a paycheck for five weeks. In week six, he brought home the contents of the home safe from his last job.

Somehow he got the safe combination. When the people went on their second honeymoon shortly after the party, he helped himself to their possessions. Aubrey badgered him for two days before he admitted hiding the expensive stolen jewelry somewhere in Aunt Gilda's house.

Then he ran off and called Aubrey for help but refused to come back, leaving Aubrey only a few days to find the missing items and return them to the burglary victims' safe before they came home and noticed. As usual, Kirk's problem was her problem. The cycle exhausted her.

Between searching the kitchen and the dining room and trying to ignore her feelings for Cole, she'd worn herself out. Sitting in a fireplace looking for a hidden compartment with one eye and watching the doorway for Cole with the other didn't help her disposition either.

The grumble of male voices downstairs got her attention. Must be another supply drop-off from Ray. She hoped so since they were running out of food.

This morning Cole had shared his breakfast without complaint. He cooked more eggs. He chatted on about the house, the weather, and a bunch of mindless topics. She sat and ate the eggs. He whistled. She ate a second helping.

What she really had wanted was four pieces of toast. Her hunger battled with her desire not to look like an absolute pig, and the hesitation cost her a shot at the food. Just as she had decided to screw it and eat her fill, Cole reached out and grabbed up the last few slices. Since he hadn't had any toast at that point, she felt petty complaining.

Now she was hungry again. So much for sharing.

She stood up and dumped Cole's flashlight back in his supply box. Leave it to him to have the better hardware. After brushing off her shorts, she headed toward the noise, which consisted of Cole's deep voice and that of another male who was not Ray.

She peeked into the living room and saw a guy staring at the hole in the wall. Great, now she'd get another lecture. This time from a preppy guy wearing khaki pants and a white polo.

As if sensing her, Biff or Kip or whatever his name was turned around. "Well, hello there."

She added dark blue eyes, short brown hair, and a mischievous smile to her list of characteristics. The guy had a cutie pie, didn't-I-date-you-in-high-school look about him. The soft southern lilt to his voice added charm.

Kind of sweet. Not threatening and not Cole, which meant no sparks.

"Hello yourself," she replied as she walked into the room and stood next to the red chair where Cole sat wearing jeans and a T-shirt. This one being lime green.

He gestured in her general direction, almost hitting her in the stomach in the process. "Aubrey, this is Adam."

Damn. She should have known by the soft accent. One of the Thomas brothers.

Her good mood evaporated into a puddle. "So, you're the greedy one."

"I prefer the term lawyer," Adam said with a broad grin.

"He's also an owner of this house. A *real* owner." Cole finally glanced up at her. "That's my shirt."

"Yes, it is." Her attention stayed on the preppy agitator. "Why are you here?"

Cole cleared his throat. "How did you get my shirt?"

"Looks good, doesn't it?" She answered Cole but never took her eyes off the lawyer.

To think she had decided the newcomer had a boyish charm. More like a barracuda's bite.

The barracuda chuckled.

"Who said you could wear my shirt?" Cole acted as if he expected a real answer to that question.

"No one, since I didn't ask for permission."

"I'm thinking that's my point, Aubrey."

She shot Cole a frustrated frown. "Get over it."

He frowned right back—a gesture he excelled at. "Did you say get—"

"You're Gilda's niece. It's nice to meet you." Adam held out his hand in welcome.

Lawyer boy's hello looked genuine. She knew better. This one had quite the reputation for negotiation. She shook Adam's hand but watched him every second to make sure he didn't try to lift her wallet.

Assessing the sparkle in Adam's eyes and the way he held on to her palm a fraction too long would take some time.

"That's enough of that." In a flash, Cole stood next to her. He reached out and separated the handshake with an abrupt tug.

"Owww." She rubbed her hand.

Gruff demeanor. Stiff shoulders. The carefree guy who sang to her at breakfast had left the building. The grumbling Cole left behind sounded as disgruntled as she felt.

"What in the world is wrong with you?" she asked.

"Yeah, Cole. Something piss you off?" Adam asked in a sing-songy voice.

"Go to hell." Cole answered Adam, but remained hovering over her shoulder.

She elbowed Cole's stomach to get a little room. Not that the move would do any good, since his abs felt as if they were protected by a steel coating.

When that failed, she tried using reason. "You're suffocating me."

"You need a keeper."

"You need a better attitude." And a less attractive face.

"You weren't complaining when I made you breakfast."

Aubrey shot a glance in lawyer boy's direction to check his reaction before turning back to Cole. "About that. I'm still hungry. If you don't like it, have your lawyer here sue me."

"I don't practice food law. Cole's on his own on this one. Sorry, man."

Cole's eyes bulged a little. "You're hungry? Again?"

"You don't need to sound so shocked. Not all women consider berries and twigs a meal, you know." And Cole could stop looking at her like that any time now.

"Cole made you eat twigs?" Adam asked.

"She had three eggs." Cole's lips moved a few times, as if he had to interrupt his food broadcast to calculate her caloric intake. "No, make that four eggs, plus toast, and all the bacon."

She'd swear on her aunt's pearls that Cole had grabbed one of those pieces. "What's your point?"

"Uh, folks?" Adam's voice stayed soft but still rose above the arguing.

"What?" They answered at the same time, her response being sharper and more pronounced than Cole's.

"As fun as this is—and it is, believe me—I actually

came here today to conduct some business." Adam leaned down and picked up a black leather briefcase.

Before she could say money-grubbing ambulance chaser, Adam flipped the thing open and dragged out a stack of papers. From the size of the pile, she wondered if he planned to have her arrested or just to bore her to death by reading all that legal crap to her.

"Shouldn't you be at work?" she asked.

"This is my work." Adam sat on the couch and patted the seat next to him.

Cole sat down on the open space before she could move. Not that she would have sat next to Adam. After all, there really wasn't enough room on the small settee for her and Adam's ego. But still, Cole's macho act had to go.

"I thought I was supposed to sit on the couch," she said.

"I'm on the couch." Cole nodded in the direction of the chair across from them. "Sit there."

Cole had the wrong woman if he thought the Neanderthal impersonation was going to work. "How 'bout you say please?"

"How 'bout you do it now," he shot back.

Whoa. Where did that come from? "I'm going to start throwing eggs in a minute."

"Can't. You ate them all."

"Get up on the wrong side of something this morning, partner?" Adam shuffled papers in what Aubrey assumed was an effort to pretend he was too busy to listen to them.

"Let's just say I encountered a problem in the kitchen last night," Cole answered.

She was pretty sure she qualified as the problem in question. Not that she felt bad about that. After all, Cole was the one who had ended the lovemaking, not her. If he regretted his hasty decision, well . . . good.

"You need me to send Ray over to handle something in the kitchen?" Adam asked.

"I can take care of *the problem* just fine." Cole stared right at her when he said the words. "Adam, tell her whatever you came here to say. Let's get this done."

Adam's eyebrows lifted. "Well, I brought over the paperwork for the house sale. It's all in order."

"Uh-huh." As if she cared about documents. Hunger pains and other kinds of pains, pains of the Cole variety, mixed together to call her attention now.

"I double-checked on your aunt. She's in her new rooms and adjusting well." Adam piled some papers in front of her and pointed to a paragraph. "Per the directions of her guardian, who happens to be an attorney and happens to be the one who acted on her behalf in the sale deal—"

"More lawyers. Wonderful. Can't have too many of those skulking around," Aubrey muttered.

Adam ignored the grumbling. "Your aunt took whatever possessions she needed or wanted and left the rest with us. We purchased the items at a steep discount and agreed to give the heirs whatever furniture or furnishings they, meaning you, want."

The lawyer's lips kept moving, but all she could hear was the rumbling memory of Cole ordering her to kiss him last night.

"Aubrey?" The harsh edge had left Cole's voice. Another emotion lingered there.

One she couldn't place. "Huh?"

"Did you hear what Adam said?"

Something about furniture, or lawyers, or lawyers with furniture. Hell, he could have asked her to clean his toilets. She had no idea. Adam was not her focus at the moment.

"Yeah, I heard him."

Adam tapped his pen against the pile of papers. "Then you know the property deal is legitimate. We treated your aunt well and fairly. She got a better deal than anyone else would have given her."

Uh-huh, fair. Whatever.

Her mind returned to Cole and the search for an explanation of why he had called a halt to the kissing. Last night, fire had danced behind his eyes. His body had curved around hers in perfect symmetry. The kiss had him breathing heavily and fighting for calm. She knew an interested man when one pressed up against her. So, why stop?

Sitting there engaged in a staring contest with Cole while Adam yammered on about something legal and boring, she needed to know the answer to that simple question.

She had to stop Adam's blathering first. "I'll have my lawyer look at the documents later."

"Didn't you hear anything I said?" Adam asked.

Hard not to hear him since he wouldn't stop talking. "Yes. Leave the papers."

A faint smile appeared on Cole's lips.

Adam's mouth made the exact opposite move. The boyish grin fell into a thin line and that southern lilt evaporated. "I just told you—"

"I know what you said." Adam didn't strike her as a guy who had trouble forming sentences. She enjoyed being the one to shove him off stride. But he had to get out. Now. "I think—"

"She needs time." Cole's voice boomed through the silent room.

"What?" So did Adam's outraged question.

"Aubrey needs a few days. We can give her that." Cole nodded his decision, then stood up.

"What the hell are you talking about? We have a done deal here."

Aubrey had to smile. Poor Adam. He'd walked right into the middle of a sensual battle and didn't even realize it.

"A day or two might not be enough." She made the comment more to tweak Adam than anything else. "Actually, I'm thinking more like a week."

Adam rose to the bait. "An entire week?"

The guy acted like she asked him to buy tampons.

"Right," Cole said with a slow, sexy smile. "Maybe two weeks."

Adam dropped his pen on top of the stack of papers. "This shouldn't take more than another half hour."

"I like to take my time. Investigate all the angles, figure out if a deal is good, before I dive in." And she wasn't talking about the law. She aimed her words right at Cole.

If the steam rising off of him were any indication, Cole caught the hint just fine. "Sensible."

"No, it's not. Look, Aubrey. This is a clear-cut case. There's nothing to assess or review. Tell me what else you need, and I'll get it." Adam's charming, practical lawyer smile came back, and the accent reappeared as if on cue.

She'd bet the grin killed Adam. Having Cole side with her probably didn't sit well either. Wait until Adam figured out she'd slept with Cole. And she would. As soon as Adam's feet hit the welcome mat on the other side of the door.

As if reading her mind, Cole started moving. He reached down and grabbed Adam under the elbow to pull him to his feet. "Time to go."

She tried not to laugh at Cole's frantic and unsteady gestures or at Adam's confused expression. Priceless.

Adam tried to lunge for his briefcase. "But, we—"

"Leave the papers. I'll call you," Cole said with a slight tremor in his voice.

This time she did chuckle. "But not for a week. At least."

Chapter Six

"That lacked a certain level of . . . What's the word I'm looking for?" Aubrey leaned against the living room door frame and stared out the open front door at Adam's retreating form.

"Speed?" Cole offered.

"More like subtlety."

Probably because he felt anything but subtle. Hot. Itchy. Horny. Ready. Definitely not subtle.

Seeing his T-shirt on her raised the red flag of his lust. The idea of her touching his clothes and snooping through his stuff should have pissed him off. Didn't. Not at all.

Knowing she lounged around his bedroom this morning sent his internal temperature soaring by fifty degrees. He had heard her moving around on the third floor earlier. If he had known she wandered up there looking for clothes, he would have rushed up there and helped. Helped her take some off, that is.

That opportunity had passed. Now he had another one.

Her. Him. Alone. Yeah, this scenario worked for him on every level.

"Adam isn't the type to ruffle easily. You had him bobbing and weaving," he said as the front door clicked shut behind him.

For the second time in two days, he walked across the

entry to get to her. Last time he wanted her out. Now, he wanted in.

"I sense your friend is used to getting his way," she said.

Time to turn the topic to something other than Adam. "We should—"

"He doesn't bully, but there's something about him that commands attention."

So much for subterfuge. "For whatever reason, the ladies like Adam."

She shrugged her shoulders at him in a universal gesture designed to confuse men everywhere. "Hmmm."

"Something you want to add?"

She shrugged again. "Well . . ."

Another female trait, one equally guaranteed to be annoying. "What do 'hmmm' and 'well' mean?"

"Adam's okay." She pushed away from the wall and walked into the living room.

The move gave Cole a front row view of her ass. Small, round, and firm. She could walk away from him any time, so long as she knew he planned to follow. Shame he couldn't sit back and enjoy it.

Sure, "okay" sounded lukewarm, but having Aubrey think about Adam at all pissed Cole off. Good thing Adam had left or Cole would've pounded his partner into the ground for that one.

At this point, Cole welcomed any release. The fact he wanted to take on Adam at all didn't sit as well. He could not think of a time when a woman ranked high enough to come between him and Adam.

If the twisting in his gut qualified as jealousy, he understood why people called it a green monster. It had the roar and fight of one.

"Adam's not my type," she continued.

Never mind that she had already answered the question. She just kept . . . Wait. Cole stopped watching her walk long enough to catch up to the conversation. "What did you say?"

She shot him a heavy-lidded look over her shoulder. One that smoldered. "I have a sudden interest in blonds."

"Do you now?"

"Most definitely."

Bingo. "We do have more fun."

He finished off the comment by tripping over a crack in the floor and nearly falling on her. Grabbing the door frame, he stopped the stumble and saved a small piece of his dignity. Very small. And only because she wasn't watching and ignored the thud as he tried to regain his balance.

"I'll take your word on that fun thing," she said.

"I'm happy to give a demonstration." Preferably one that did not include falling and cracking his head open on a historically protected doorknob.

"You sure Adam won't be back?" She stopped and sat on the arm of the chair with her hands balanced beside her.

"Not if he wants to live."

"My sense is that the Thomas brothers give orders and people follow them."

"True." He sat on the coffee table in front of her with his elbows on his knees and his legs straddling hers. The position put him in close and intimate. His hands fell into the empty space between them. Perfect for what he had in mind.

The mundane conversation contrasted with the heat spiking all around them. She talked about normal, everyday stuff. The kind of get-to-know-you stuff reserved for first dates and fill-in conversation. He had moved way past this step.

His mind wandered to her smooth, tanned skin. To running his hands over every inch of her. To seeing her dark hair spread out over that red bedspread in his room. Fiery and alive. That's how he saw her.

"No wonder you're in business together," she said, proving she wasn't quite ready to focus on his hands or any other part of him.

"We make it work. Yelling helps."

"You're very similar."

She was fishing for something, but Cole could not figure out what. "I guess."

"Like siblings, really."

Wrong. Family was the one thing he no longer had. But a significant loss like that would never register for Aubrey. She tossed the concerns about her aunt aside without a second thought.

Aubrey took family for granted. Ignored its value. The idea left him feeling restless and a bit disappointed in her. But, this was sex. Only sex.

"Cole?"

"No relation."

She tilted her head to the side as if she were studying him for a scientific experiment. "Are you afraid to admit that you're close to Whit and Adam?"

She must have mistaken the sharpness of his voice for something else. "No."

"Is caring about them too feminine or something?" Her smile lit up her face, giving her skin a warm glow and her eyes a soft shine.

Watching the sensual awareness fill her killed any thoughts of disappointment. Aubrey could handle her family however she wanted. That was her business. What he wanted was her. Right now.

"I'm feeling anything but girly at the moment."

Her smile turned from warm to simmering. "Tell me all about how you feel. Every last detail, nice and slow, in that sexy deep voice of yours."

The room tilted. The topic finally switched to something he could handle. Wanted to handle. Them.

"Hot." The word didn't come close to describing the inferno welling inside him.

"Anything else?"

Yeah, something else. Something he could not describe or name. "Overdressed."

Her gaze traveled over his shoulders in a slow, lazy line. "Not on my account, I hope. Feel free to strip."

"Alone?" His palms skimmed over her knees and grazed the area right above.

"You're wearing more than I am." She tightened her grip on the chair's arm until he thought the antique piece would disintegrate under her fingers.

"True, but I can fix that."

One hand smoothed over her leg from knee to the very tip of the shorts riding high on her thigh. The other reached to his waist. With his tee bunched in his fist, he pulled the cotton up to his shoulders and over his head, breaking contact with her skin only long enough to disrobe.

"Very nice." Her gaze lingered over his chest then dropped to his stomach and below. "Even better."

He leaned forward, sliding his hands under the edges of her shorts, letting his fingertips brush against her underwear. Cotton and too big, as if she were wearing another pair of shorts. If so, fine. He'd strip those off her too. He'd keep going, peeling away layers, until he found the soft, heated center between her legs.

"Still hot," he said.

"Me, too."

"Let me see for myself." Feel for himself is what he really meant.

"Yes," she said in a husky whisper.

Her head fell back, exposing a sultry line of perfect neck. The higher his hands ventured, the more her legs relaxed and fell open. When his fingers moved to her zipper, she loosened her hold on the chair and lifted her thumb to rub against the scruff on his chin then over his lips.

The gentle caresses ignited something inside him, snuffing out the previous cold. He wanted her just as hot as he was. Everywhere. When his hands stroked the very top of her thighs, he got exactly the reaction he wanted. Her nails scorched a heated path down his arms and back again, encouraging him to go further.

His forefinger brushed against the crotch of her underwear. Damp and pulsing, the rhythm inside her matched the frantic thudding of his heart in his throat.

The way her body responded both humbled and inspired him. "You're on fire."

"Burning. For you." Her whisper echoed next to his ear.

That was all the encouragement he needed. Trying to keep his moves slow and sure, he slid her zipper down, revealing inches of stark white underwear. His underwear.

"I'm sure there's an explanation."

Not that he cared. No. Seeing her open and willing, wearing his clothes against her bare flesh. The sexy, feminine way she stretched and curled. All of it made him burn to have her. Right there. Right now. The why did not matter at all.

Her lips hovered above his. Her fingers brushed through his hair. "I wanted to be close to you."

"Not with these in the way." He flattened his palm over her shorts and against her flat stomach.

"Then take them off."

"About damn time," he muttered in a voice gruff with need.

"We've only known each other a day."

"And I wanted you every second of it."

His hands took over, lifting her hips to ease his way and stripping the shorts down her inviting thighs. Instead of setting her feet back on the floor, he folded her legs over the tops of his thighs and perched her butt on the tips of his knees.

Even without contact with her bare skin, he could feel the tremors running through her. Smell the excitement building in her.

Her unique scent intoxicated him, filling his head until he drowned in it. The desire to taste her, to abandon all reason and lose his body in hers, swamped him. In a flash of common sense, he reached into his back pocket and fished out the condom he had put in there in an earlier moment of positive thinking.

With the foil packet behind him on the table and her in front of him, he had everything he needed. Almost.

As if reading his mind, she kissed him. A deep, open-mouthed kiss full of heat and promise. Every inch of him ramped up. Adrenaline churned. His body careened at warp speed as his erection twitched and begged for completion.

With his hands against her back, he pulled her down until her legs fully straddled his waist and her upper body crushed against his chest. The kiss continued and heated there on the coffee table as his fingers untied the knotted tee and dove underneath to unhook her bra and cup her soft, round breasts.

A low, throaty moan vibrated against his ear as he massaged her firm skin. Thumb over nipple. His palm tracing every inch of her ample flesh. Desperate to get closer, he lifted her shirt trapping her arms and leaving her breasts open to his gaze and mouth.

The table creaked under their combined weight as their bodies moved and shifted. He unleashed a gentle assault, first on one breast then the other. With a tiny trail of kisses, he outlined every inch of skin. Learned every curve.

Aubrey did some studying of her own. Fingers roamed his head before traveling down his neck, across his shoulders and down his back.

She rimmed his ear with her tongue. "We need a bed."

Wrong. Needed the condom. "Never gonna make it there."

"You aren't stopping?"

"Just starting. Forget the stairs."

She bounced lightly against his knees making him groan and his cock jump. "This will never hold us."

"Not for what I have in mind."

Damn. The where didn't matter to him. Only the timing and it had to be now. He lifted the shirt over her head and threw it and her bra on the floor. When his mouth settled over her breast again, his tongue licking between gentle bites and the soft sucking of her skin against his lips, she gasped.

"Cole. We need—"

"This." His hand slipped under the waistband of the underwear in a direct line through her soft tuft of hair to her slick wetness.

He forced his body to slow down, to enjoy every second. Before he slid inside her, he wanted to see her. Watch her find pleasure at his hands. In his arms. With his mouth.

His fingertip circled and teased her clit. Rubbing and caressing until her hips bucked and her nails dug deep into his shoulders.

"Yes," she said as her head fell back again.

Her body was wet with excitement, slick with desire. He eased first one finger then a second inside her channel. Internal muscles clenched against his fingers, drawing him in and fighting against him as he pulled out.

He pushed into her a second time, then a third, watching her upper body lift off his lap, feeling the clench of her thighs next to his waist. The sensual touch forced a long, deep groan from her parted lips.

Tension poured off of her as she strained to come. "Cole . . ."

When he wasn't kissing her mouth, he was sucking on

the tip of her breast or dipping his fingers inside her. His body stayed in constant motion. Hands and mouth moving. Every muscle aching from restraint and want.

His erection swelled to the point of pain as her body responded, creaming to his touch. Her olive skin darkened and glistened with sweat.

"I. Can't. Wait." He forced the words out through thick, choking breaths.

"Take me." Her hands went to work before the words left her mouth. She wrestled with his belt, dragging it through the loops and flinging it into the fireplace. The first button to his fly popped. Then another.

"Faster, honey." His control faltered. The muscles in his legs shook from holding back.

With three buttons opened, she slid her small hand inside. Right down his jeans and boxers until she palmed his flesh. With her hand folded around his cock, she pressed up and down, inflaming every cell and destroying his last hold on his sanity. He hung onto the edge by his fingertips.

"Aubrey, don't—"

Her tongue licked across his nipple. "The floor."

The haze wouldn't lift from his mind. "What?"

"On the floor." Her tongue circled. "Now."

A woman who knew what she wanted. He could not think of anything sexier.

Until she slid off his lap.

Naked to the waist with her arms stretched high over her head, she lay on the hardwood floor at his feet. With her heels flat against the floor, her knees bent at the perfect angle to give him a clear view of the white cotton between her legs.

Open. Wild. Ready.

Yes.

With less finesse than he hoped and more control than he felt, he rolled off the table and settled on his knees between her open thighs. He slipped his underwear off her heated body. Inch by inch, exposing miles of bare tanned skin and a thatch of dark damp hair.

Her stomach rose and fell with sharp jerky moves in time with her shallow breathing. When the last of her clothes came off, she tugged his jeans down to his hips.

Her legs shifted. She was shielding herself from his view. He didn't tolerate that. His palms on her inner thighs, he pressed her legs open again and slid forward, reaching over her to retrieve the condom from the table. The process freed his jeans from his hips. In two seconds, he had them off.

He clenched the foil wrapper between his teeth and ripped it open. In a few rough moves he kneeled in front of her sheathed and ready.

Need snapped at him to move. To plunge deep inside her. The craving won out over his desire to stare at her. His hands slid under her thighs until the back of her knees balanced over his forearms. The position spread her legs wide and open.

Her scent curled into the air drawing him closer. He moved forward until his stiffness pressed against her wet opening. Easing his hips forward, he dipped inside an inch at a time. The slow torture let her adjust to his size and let him focus on the friction between their lower bodies.

Finally, his hold shredded. Pressing forward, he slid deep and long inside her ready body. Into her tight warmth.

"Aubrey . . ."

"Now," she choked out as her head rolled from side to side and her hands grabbed at his arms. "Please."

All pretense of control vanished with her begging. His palms against the floor, and her legs in the air, his body set a steady beat. He plunged in and out of her with increasing speed and even greater need.

As the pressure built inside him, her body trembled beneath him. The combination made his limbs tighten and every organ slow to a near stop. He fought to drag more air into his body.

Aubrey expressed her dissatisfaction with the slower rhythm by grabbing his hips and forcing his body down harder and faster. Her urgency set a new tempo.

In finding her ecstasy she grew even more beautiful. Her lips fuller, her eyes wider, her body softer. Dark curls framed her face and spread out across the floor. Her thighs tightened against his rocking hips.

The feel of her hands, of her hot body wrapped around him, started his arms shaking. Black spots exploded at the back of his eyes as he struggled for one last gulp of air. As he did, the tension inside coiled tight, then sprang loose.

When the orgasm ripped through him seconds later, it wiped out the stiffness crushing down on his body, and he collapsed to his elbows. With one final push, he shouted her name and unloaded inside her.

If she heard him, she didn't show it. Her shoulders were too busy convulsing off the floor as she engaged in some shouting of her own.

Chapter Seven

Seventeen hours, one meal, a long nap, and six orgasms later, Aubrey lay in a diagonal sprawl across Cole's red bedspread, with her back balanced against his chest and her head against his bare shoulder. Her feet rested on the stack of pillows at the top of the bed.

Seeing her bare legs had her pulling a thin blanket over her naked body from breast to thigh. No need to go all crazy and forget the one thing that made her eating habits possible—clothes. She had always found that a piece or two of well-placed cotton could hide a multitude of sins or, in this case, overeating for two days.

When nervous, she ate too much. Cole made her nervous.

"Don't cover up on my account." Cole's speech slurred in what she hoped was a sign of satisfaction and not laziness.

"You're sounding a little rough around the edges, big boy."

"So, size does matter." Other than stroking her hair with a brief detour or two down her cheek, he didn't move.

"In that case, using the word 'big' seems inadequate, doesn't it?"

"If I could move my head, I'd kiss you." His shoulders rose a fraction then fell against the mattress again. "Damn, I'm exhausted."

"From too much moving last night, I guess." She shifted until the back of her hand rested against his chest.

"That's not quite right, but I don't have the energy at the moment to give you a demonstration."

Amazing what hours of lovemaking could do to a guy's physical strength. Right now, he lay there, half-underneath her and half-beside her. All nude. The only thing covering him was her.

"But I can lift my hand and remove that blanket. It's blocking my view of your hot little body."

She stayed still to encourage more gentle caresses. The more he touched, the sweeter the sensation.

"I got chilled." More like she started feeling a bit too naked.

"You've got to be kidding. It's three hundred degrees in here."

She tried to look out the window behind her. Since his arm trapped her long hair against the bed, that didn't work. The small lamp by the fireplace didn't cast much light. A fact she had appreciated earlier when she straddled Cole's lap and rode him with an abandon she'd never felt before.

Now the darkness disoriented her. "What time is it?"

"Maybe three or four in the morning. Somehow it's still three hundred degrees in here."

"One of the hazards of an older house. No air-conditioning."

Lounging around naked with a virtual stranger was not her usual operating procedure. Actually, naked with a stranger in any position was not her thing. Quickie sex sessions always struck her as dangerous and dumb. Women in Washington, D.C., or any city or anywhere, really, had to be a bit smarter than that.

But with Cole something changed. Time moved faster. The rules changed. Attraction blossomed out of control before she could focus on the task at hand and block him out.

She had never chosen a man over Kirk before. Never chosen anyone over family except for during the last few hours.

She did not regret her decision to put her needs first for once, but it was a strange sensation.

This moment, these hours, were only for her. Alive and strong in her sexuality thanks to Cole. This feeling of vibrant femininity was a gift. A compliment she had not even known she needed.

"Cool or no," he stopped in mid-sentence to drag her close for a quick, hot kiss. "You and naked are a good match.

"Gee, Cole. With words like 'good' you'll turn my head. Sure it wasn't just average?"

"Babe, if the last few hours only rose to the level of good for you—"

"Did you say rose?" Her hand slipped from its resting place on his chest to his stomach, then below.

"Vixen." A hiss escaped through his teeth, dragging the "x" for a few syllables.

Her fingers circled him. Squeezed him against her palm. The touch set off an immediate chain reaction, from his hardness to the waves of adrenaline pounding through her veins.

"I was thinking more like temptress."

"Works for me. And, for the record, we exceeded 'good' way back before the clothes hit the floor. Hell, we'd have to look in the rearview mirror to see great."

"Aren't you sweet."

"Any better my heart will explode."

"Now you're trying to impress me."

He held her hand against his stiffening cock. "Is it working?"

From the hour after she met him. "Men."

"Yeah, we suck."

She squeezed, feeling him stir and lengthen beneath her palm. "Knuckle-dragging caveman."

"Yet you're attracted."

"Apparently." Judging by the hardness under her hand, she was not the only one suffering from a flash of desire.

She rolled over on her side and snuggled into the space under his arm and against his side. One hand curled into a fist on his broad chest.

Warm and cozy, she could sleep like this forever. "Now this feels good."

An ambulance siren screamed in the distance, breaking the relative quiet of the early morning street below. The whistle sounded foreign as it echoed through the old house. When inside, she forgot the property sat in the middle a thriving brownstone and retail area.

"Does the fact that your hand left my dick mean we're stopping?"

She could not help but smile at his disgruntled tone. "We need rest."

"Damn, woman. Did you lose feeling in your fingers or something? I'm wide awake and raring to go."

"You couldn't lift your head a second ago."

"Everything's ready for liftoff now."

"What a lovely sentiment."

"I vote we skip the rest."

"For a thirtysomething guy, you sure have a lot of stamina."

"Thirty-five."

"And a very well-preserved thirty-five." Her tongue flicked out over the damp skin of his chest. Back and forth across his nipple.

"Aw shucks, ma'am. You're making me blush."

"You can't sell the humble act here, mister. Don't try."

"Fair enough." He leaned over and treated her to a second kiss. This one longer with a touch of sweetness behind it that made her breath stop. "And, if you're exhausted, blame yourself. You were on fire. Pure magic."

A line, but he delivered it with such conviction that she

wanted to believe. For just a few minutes, she closed her eyes and gave in to the temptation to forget her problems.

As if sensing her need, he tucked her body close to his. Without warning a wave of contentment swept through her. Life rarely brought this level of peace. The comfort of the moment highlighted the discomfort of all the moments that passed before.

Her father operated with a total disregard for rules and family. When a jerk had refused to let her dad cut over into the next lane and get off at the right interstate exit all those years ago, her dad showed him. He engaged in a car chase and subsequent fight that left the jerk dead and her dad in jail serving out a lengthy sentence as a public example of the dangers of road rage. A second murder in prison, this time of a guard, sealed his fate. And hers.

Her mother died soon after her dad left for prison. Her car had plowed into a tree. The police said accident. The dry roads and absence of skid marks suggested something else.

But those were all facts hidden from her during her tender years. She had uncovered the truth later, in high school, as she searched through newspaper and court records looking for some explanation of and insight into her baby brother's increasingly reckless and unlawful behavior.

On the day of her father's second sentencing, she earned the unofficial title of family conscience. She became the sole voice of responsibility and Kirk's keeper. Being so young, he never recovered. No matter how hard she tried to fill the void of their lost parents, she failed.

Thinking of family made her think about some of Cole's earlier comments. "Can I ask you a question?"

"Two."

She lifted her head up as far as his arm would allow and stared at him. Eyes closed, he looked peaceful and serene.

Hardly the same guy who begged her take him into her mouth fifteen minutes earlier.

"I can ask two?"

One of his eyes opened. "We have two condoms left."

"That wasn't my question."

"Why not?"

"Cole . . ."

"Fine." He sighed with enough dramatic flair to blow her hair around. "Go ahead."

"There's more to life than sex."

"That's blasphemy, woman." With a light touch, his hand swept across her forehead and released her hair from its imprisonment under his elbow.

In the safety of his arms, she decided to broach a difficult subject. One she never discussed and rarely acknowledged. She wanted to open up to him. She craved that level of intimacy with Cole. But, he refrained from spilling any personal information. He turned terse when she asked questions about Adam and Whit, and their company.

Maybe she wasn't the only one with secrets. She focused on the rise and fall of his chest. "Let's get back to my questions."

"The ones not about condoms?"

She pressed her palm against the chiseled muscles of his stomach. "Tell me about your family."

His hand stilled in her hair. "Why?"

"You haven't said anything. You're obviously close to the Thomas brothers, but I don't know if you have one sister or forty of them."

He shifted to the side, separating their bodies a short distance and bringing a wave of coolness between them. The sleepy satisfaction of sex vanished from his eyes. He was wide awake and ready to rumble.

"I'm an only child. Whit and Adam are friends as well as

business partners. That's about it." A clipped tone replaced the warmth in his voice.

A strange reaction. "Anyone else qualify as family?"

He sat up and drew the corner of the blanket over his thighs and up to his stomach. The position put him above her, looming and dark in the faint light of the room.

"Aubrey, what is this about?"

"Just talking."

"Feels more like fishing." He wiped a hand through his hair. "Why the big change? Why do you care about any of this all of a sudden?"

She sat up and leaned her weight on her elbow. "Seemed natural."

"Because we're in a bed?"

Because she wanted to know about him. That was the real answer. The one she could not say. "I've talked about my aunt and grandmother. You haven't said anything about anyone. I'm just wondering about your family. About you."

"About me." Somehow he made two little words sound like an accusation.

"Well, yeah."

He crossed his arms over his bare chest, all signs of the carefree Cole gone. "Not about anything else?"

"Like?"

"You tell me. Ten minutes ago you acted as if you didn't care about anything other than having sex."

She toyed with the idea of making up an excuse, of not opening the door. But, she had started down this road and needed to finish. Understanding what happened inside Cole mattered to her.

"I asked because family is important to me."

"Oh, come on."

She sat up straighter. "What?"

He barked out a harsh laugh as he stared at the bedspread. "You really expect me to believe that's what this is about?"

She ignored the shot of pain his defensive reaction set off within her. "The idea of being fiercely protective of the ones I love is natural. I just wondered who, if anyone, meant something to you."

"You're saying you care about family and want to know if I care about mine."

Seemed a natural response when a woman slept with a man. Well, natural to her anyway. "Basically."

He peeked up at her with those clear blue eyes. "So this isn't about my family in the sense of its money."

Somehow they skipped from a simple conversation about family to one much more sinister. "What are you accusing me of?"

"Aubrey, you don't need to pretend. You're not exactly the poster child for family values."

She shifted to get a better look at him so she could see his face when he answered her. "What is that supposed to mean?"

His peek turned to a scowl. "Aunt Gilda. You're sitting there, giving me a lecture. You who are so tied to your family, so concerned about your dear Aunt Gilda's well-being, that you're screwing the guy you think scammed her."

"How could you—"

"Forgive me for thinking there's a motive other than love of family at work here."

The blow came out of nowhere. The punch so swift and hard, Aubrey never saw it coming. "You don't understand."

"I think I do. You figured out there was money to be made here. Maybe you knew that from the moment I walked through the door."

His words shook her to the core. "You found me, not vice versa."

"And instead of fighting or suing, you stripped my pants off." He spread his arms wide in a move that highlighted his nudity. "As soon as Gilda was out of here, she was out of your mind. Not the most impressive demonstration of loyalty I've ever seen."

Aubrey yanked the edge of the blanket up to her chin. She wanted to shove him off the bed. "You don't know what you're talking about."

He had mixed up everything. She held back some facts, but his conclusions were horrible. Degrading. Made her sound like a heartless gold digger. Or worse.

"Hey, it's your life." He threw his hands up in mock surrender. "Screw who you want. Me, your aunt, whoever."

"You're acting as if I used you." Sure, she faked her way into the house, but that didn't have anything to do with Cole.

"It's none of my business how you handle your aunt, just don't lecture me about family and don't pretend to quiz me for the sake of getting to know me better."

Aubrey's palm itched to slap him. "How dare you judge me."

With a hard tug, Cole pulled his end of the blanket closer to his body and trapped it there by folding his arms over his stomach. "You started down this road."

"I was making conversation. Trust me, I'm sorry I bothered." She jerked on her side of the blanket again. Being naked in front of Cole at the moment—in any moment—was not going to happen.

"Give me a break." He snorted in derision. "You fed me a line about family meaning so much, all while suggesting I don't have the same level of commitment you do."

Rage and disappointment battled inside her. Here she was, trying to have an emotional and real conversation after hours of lovemaking, and he ruined it all by flinging accusations around. Sat there all indignant and . . . Something wasn't right.

Her gaze toured his face. Red splotches covered his cheeks. His hands were balled into tight fists. Clenched jaw. Dead eyes. She could see the anger, but something else lingered behind the sudden left turn in his behavior.

"Did something happen to your family?"

"They are around." He emphasized each word with a tiny explosion of feeling. "Hannah is with Whit."

The mention of another woman caused a spike in Aubrey's heart rate. "Hannah?"

"My cousin. Whit's wife." Cole blew out a ragged breath. "What's with the psychological scrutiny?"

Too sensitive. Each response increased in volume and was more defensive than the one before. "I asked a simple question. You're the one who blew it out of proportion. A problem you seem to be having this morning."

"Then let's get back to something that doesn't make us fight."

"I'm not sure what that would be, since we seem to be fighting about everything at the moment."

He slapped the side of the bed next to him where her upper body had rested a few minutes ago. With his anger, the pat turned into more of a slam against the mattress.

"Let's go back to bed," he suggested. "We do fine there."

She didn't need a mirror to know her mouth had dropped open. "You can't be that much of an idiot."

He shrugged. "Just a suggestion."

"If I'm so horrible why would you want to take me to bed?"

"Because talking isn't getting us anywhere."

The way he compartmentalized the pieces of his life confused her. Saddened her. He took their time together and cut it down to a physical release, separate from anything else. As if she barely mattered.

"And sex isn't happening, Cole."

"Your choice, but get-to-know-you time is over."

"Yeah, well, so is our time in bed."

As his lips stretched in a thin, flat line, his gaze wandered over her face. "So, that's it?"

"Yes." Until she could figure out another way to tackle his sensitivity and find out what set him off.

"Why?"

His stupidity knocked her speechless. She couldn't put together a sentence.

He shrugged. "What, a guy can't ask a question?"

If her mouth dropped open any farther it would be hanging under the bed. "If you think real hard you should be able to figure out the problem."

"I guess you have something better to do."

The man was obtuse.

"Yeah, that's it. My schedule is full," she said with as much sarcasm as possible.

"Being so devoted to family and all, I thought maybe you needed a break to call your aunt and check on her." A smug smile played on his lips. "Or have you forgotten about her again?"

Frustration bubbled up inside her and spilled out. She didn't even think. She just slapped her hands against his chest and shoved.

He flapped his arms but couldn't regain his balance. He floundered and gestured, kicked his legs out, and went all bugged-eyed. And fell right on the floor on his big, dumb ass.

"Hey!"

"Serves you right," she muttered under her breath as she stood up and wrapped the blanket around her.

Cole was correct about one thing: men sucked.

Chapter Eight

The politics of apologizing were lost on Aubrey. Cole made that decision four hours later while sitting alone at the kitchen table slumped over a second cup of coffee.

She started with all those questions, searching for personal information and suggesting *he* had family issues. *She* was the one with the messed up priorities, not him. Accused him of being a thief yet slept with him. Yeah, right, he was the one with the problem.

He could hear her banging around in the living room right now. He'd heard almost every move she made from the time she stormed out of his bedroom and ran down the hall to now. From her shower, to the way she clanked dishes around while making toast after, to her current stomping on the hardwood floor.

The woman weighed next to nothing and clomped around like a herd of buffalo. Clomped everywhere but near him.

He waited for her to apologize for the bedroom interrogation. To admit that she neglected her aunt. To admit she knew something about his family's money and agree to leave his personal life and finances out of their relationship.

Not relationship exactly. They had . . . Hell, he didn't know what they had but it amounted to something whether she liked it or not.

Her groveling should have happened within minutes of

their fight. Hours had passed. So, being a patient man, he sat there.

And sat there.

And sat.

Glancing at the clock he made the decision not to spend hour five fuming over her. Not when he could walk into the next room, explain why family mattered, demand an apology for her behavior, and decide whether or not to forgive her.

Good plan.

The chair legs squeaked against the old floor as he got up. He would have thrown the mug into the sink and enjoyed the release of the crashing of glass against porcelain, but that kind of thing would ruin any chance he had of surprising Aubrey. He needed some form of leverage here.

Making as little noise as possible, he walked down the hall to the living room. Bright sunlight blared through the windows and bounced off the chandelier. He scanned the room. At first he didn't see her.

Pillows thrown on the floor. Rumpled white lacy things piled on the coffee table. An overturned chair. Yeah, he saw all that. No idea what the chaos meant, but he saw it.

"Ouch!" Aubrey's head popped up behind the couch. Sitting on her knees and facing the window, she did not notice his entrance.

That kind of thing appeared to be a habit with her. Not very flattering. She could destroy a man's ego without saying a word. Could ruin a sexual mood, too.

From his side view, he watched her suck on her thumb. Noticed she had stolen another one of his T-shirts, this one light blue and his favorite. Explained why a white undershirt was the only one left for him to wear this morning.

"What are you doing?" he asked to the quiet room.

At the sound of his voice, Aubrey yelped and ducked back down behind the couch.

Rather than wait for an explanation, he went in search of one. He walked across the room and around the couch to stand over her. Over the big hole in the floor.

More damage. Aubrey counted as a one-woman wrecking crew. "What the hell is going on in here?"

And where did the crowbar sitting next to her come from?

"Nothing." She tried to cover the mess by piling broken pieces of hardwood over the hole.

When she kept moving the shredded boards around, trying to fit them together in a logical pattern, he dropped to his knees and grabbed her hands. "Stop."

She finally looked at him. "I'll fix it."

The tremble in her voice and glassy shine to her eyes stopped the flow of his anger. He pulled back and studied her. She was a mess. Tiny cuts covered her hands. Her long hair must have been pulled back at one time. Now it hung in clumps around her round face.

"Did you hurt yourself?" The thought of her out here injured and needing him while he sat in the kitchen grumbling made him swear under his breath.

"I'm fine."

"You don't look it."

"Thanks." She sat back on her heels and wiped her hands on her shorts.

Their knees touched, but he didn't reach out to her. "The thought of you using tools makes me worry about the house. I'm not sure it can withstand another pounding by you."

"I give up."

So much for his attempts at trying to lighten the mood. "On what?"

Her shoulders sagged low enough to drag on the floor. "I can't find them."

He wondered if he had missed part of the conversation.

"Does this have something to do with our conversation this morning?"

"No."

For a woman who ruined good sex in order to poke around his private life, she did not appear all that interested in sharing. "Aubrey, I have no idea what we're talking about."

Dejected was the only word Cole could think of to describe the limpness of her body and the sudden paleness of her skin. The sadness in her eyes spoke to defeat. Her chest fell as she let out a long breath.

He stood up and reached a hand down to her. "Give me some idea of what this has to do with my house."

"We're back to the ownership issue again?" She jumped to her feet without any help. "Yesterday you said I could have a few days for my lawyer to review the papers."

She could not be this clueless. "Only to get rid of Adam. Hell, I would have said anything to get him on the other side of that door."

She frowned. "Why?"

That settled it—clueless she was. "To be with you."

"For sex."

Having her boil down their time together to a simple act and nothing more made him furious. When she tried to walk around him, tried to run away, the fury turned into something else. Fear.

Cole grabbed her arm and forced her to look him in the eye. "I didn't say for sex."

"You didn't deny it either."

He didn't but he should have.

Shock registered in his gut at just how easy it was to travel down this road. To care about her. To hate the thought of having her walk away thinking she satisfied his lust and nothing more.

"Last night wasn't only about sex." He tried to work the edge out of his voice. "You know that."

Wariness danced behind her dark eyes. "How am I supposed to know that? You were too busy accusing me of being a gold digger this morning for me to notice anything."

Sure, he wanted her on her back and between the sheets. The semi-erection he sported almost from the moment he met her made that part obvious. But his interest did not stop there.

If all he wanted was sex, how she treated her family would not matter to him. Her prying would not have set off a warning bell in his head.

When he said he wanted to be with her, he wasn't lying. He did. To hold her, touch her hair, talk to her. Last time he saw a guy act this dumb was Whit. And that poor bastard was married now.

The reality of that thought staggered his step, but Cole held his ground. With his hand against her lower back, he guided Aubrey to the couch and sat on the coffee table facing her.

"If staying here with you were about babysitting then Ray or someone else could have played that role. I didn't let that happen." Because the thought of another man touching her made Cole want to tear the house down piece by piece.

He refused to believe that what existed between them amounted only to an attraction of opportunity. That he was interchangeable with any other guy who could have walked in the door first. Adam could have drawn this work duty and been the first one to meet Aubrey. . . . Cole's mind rebelled at the thought.

"You think I'm out for money."

"I shouldn't have said that."

"I'm not sure what set you off, but the questions were innocent. I have no idea about your background or money. And, frankly, I don't care."

"My family—"

She pressed a finger against his lips. "I said I don't care."

Her words sunk in. From the determination in her dark eyes to the firm hold on his hand, he sensed the truth. Interest, not money, drove her questions.

His past, his life, didn't matter except to help her understand the guy sleeping next to her. The same giant jackass who jumped all over her for no good reason, who judged her relationship with her aunt without bothering to ask her about it.

"About this morning. I, uh, wasn't—"

"Thinking?" Aubrey chuckled. "Yeah, that much was obvious."

He expected a thundercloud or lightning or something. Not a sudden clarity. The simple answer was that she blindsided him. Crawled right into that empty space inside him before he could throw up a wall to keep her out.

He pressed small kisses on her palm and down her wrist. "I lost my head."

"Just so you know, I prefer cuddling to arguing after spending the night together."

He gave in to that kiss he craved. Letting his lips wander over hers, rekindling the memory of their time together, he tasted every inch of her mouth. Her smell, her essence, filled his senses a second time, pushing out the bad feelings between them.

"Remind me not to piss you off," he said against her lips.

"I have a feeling you excel at that sort of thing."

Now that his equilibrium had returned, he debated throwing her on top of the stack of pillows and showing her just how special lovemaking on the floor could be. But first, he needed answers. If they planned to move forward—and that was his only plan at the moment—they had to back up a step or two first.

"So," he glanced around the room. "Why were you in here digging holes in the floor?"

Her back stiffened as she leaned away from him. "I wasn't."

The defense shield came down with a snap. He could feel her shutting down. He resented the distance she put between them and how fast she could do it. "Still hiding, huh?"

"It's nothing."

Getting eye contact from her proved impossible until he lifted her chin and forced the issue. "Then tell me."

Aubrey swallowed hard enough for him to see it, but finally started talking. "I lost some jewelry."

Relief washed through him. Nothing serious. This he could handle. "I'm sure it's here. Your aunt left some stuff with us. You could look it over and—"

Aubrey let go of his hand. "The items don't belong to Aunt Gilda."

Whatever was going on in Aubrey's head had her fidgeting, rubbing her palms together, and biting on her lip. Tension crackled off of her.

"Just tell me what's going on. I can't help if I don't know."

"I'm not asking for help."

He should have expected her independent streak to flare to life, but it caught him off guard. "I'm not trying to take over. I just want to understand."

She watched him for another second. "I need to track the pieces down and get them back to the owner."

"For some reason I think you're forgetting a big part of the story. Like, why someone else's jewelry is in your elderly aunt's house and why you're sneaking around to find it."

When Aubrey stood up, he thought she planned to evade the topic again. Then the words started pouring out of her.

"My brother. He took some jewelry that wasn't his and hid it here." She stared into the fireplace. "The owner of the jewelry comes home soon. If I don't replace it, Kirk will be in huge trouble."

Cole spun around on the table to watch her. Her upper body sagged as if her chest had collapsed in on itself. Instead of the vibrant, sexy woman he knew, he saw one overcome by fear and doubt.

"So, this was never about thinking my company screwed your aunt. And it was never about money." Cole knew without asking that his conclusions were true.

"I swear I don't know anything about your family or its money."

No, of course not. He had walked in on her. She never set him up or acted as if she wanted anything but to be with him.

"I'm sorry." For the first time in his life, he felt the words down to the depths of his stomach.

He had uttered the words before but always as a way to end a fight or get what he wanted. This time was different.

"Yeah, you are," she grumbled back at him.

He stood up and went to her. "Really, Aubrey. I'm sorry for not believing in you. For accusing you."

"How about for being the biggest jerk ever?"

He soothed his hands up and down her arms. "That too."

"You're awfully agreeable all of a sudden."

"I was wrong. If I could take back the words, I would."

From the way her gaze scanned his face and her eyes softened, he knew she understood his genuine regret. "Is that like saying you would have my period for me if you could?"

"No, because that would be a lie. I have no idea how you women tolerate that."

Her lips rounded into a small smile. "We're the stronger sex."

"No question."

Aubrey's smile turned sad. "I do love Aunt Gilda, you know. She needs to be with nurses and doctors and other people all the time. Being alone is wrong for her."

He thought about saying something, about agreeing, but he wanted Aubrey to keep talking. To get out whatever it was that haunted her.

"I fought it, but I know it's true. I can't be here every minute to make sure she doesn't get hurt or injured," Aubrey said.

Cole closed his eyes in a mixture of relief and remorse for having thought the worst of her. For a guy who fought against the expectations everyone else placed on him, he sure did rush to make judgments about Aubrey.

"Okay, now that that's settled, tell me where Kirk is right now." Cole knew they had to talk about Kirk if they wanted to move on.

And this time she did not fight him. "Hiding."

Cole exhaled the breath he was holding. "There's a wrong strategy."

"It's the only one that will keep him out of trouble."

If she shook her head at him one more time, he'd . . . Well, he didn't know what he would do, but something. The pinched look on her face had to go, too.

"Let me get this straight. Your brother did something stupid and dangerous, and instead of fixing his own mess, he's depending on you to do it."

"It's not that simple."

"It sure as hell seems simple."

"It's my job."

"He's a grown-up." When she started shaking her head again, Cole changed directions. "He's not?"

"He's twenty-six, but that's not the point."

"It should be." Cole dropped his hands to his sides to

keep from shaking some sense into her. "Damn it, Aubrey. What if you get caught putting the stuff back?"

"This is what I was trying to figure out this morning. If all you have is a bunch of pals to hang out with on a weekend, then you can't understand how important family is."

Her strike hit its mark. "This time you're the one jumping to conclusions."

"That's why I asked the question. To see if your life amounted to anything more than a series of no-strings attachments. To see if you would understand." She aimed a finger at his chest. "And you don't."

Since he acted like a jackass this morning, he was willing to cut her some slack now. But she did need to understand reality. "We don't all get handed a happy, sunny life, Aubrey. Maybe some families aren't all that worthy of sacrifice."

She scoffed. "Sunny? My mother killed herself. My father is in prison, and my brother is headed that way. Yeah, it was a laugh riot at my house."

Cole felt his anger deflate. "Jesus, Aubrey."

"I don't want pity." She practically screamed at him. "But don't hand me your sob story, Mr. Prep School. Having too much money isn't a trauma. Get over it."

Her snotty attitude helped hold the sympathy at bay. Killed it off, actually. "Money isn't family, Aubrey."

"I know." The words snapped out of her but the heat behind them faded. Color returned to her knuckles as she loosened her fisted grip.

"I don't have one. Not a biological one. Not really." He shrugged as if it did not matter, even though on some level it did. "My acceptance was always a bit tenuous since I didn't fit into the country club role. But when I stuck up for Hannah's right to start her own business, I crossed the line."

"That doesn't make sense."

"I agree. My job, I've been told, was to blackball Hannah

along with the rest of the family members and refuse to support her marriage to Whit."

Confusion showed in Aubrey's eyes. "They don't like Whit?"

"They don't like independent streaks or family members who don't do what they're told. Whit expressed a love for Hannah, not money, and that wasn't good enough."

"Your family needs therapy."

"They've had it. Therapy is more or less a birthright."

"Do you have a relationship with any of them?"

"I'm disinherited, which doesn't matter much to me, but they think it should."

"I can't imagine being left alone." She closed the distance between them and smoothed her fingertips against his cheek.

The gentle touch sent a shot of need straight to his head. He expected desire. An erection. A tumble. Lust. Not a deep, sharp craving that she reach into every part of his body including his heart and mind.

"I'm not. Adam and Whit may not be blood, but they're family."

Her smile was one of encouragement and support. "You'd do the same thing again, wouldn't you? Even knowing the consequences."

"Sure." He did not have to think about his answer. With bone-chilling certainty, he knew he would support Hannah and Whit regardless of the consequences.

Aubrey leaned in and kissed him. "So, you understand how I feel about Kirk. I can't abandon him."

"You can't rescue him either."

Chapter Nine

Aubrey knew the conversation would circle back around to her problems. Watching the light move into Cole's eyes, seeing the color rush into his cheeks, gave her hope. He could feel and feel deeply. Which was good since she had fallen for him.

Hearing about all he was willing to give up, because he knew it was right and because he loved his cousin, sent Aubrey's heart flipping in her chest. The name for the feeling blossoming inside her wasn't really a secret. Love. She was falling in love with Cole.

And it terrified her.

"Kirk is my brother, Cole. I'd do anything for him."

"If my guess is right, you've been rescuing Kirk his entire life."

"That's my—"

He stopped her words by putting a finger to her lips. "Don't say job. He's not. He's a grown man who needs to take responsibility for his own actions."

"And he does."

"When?"

She searched her memory for examples but nothing came to her. Standing there she couldn't think of a time when Kirk had pulled himself out of trouble.

"The hesitation is your answer, honey." His voice grew even softer. "Never, right?"

The warmth of Cole's smile seeped into her, filling up all these strange little holes she did not even know she had until that moment.

"But Kirk needs—"

"To be a man." He took a deep breath. "And don't get all huffy. This isn't a male thing."

"Sounds like it," she muttered.

"It's a maturity thing. He needs to have a serious relationship, hold a good job. Have a full life."

"He does."

"Really?" Cole's eyebrow inched up in question.

"Sort of."

"That's what I thought. Look, it's okay to help. It's not okay to assist in his arrested development."

The words whipped against her, but she fought against them. "That's not what I'm doing."

"Honey, it is." Cole wrapped his arms around her waist and pulled her in close.

She inhaled the clean scent of his shirt and musky smell of his body. There cocooned in his warmth, she felt safe. She wanted to stay right there and ignore everything else.

"You're his safety net. Why should he work for anything or be anything if he has you to pick up the slack?" Cole's deep voice rumbled in his chest and against her ear.

Some of the fire left her argument. She experienced twinges of concern about that from time to time but pushed them to the back of her mind. Someday Kirk would figure it out. Right?

"His life's been hard," she said.

"You had the same life. You moved on. Kirk uses history as his excuse, or he lets you do that for him." Cole pulled back and stared down at her with a mixture of compassion and longing that made her chest expand with joy. "See, he acts like a kid because that's all you've ever forced him to be."

"This is my fault?"

"No. He has to take responsibility. You have to learn to let go."

Desperation to have Cole understand clawed at her insides. "Without me he can't—"

Cole gave her a little squeeze. "Listen to yourself. Kirk should be able to live without you."

She knew that on one level. On another, what Cole suggested seemed impossible. "I just want to help."

"Help Kirk now by making him figure this out. We'll go get him, bring him here, and make him fix his own mess."

"He'll get arrested." The word sent a tremor down her back. If Cole had not been there holding her up, she would have slipped to the floor. Probably would have stayed there for hours.

"Not if he does the right thing. But, and I mean this, it has to be Kirk's choice." Cole kissed her forehead. "Trust me. I'll be there with you every step, helping you handle whatever needs to be handled."

Her heartbeat kicked up. This time excitement, not pain, fueled the racing of her blood. No one had ever offered to be there for her. Being in charge, fixing the mess, had always been her sole responsibility. Having someone offer to share the burden filled her with a mix of confusion and relief.

"All I'm asking is that you try." The corner of Cole's mouth pushed up in a flirty smile. "Speaking of handle, can you handle me?"

The weight lifted from her chest, leaving room for a rush of other feelings. "Stud, I've handled you. You don't scare me."

"What if I threw you on the floor and made love to you until you couldn't see? Because, damn, I've been thinking about it ever since I saw you strutting around the room in those tiny shorts yesterday."

"I'm not stopping you."

She squealed with delight when he grabbed her and brought her down to the floor on top of him. The pillows were scattered underneath him. She was on top just where she wanted to be.

Except that Cole frowned and kept on frowning.

Not exactly the reaction she wanted. Not a reaction any woman would want a guy to have to a seduction.

She straddled his waist and sat up with her hands resting against his forearms. "Did you hurt yourself?"

"Uh, no." He shifted his weight, moving to the side a short distance.

"Your back?" Her hands smoothed over his sides.

"Not quite."

"Then what's with the look?"

"I think I found the jewels."

She straightened, accidentally grinding her hips against his pelvis. "What is it?"

Cole half-groaned, half-whined. "Damn, woman. We'll need those body parts later."

"Forget that."

"Are you insane?" He practically squealed in outrage.

"Later."

He grumbled something about ungrateful women.

"Uh-huh. Tell me about the jewels."

"And women say men have one-track minds." He sighed the sigh of the sexually frustrated male.

"You do. We'll get back to that track as soon as you start talking."

"The pillow under my ass has something hard and lumpy in it. I thought your aunt used her biscuits to fill—"

Before he could finish, she tore the square out from under him. The move smacked his head against the floor.

"Um, owww." He scowled up at her. "Might need to use my brain again sometime, too."

"Sorry." She ripped open the case and found the bubble wrapped bag. "I'll be damned."

"I may never move again."

A scream of excitement rattled around in her throat. Seeing the blank look on Cole's face killed it. "What?"

"What do you plan to do with those?"

"Well, I . . . uh, thought . . ." The answer eluded her. She looked at the bag, turned it around in her hands, and stared at it some more. "I'll take it back—"

"Or?"

"But I can save Kirk."

Cole sat up and rested his hands on her hips. "The plan is to let him save himself."

She just knew Cole would say something like that. "You know how to kill a moment."

"Since I'm the one with the unrequited erection, I think you have our roles confused."

She patted his chest. "Poor baby."

"Patient baby is more like it."

"So what do you propose?" When his hands started wandering, she clarified the question. "About Kirk."

"Oh, him."

"Yeah, him."

"We call Kirk, get his butt over here, and give him options." Cole slipped the package out of her hands and set it up on the table. "Either way, I have a talk with him."

"That sounds like scary male stuff." Not scary at all actually. The idea of Cole's having a man-to-man chat with Kirk filled her with a sense of relief. She was ready to start living her life rather than spending the rest of hers fixing Kirk's.

Cole's fingers wandered around to her back and pulled her lower body down flush against his. "If Kirk does the right thing, then we take it from there. He'll spend some time in my office or out on the job with Ray. We'll get him into shape."

She bit back a smile. "And if he doesn't do the right thing?"

"He will." Cole nuzzled his nose against her ear.

"Now who's in the saving business."

"The jails are full enough without adding Kirk. But it's time for him to get his act together."

"You're the guy to help him do that."

"Damn straight."

She folded her arms around Cole's neck. "Sounds like a very family thing to do."

"I've always been the family type."

She kissed her way down his neck to his collarbone. "Guess we should call Kirk now, huh?"

"He's probably not up yet." Cole's hand slid under her shirt and up to her bra clasp.

She felt a tug and then freedom. Next came his hands on her breasts. "Then we'll call later."

"Half hour," Cole mumbled against her lips as he rolled her to her back. "It will take me that long to tell you how I feel about you."

"Take an hour and show me."

Cole's rich laugh filled the room. "You're on, honey. Let's see how much action this floor can take before it caves in."

"You're on."

ALL ABOUT ADAM

Chapter One

"Someone spit in your coffee this morning?" Adam Thomas balanced one ankle over the other on top of his desk and watched his job foreman Ray Hammond cross the threshold of his office.

Ray's stark look broke long enough to flash a smug smile. "My overnight guests have better things to do with their saliva."

"I really hope you're talking about sex."

"Oh, yeah." Ray nodded as if lost in thought. "Damn good sex."

"You better mean with a woman."

"All woman. Five-nine, blond hair, blue eyes, and—"

"She got a sister?" Adam dropped his pen on his blotter with a bit more force than intended. A lot of stress and very little sex did that to a guy.

"Not one I'm ready to share."

Adam laughed despite the punch of envy over his friend's sexual freedom. Running a construction company, handling his family's business and continuing with a boring but thriving legal practice left Adam with few opportunities for saliva-draining sex. For any kind of sex, for that matter.

Sure, he got his share of action. He'd slept with the usual array of workaholic women over the past few months. A financial planner, two stockbrokers, and a psychologist. All of it mediocre. None of it memorable. Some if it just plain scary. The psychologist to be exact. His dick withered just thinking about that woman and how she cried during foreplay.

She had killed off the mood along with any chance he'd ever date a psychologist again. He thought about ruling out pharmacists and all the other professions starting with *P* just to be safe. And he had skipped even mediocre sex since then.

Thirty-one days and counting. But who was counting.

Ray kept glancing over his shoulder at the outer office. His large frame filled the doorway, blocking Adam's view of whatever might be so interesting out there.

"For a guy who got laid last night you don't exactly look relaxed." Adam tried to make light of Ray's serious expression.

"I was fine until about ten minutes ago." Ray closed the office door, shutting out the dull buzz of chatter and phones behind him. "We have a problem."

Ray's demeanor seemed a bit too cloak-and-dagger for the relaxed atmosphere of T.C. Limited. Adam listed the open-door policy as one of the benefits of going into business with his brother Whit and best friend Cole Carruthers. The other benefit being the lack of death threats since leaving his criminal law career behind.

"You know lawyers live for problems. Hit me with it." Adam dropped his feet to the floor and sat back in his oversized blue leather chair.

A rush of adrenaline surged through his veins at the thought of resolving a meaty issue. The familiar churning built in his gut. Nothing recharged his batteries or fueled his system like a solid battle. Like arguing and posturing until he got the best deal for a client.

Not that the current excitement would last. Recent experience told him a fizzle lingered on the horizon. His glory days of courtroom action were over. Now life consisted of negotiating deals and telephone calls. Contracts. Boring damn contracts.

For the hundredth time he debated his decision to leave the criminal defense world behind. If his life were the only one on the line things might be different. But the problem was bigger than that, so he would continue to sit behind his big mahogany desk and stare out the floor-to-ceiling windows behind it. The same windows with the impressive view of the Potomac River and the waterfront park that ran through this part of Georgetown in Northwest D.C. From this vantage point, he could see Virginia across the water and the infamous Watergate Hotel and condos to the south.

Despite the view, all the fancy antique furniture, and the soothing beige carpet of his current workplace, he'd rather be standing in front of a jury. If that meant spending long hours preparing in a cramped office on the third floor of some run-down building, then that was fine with him. The trappings of an upscale practice did not mean anything to him anyway.

Adam exhaled, trying to drown out the doubts and regrets. "So, is the problem yours or mine or both?"

"The Shipman Project."

Adam bit back the barrage of questions stuck in his throat. The Shipman Project had been his one hope. The possible answer to his growing obsession. "What's wrong at the house now?"

"What's right?" Ray shook his head. "I trust your judgment, Whit's judgment, but I don't understand why you wanted this house job so bad."

Adam had his reasons. Reasons he was not quite ready to share. "It's mostly Cole's fault. He stopped being helpful once he moved Aubrey out of the house and into his bed on a full-time basis. I can't believe the change in him in just six weeks."

Ray threw an arm over the back of a chair and settled in. "Can you blame him?"

"Actually, yeah. Aubrey is one scary lady."

"She hates lawyers. You're a lawyer. You didn't stand a chance with her."

"You'd think the fact that I cleared up her brother's criminal record would buy me some gratitude."

"She doesn't strike me as a woman who can be bought. Besides," Ray shrugged, "she likes me."

"She'll grow to like me."

"Speaking of trouble." Ray ran his hand under his chin. "I have two words for you."

"Termite infestation?"

"Worse. Rebecca Carter."

Adam's throat dried out. The desertlike conditions affecting his head must have messed up his hearing because he thought Ray said . . . "Did you—"

"Yeah." Ray included a firm nod for emphasis. "The woman you've been checking up on. You were worried she might show up, and she did."

Not worried. Hoped.

"You're sure?" After so many near misses and almosts, Adam refrained from getting too excited.

"She's sitting in the third conference room now."

Only a few feet away. He had been hunting the woman down for eight months, and all he had to do was set the trap and wait for her to walk right into his lobby.

Adam forced his feet to stay put. Tracking Becky down was one thing. Running after her like a hormonal boy trying to get to first base was another thing altogether.

"Did Becky say what she wanted?"

Ray's eyebrows lifted. "You call her Becky now?"

"That's her name."

"Interesting," Ray grumbled under his breath.

"Got something to say?"

"Just that it sounds as if your interest in this woman is a bit more personal than I thought."

Ray knew part of the story. Adam was not about to fill in the blanks. Not now. "Let's just say Becky and I have some unfinished business."

"I knew you guys had a fling, but—"

"That was conference room three, right?"

"Yeah." Ray's smile returned at full wattage. "Think she'll recognize you with your clothes on?"

Chapter Two

Adam walked out of his office and strode halfway down the hall before Ray's question registered. Yeah, Becky would remember him. Six days, seven nights with no clothes, no rules, no inhibitions, and no one but each other. People didn't forget something like that.

Of course, most normal people didn't run from sex that amazing. Most stuck around until the electricity stopped arcing. Not Becky. No, she ran out like her ass was on fire.

In that hotel room with Becky eight months ago, he had felt a spark of interest in something other than a novel legal argument. Then she left him cold.

Now she sat in his conference room.

Karma had a hell of a sense of humor.

He picked up his pace and hit the corner at a near run. With a two-handed shove, he pushed open the frosted glass double doors and rushed inside the conference room. His speed carried him across the threshold, then momentum took over. If Ray hadn't made a last minute grab, Adam would have slammed stomach first into the long boardroom table.

Not the coolest entrance of his life. Then again, everything around him coasted out of control these days.

Becky glanced up from the papers spread out on the table in front of her—confidential contracts that were none of her damn business—as he slid to a stop four feet away from her chair.

"Adam?" She frowned in concern when she asked the question.

Same deep throaty voice.

Same wide, chocolate brown eyes touched with sadness.

Still beautiful, but changed. The once flirty smile carried a serious wisdom, deeper than before. Soft brown hair shorter, now resting on her shoulders and tinged with streaks of blond.

A more refined and sophisticated look. Very put together, but all signs of a meaningful life outside of work gone.

Adam pulled his fragmented thoughts back together into a big ball of nothing. "I tripped over something on the carpet."

"Like your dignity?" Ray muttered the question from behind.

When Becky stood up, Adam tried to look away. At the very least look uninterested. Hard to do when his eyes conducted an involuntary roam over all five-feet-ten of her. Tall and lithe. He never knew how attractive tall and lithe could be until he met Becky.

With one hand she smoothed down the blue blazer of her slim-fitting pantsuit. The other extended in greeting. "Hello, Adam. It's good to see you again."

So calm. She acted like they had talked on an elevator for a few minutes one time years ago. Nothing but an acquaintance. No one would ever know he'd touched and tasted every inch of her.

And women said men compartmentalized their feelings.

"Becky." Adam folded his hand over her ice cold fingers.

Cadavers gave off more body heat. Maybe Ms. Smooth wasn't quite as unaffected as she pretended.

"This is my foreman and general contractor, Ray. Ray,

meet Rebecca Carter." Adam motioned somewhere in the general vicinity of where Ray last spoke.

Adam did not need to look back and see if he had come close to pointing Ray out, because Ray picked that moment to inch between them. A mix of appreciation and awe showed in his eyes. "Nice to meet you, ma'am."

Adam figured Ray had ten seconds to wipe the dumb-ass grin off his face.

"Definitely a pleasure," Ray said with a nod.

Maybe not even ten. Adam started counting.

"I've heard a lot about you," Ray continued.

Becky's smile froze.

So did Adam's insides. He could host the Iditarod on his stomach.

"Really?" She looked far too pleased at the thought of being the subject of office chatter.

Adam knew ten counts were too many. Where was a muzzle when a guy needed one? "Ray, why don't you go—"

"It was all good stuff." Ray shook Becky's hand with both of his and leaned in for a conspiratorial whisper. "Well, mostly good."

Forget the muzzle. Adam decided he needed handcuffs and a soundproof prison cell to stop his supposed good friend from acting like a gossipy old woman.

"What were the not-so-good parts?" The shine in Becky's eyes suggested she really wanted to know the answer.

All the more reason for him to stop this racing train, Adam thought. "Nothing worth mentioning."

That killed the conversation. Finally. But the handshake kept going, as if Ray and Becky were aiming for a world record.

Adam thought about tracking down a crowbar to separate them. "What brings you here, Becky?"

When she switched her eye contact from Ray to him, Adam decided to let Ray live.

"I think you know."

He did. "Not really."

"Fine. We'll play it your way. I'm here about the McHugh rehab contract."

"Who?" Ray asked.

Becky cut off the handshake and threaded her fingers together in front of her. "The three-story historic Victorian home in Dupont Circle. This company sold the property to Erin McHugh. Gilda Armstrong last lived there. Any of this ringing a bell?"

"I know the property." Ray looked too spooked to say much else.

"Certainly you haven't forgotten about the company's newest project so soon."

"Of course not. You mean the Shipman property." Ray nodded in understanding.

Becky responded with a flat-lipped stare. "The Shipmans haven't lived there or anywhere, for that matter, for about a hundred years."

"Uh . . ."

Adam smiled at Ray's sudden inability to finish a sentence. Becky had that effect on him as well. "Now that we've established the Shipmans are dead."

"Right. My client's name is Erin McHugh. The former Shipman property is now the McHugh property."

Adam grabbed the conference room chair in front of him to keep from lifting his fists in victory. "The house is listed as a protected property under the Shipman name."

"For now." Becky hitched her chin up. Any higher and her head would bounce off the ceiling. "In that vein, from here on out, I'll be your opponent on the contract deal."

"Damn." The awe had moved from Ray's eyes to his voice.

The plan had worked. On the inside Adam wanted to celebrate. On the outside, he stayed calm. "Since when do you represent Erin?"

The corner of Becky's mouth kicked up in a smile. "Since right now."

"Erin didn't tell me she'd retained counsel." But he had hoped. First he acquired the property. Then he lobbied Erin to buy it. All the time knowing Erin was his ticket to Becky.

"She has." Becky tapped her thumbs together. "Me."

The memory of what she could do with those slim fingers slipped to the forefront of Adam's brain. He shoved it right back as he tightened his grip on the red leather.

"Erin and I have been going back and forth informally. Everything seems to be on track without involving additional lawyers," he explained.

"From now on, deal directly with me."

Exactly what he hoped Becky would say. Forget that the last time he slept with an opposing counsel it did not end so well. He won the case but lost his wardrobe when his bed partner of three weeks burned his suits on her front lawn. Kind of killed his desire to sleep with the enemy. Or any lawyer anywhere in any place throughout time.

But the fire incident had happened long before he met Becky. He had made an exception to the lawyers-keep-out rule for her, thinking they would never be on opposite sides of a case. Not when she practiced corporate law, and he spent his days with alleged criminals.

But times had changed. Now he needed her on Erin's side.

"I consider this a friendly meeting between like-minded individuals." A flush of heat swept through Adam as he remembered their last friendly meeting.

Ray's snort earned him a glare from Becky. "Sorry. Don't let me interrupt."

Becky stared at Ray for an extra beat or two before continuing on in her rational lawyer way. "We have different interests in this matter."

"You make negotiation sound like a negative thing."

"Is there something positive about a bunch of lawyers gathered in one room?" Ray asked.

Adam could not figure out what amused him more—Ray's fallen smile or the red burn on Becky's cheeks.

"Are you about to tell a lawyer joke?" Becky asked the question in a tone chilly enough to ice the wall of windows framing the far side of the room.

Ray looked as if he would rather be thrown under a bus than stand there. "Uh, no."

"They're not funny."

Adam smiled. He'd never seen a woman back Ray down before. Ray charmed and sweet-talked. He lured women into bed like the Pied Piper of Skirts. Becky was not buying a second of it.

The realization filled Adam with a lightness he had not felt in . . . well, in the eight months since he had last been with Becky. The carefree sensation surprised him. No doubt about it, eight months was too damn long to be weighed down by anything.

Ray shook his head. "No jokes."

Adam decided to perform a rescue since Ray, the poor guy, looked a bit green around the mouth. "Becky, we want the same thing here."

"Then you also want Ms. McHugh to get the rehab project done at the lowest cost possible and in the fastest conceivable time?" Becky lifted an eyebrow in a perfect impression of a humorless law school professor bent on humiliating unsuspecting students.

Not a good look in Adam's book. "Okay, maybe not the *exact* same thing."

"Score one more for Becky," Ray said.

Adam realized he was shifting his weight from one foot to the other and stopped. If Becky sensed weakness, she would crush him. "Look, we both want to put Erin in a renovated property that suits her needs."

"To that end, she has a list of demands."

He talked right over Becky's interruption. "At the same time, the National Trust has a list of requirements that must be met in order for Erin to receive all the credits and grants she expects to fix up the house."

"I've read the sales documents. You don't need to summarize them."

Adam's palms ached from his death grip on the chair. "We at T.C. Limited have the task of smoothing out all the wrinkles between the two parties and their, at times, divergent interests."

The phrasing pleased Adam. Always amazed him how many words he could use to say almost nothing.

"Wrong." Becky sounded anything but pleased. Not too impressed with his speech either.

"Uh-oh," Ray said as he took a giant step back toward the door.

"Why are you involved in this deal?" Adam really wanted to ask what took her so damn long, but he refrained. "Erin's not a bank or a corporation or a big money client."

"I have another interest."

"Driving me insane?"

Somehow Becky's lips thinned even more. "Excuse me?"

"Nothing."

"Well, nothing he could say a second time and live." Ray chuckled at his joke but no one else did.

"Erin is my sister." Becky's smug smile suggested she thought she had dropped a bombshell.

Not even close. Adam knew all about Becky's background. Hell, he had tried to track Becky down every other way he could think of before going through her sister.

"Anyone ever tell you to keep your personal and business interests separate?" Never mind the fact their last meeting depended on the mixing of business and pleasure.

"No, but I do know the difference between an attorney and a pit bull." Becky's dark eyes focused on Adam.

"Wait a second. I thought lawyer jokes were off-limits," Ray said.

Becky smiled over Ray's confusion but kept staring at Adam. "Only when told by non-lawyers."

"The answer to the joke is jewelry." Adam nodded at her wrist. "Nice watch, by the way."

"On that note," Ray backed up until he slammed against the door. "I'll be going."

"My sister is in the other room with the work plans."

"Right." Ray nodded. "I'll go talk with her. Seems safer."

Adam waited until the door clicked shut and then sat down in the chair he had been strangling for the last ten minutes. "It's just us."

Her smile lit up her face. "Just like old times."

How she could smile was beyond him. "I see you still know how to kill a good mood."

"And you still know how to sweet-talk the ladies."

Shame he could not use that skill to find a smooth way out of his current situation.

Chapter Three

"You didn't have any complaints about us being together eight months ago." Becky regretted the words a second and a half after she said them.

She would rather talk about any topic in the universe, anything other than their history. Yet there she was, opening the door and inviting Adam to walk on through.

Before she could fix her mess, he grabbed on to her throwaway line. "I'm impressed, Becky."

She slid into the closest chair, the one at a ninety degree angle to his, and waited for his smart-ass comments to start. "About anything in particular?"

"Opening the dialogue. You said you want to talk about what happened at the hotel. I'm game."

"I didn't—"

"Go ahead. Let's talk."

The guy sat at the head of the conference room table and acted as if he ran the place. Technically, Adam did run the place. He just did not run her.

She cleared her throat. "I'm not here to relive old times."

"That's disappointing."

"We have work to do."

"Then your plan is to run away again."

Okay, she deserved that. Not that Adam had a right to say it in such a snotty way. "Do you see my feet moving?"

"No, and it's a nice change." He leaned back and folded his hands across his flat stomach. His long legs stretched out under the table until they bumped hers.

The height thing attracted her from the beginning. Being tall, she spent her life looking over the heads or into the recessed hairlines of men. Not with Adam. No, he was just as she remembered. Six-feet-something of adorable, with short brown hair, navy blue eyes, and the same cocky, sure attitude that had dragged her under the first time she saw him all those months ago.

Becky's vision blurred around the edges. It took ten more seconds before her breathing restarted. To hide her discomfort, she grabbed up the papers thrown all over the table and put them in a nice, neat stack. She had no idea what the documents said, but at least everything looked nice and organized now.

"You okay?"

"Sure."

"You seem frazzled." And he sounded damn happy about the possibility.

"Hardly." Once her eyes focused again, she scanned the notes Erin had left in the margins of the draft. "We need to go back to the beginning and review some of these contract provisions."

He interrupted her with a laugh. "You've got to be kidding."

"Rarely."

"You actually came to talk about contracts?"

She had no idea why she was there. To help her sister, sure. But Becky had walked into the building knowing Adam would be sitting here, tough and in charge. After months of deflecting, she put her body right on the firing line.

A dumb move for a usually smart woman, but Erin's decision despite warnings gave Becky little choice. Or that's what she kept telling herself. "Absolutely."

"This is business only?"

She crossed her legs to keep from squirming like a grade school kid caught stealing another's lunch money. "Yes, business."

He stayed quiet, staring straight at her, no response coming from that irresistible mouth and those full lips. No emotion lingered behind those bright, unblinking eyes. Smoldering sexuality, yeah, but not quite the anger she expected.

Picking the pen out of her suit pocket, she tapped it against the glass tabletop. The move cut through the silence and gave her hands something to do, as she pretended to read the tiny lines of black print in front of her.

The letters smeared together into a dark blob, so she grabbed a detail from her memory. "For example, if you look on page three you'll see—"

"Becky?" The soft way he said her name made her lift her head.

"What?"

"No."

That's all he said. Simple, and delivered with all the excitement of the weather report.

She had no clue what he meant. "Excuse me?"

"I said, no."

"What question do you think you're answering?"

"The one in my head."

"Maybe you should see someone about that issue. I hear D.C. has many good therapists."

"The 'no' was to your business proposal." He smiled.

"I didn't say anything yet." Hell, she could not focus enough to read the damn contract, let alone phrase a sensible question.

"You don't have to. Answer's still no."

She started to wonder if she missed a big chunk of the

conversation while daydreaming about his bedroom expertise. "To what, exactly?"

Adam spread his arms wide. "Anything."

The word hung there until she put together a response in her head that did not include swearing and name calling. Not the easiest task, but she did it.

"Let me get this straight," Becky said the words nice and slow so they both could follow along. "No matter what I say or suggest about Erin's contract you plan to say no."

He winked at her. "Now you're getting it."

"You seem to have a tic." She pointed. "Your eye is jumping around."

"That was my way of agreeing with you."

"About the 'no' thing?"

"Yes."

From the wide smile it was clear Adam enjoyed this confusing round-robin a bit too much for her liking. She threw down her pen in frustration. When it bounced and started rolling toward the far chair, she bent over the table and made a grab for it.

"Need some help?" He sat up and asked with more than a spoonful of fake concern.

"I'm fine." Except from where the edge of the glass table dug into her stomach.

"You don't look fine."

With as much dignity as she could muster, and at the moment that was not very much, she settled down in her seat and tugged her jacket back into place before it crept any higher and strangled her.

"Your negotiating posture is ridiculous." She let the anger seep into her voice. "Not to mention unprofessional."

"Uh-huh." He looked at his watch then clasped his hands together over his stomach again.

She just sat there. Kind of hard to know where to go from there. She would bet cash Adam did not make a habit of saying 'no' to women. Not in her experience anyway. But he had no problem repeating the word to her.

A sharp contrast to their previous time together. She certainly had heard a whole lot of "yes" when they slept together then.

Rather than argue, Becky went for reinforcements of the liquid variety. Coffee brewed in the kitchenette at the opposite end of the long rectangular room. The earthy smell mixed with vanilla and tickled her senses from the minute she opened the door.

Screw restraint, she needed something other than anger coursing through her veins. Something stronger, like caffeine. If the pressure rose any higher her head would pop off her shoulders. The move would ruin both the professional image she intended to project and her pretty new Wedgwood blue pantsuit.

She pushed up from her seat and thanked the heavens her legs held her. Falling in a pile on the floor in front of Adam would not be all that satisfying either.

With every step, she could feel his gaze burn into her back. On her ass, actually. Adam was not the kind of guy to let a free look get by him.

The glass pot rattled as she tried to fit it back on the metal stand after pouring. After two clanks, the stupid thing slid in.

"Another problem?" He didn't even try to hide the amusement in his voice.

"No, I'm good." Except she should have stuck with decaf.

"Oh, that I know."

The opened pink packet of sweetener slipped from her fingers and spilled all over the floor. "Damn!"

"Now would you like some help?"

"No." She pushed the grains into a tiny white pile with the toe of her shiny pump then grabbed a second package off the counter of the breakfast bar.

"How about a broom?"

Becky hoped the comment spoke to the mess on the floor and not a suggestion about her status as a witch. "You don't strike me as the guy who knows where the cleaning supplies are kept in this place."

It was Adam's turn to stand up. He walked to the small closet off to her left, the one she had not even noticed until he stood next to it.

He looked every inch the successful lawyer in his charcoal gray suit, crisp white shirt, and navy blue patterned tie. Lean and put together, with confidence radiating off of him. He was a man comfortable in his element and in his skin.

That self-assurance mixed with his shy-boy charm had proven her downfall eight months ago. Two drinks into a pity party, she had sat at the hotel bar ready to pick a fight with anyone who coughed in her direction. Adam took her mood as an open invitation. About an hour after that, he offered one of his own. One she did not refuse.

He had showed her what a real man could do in a bedroom. A man who knew exactly where to put those fingers and that full mouth. When to push and when to hold back. Charm and grace, yeah, he had it all.

Great characteristics for a litigator. For him to be successful in the courtroom—and by all reports, he was—juries had to love him, feel they could trust and believe in him. Not that different from the skills he used on a woman when he wanted to engage in a one-night stand. Or, as in her case, a one-night stand lasting seven nights.

Adam turned back around from the closet, broom and dustpan in hand, and treated her to a wide grin. The kind that took a woman's long-held inhibitions and buried them deep underground.

She glanced at the items in his hands. "You know how to use those?"

"I have skills you can't even imagine."

With a rip, her newly manicured thumbnail poked through the side of her Styrofoam cup. She jumped back to avoid the inevitable splash of liquid. "Crap!"

"What now?" He dropped the supplies and vaulted over the discarded items. The wooden broom handle thumped against the floor as he stalked toward her.

She tried to wave off his assistance even as the hot coffee dribbled down her hand and dripped onto her pants. She held the cup as far away from herself as her arm would stretch, hoping to limit the dry cleaning damage and keep the wounds to a minimum.

"Damn, Becky. Did you burn yourself?"

"No." At least not in the way he meant.

"Let me see your hand."

She shifted until he faced her back. "I'm fine."

This time he grabbed a fistful of blazer. Just enough to drag her back to him. "Stop being stubborn."

"I'm not." Okay, she was.

"Let. Me. See." He put his hands on her shoulders and turned her around. The stern look on his face suggested she not argue.

Since he had broken out his commanding lawyer voice, she gave in. Not as if she had a choice to do anything else since he outweighed her. Not to mention he was more ornery by a factor of ten.

"Here." She shoved her throbbing hand in his face.

His head snapped back. Probably his way of keeping from getting smacked. Smart man.

Hovering over her, he shrugged out of his blazer. "I can't actually see anything with your fingers up my nose."

With the jacket off, his broad shoulders filled her vision. Looking up, she saw only yards of white. She was a sucker for a well-dressed man in a snappy pressed shirt. For some reason, her soft spot grew even softer when it came to Adam.

"I didn't—" Becky's words cut off when his thumb smoothed over her skin.

The gentle touch, with her sore hand cradled in both of his, scrambled her thinking. Sent her brain waves racing in a hundred different directions before crashing into each other.

Memories of their time in the hotel room filled her head. Of the hours spent naked, sweaty, and all over each other.

The tensions of the last few weeks washed away. Harsh breaths raced up her throat as her stomach flip-flopped, bouncing off every other internal organ. With a tug, he pulled her toward the sink and stuck her hand under running water.

Her back rested against him as he sandwiched her body between his hardness and the counter. Heat pulsed off his chest and seeped through her jacket, in sharp contrast to the cool water running over her hand. The citrus scent of his cologne wove around them, making her dizzy.

He gently rubbed and caressed, easing the pain from her skin. Liquid splashed, soaking her blazer sleeves and wetting the silky camisole underneath. Oblivious to the streams of water running down his arms and onto the black marble counter, he kept soothing her.

The sound of the trickling water hypnotized her. Then a flicker of hot air blew across her neck making her shiver in reaction. Adam tucked her cropped hair behind her ear before a fresh breeze shot across her skin.

At the intimate contact, everything inside her grew soft and squishy. Her knees weakened, threatening to give out.

"You okay?" His husky whisper, so close to her ear, echoed through her body.

More than okay. More like sleepy and relaxed despite the thumping in her hand. Sliding back into his embrace, into the safety of his arms happened without thought. She dropped her head against his strong shoulder and let her eyes fall shut.

"Told you I had skills." This time his voice rose above a whisper.

Becky's eyes popped open as her shoulders stiffened away from his chest. "What?"

"You heard me."

Heard and registered. Something about this guy made her stupid. She did not appreciate the sensation, the feeling of being out of control and headed for a huge crash, one bit.

She had smashed and bumped into enough problems lately, thank you. She did not need to go looking for more trouble.

At thirty-one she should have been past the age where a man could take her world, whip it around, and dump it upside down. Not that Adam held any power over her. No man did. Not even the idiot male partner who had derailed her from the partnership track at her prestigious D.C. business law firm. Her now former law firm.

Time to set a new rule: no touching.

She slipped her hand out from beneath Adam's caress and stepped away from the warmth of his arms. "We need to get back to the contract."

To work out some of the energy sparking inside of her, she reached over, grabbed her cracked cup, and dumped the part of the drink she was not wearing into the sink. The empty cup crunched as she crushed it in her fist.

She had faced down yelling law professors, annoying fellow attorneys, pontificating judges, and the most insane of clients. After all that, seeing Adam Thomas felled her. Turned her into a shivering wimp.

Correction: a shivering wimp with stained pants. Hard to be professional with wet pants.

Inhaling deep and long, she walked back to her chair at the table. The paperwork still needed attention. Adam had to know that. Had to know Erin would get an attorney. Ignoring the problems would not get the deal done. And this deal needed to be done so she could go away before she did something self-destructive with Adam. Again.

"I thought you wanted to talk." Adam asked the question without moving from his station at the sink.

"I do." She sat down and spun the chair sideways on its casters so she could watch his every move. "Ready?"

He leaned against the counter. "Hit me with whatever you're ready to say."

"There's a typo on page three."

"What does that have to do with us?"

"There's no 't' in the word 'wherefore' as far as I know. We need to fix that."

One of his eyebrows lifted. "You're still talking about the contract."

"Of course."

"And not about what happened between us."

"There is no *us*."

"I thought I'd made my position on this subject clear. No editing discussions about the contract."

"Then we're at an impasse."

"Guess we'll have to find something else to do."

"Right." She slapped her hand against the paper stack. "While you work on that, I'll be in the other room with Ray and Erin."

Chapter Four

The next day Becky walked through the now McHugh, formerly Shipman, property with Erin. Just the two of them in a quiet, falling down house that smelled like an old shoe.

Old furniture. Dark wood. Musty dampness. All in all, not Becky's first choice for a fun sisters' Saturday activity.

Becky regretted her choice of attire as well. The slim black pants and royal blue cardigan sweater had seemed like a good choice a few hours ago. Not so much now. It was only a matter of time before the thick layer of dust covering every surface transferred to her dark clothing.

She should have followed Erin's lead and gone with the outfit of jeans and a long-sleeved tee. The relaxed wardrobe fit Erin. She worked with her hands. Designed and built furniture.

But that did not explain why Erin fell so hard and so fast for the three-story monstrosity destined to take all of her money like a huge sucking drain.

"Tell me again why you bought this place." Becky picked a discarded doily off the floor and spread it over the arm of a big red chair in the living room.

"Can't you tell?"

"Frankly, no."

"It's perfect for a furniture design studio. Just envision the possibilities."

"I'm having a tough time imagining floors you can walk on without falling through to your hips."

"Very funny."

"You're the artist. I'm the lawyer, remember?"

"The bottom level of the house will work as a showroom for my work and the works of other artists. The top floors are big enough to serve as living quarters without any fear our privacy will be invaded." Erin walked every corner of the large room. She stopped in front of a drywall patch and wallpaper void near the fireplace.

"The place is falling down," Becky pointed out.

"It's perfect."

Becky felt the excitement pulsing off her sister and thrumming through the room. Must be nice to have that kind of passion for something. Becky tried to think of a time when all that loomed ahead of her was opportunity.

Not while growing up with eccentric parents.

Not during her hasty marriage and rushed divorce.

Not when she embarked on her legal career.

Not in those moments when her career climbed and the money and offers poured in.

Certainly not when she figured out her boss planned to scuttle her career. Then did.

"You know what else I hear is perfect?" Erin smoothed a hand over the wall in a loving gesture.

"A hotel?"

Erin laughed as she dragged a rag out of her back pocket and started dusting the fireplace. "Guess again."

"How about a brand new condo in a security building?" Becky brushed off the chair cushion so she could sit down.

"Adam Thomas," Erin said.

Becky almost fell into the seat. She stood up straight instead.

After a few deep breaths she figured she could talk without sounding like a strangled chicken. "What?"

"I've heard some stuff."

This time Becky slumped into the chair ignoring the dust that puffed up and threatened to choke her. "I'm guessing you're not talking about his courtroom work."

Erin finished her impromptu housework. "I'm talking sex."

Becky swore under her breath.

"A woman I know from the auction house, the one who is going to take some of this furniture off my hands, well, she has a friend." Erin stopped and frowned. "Wait, maybe it was a relative?"

"Erin—"

Erin waved her hands in a dismissive gesture. "Anyway, the friend or relative, whichever it is, has a cousin who's a lawyer—"

"Anytime now."

"I'm getting to it."

Becky tried to brush the grime off her pants. The harder she brushed, the more obvious the stain became. "This explanation is exhausting."

"But worth it." Erin walked over and straddled the coffee table in front of Becky. "The bottom line is this lawyer cousin slept with Adam and said he's wild in—"

Becky held up her hand as much to stop her sister's explanation as to stop the memory filling her brain. "I get it."

"What's wrong with you?"

Nothing other than the fact she had personal experience with Adam and could swear a blood oath about his wild nature in the bedroom. That was a subject for another day, another time, maybe even another life.

"He talked me into buying this house, you know."

A warning light flashed on in Becky's brain. "Adam?"

"Yeah. He approached me with the opportunity. The place is perfect. I couldn't resist."

"I wonder how he knew you were looking."

"Through my real estate agent." Erin's smile faded a bit. "Then there was the newspaper article that mentioned my work."

"I'm sorry about that."

Erin waved her off. "No big deal. So, tell me why you're so anti-Adam when the rest of the female population appears to be very pro. Is it a lawyer thing?"

"Something like that." Time to throw Erin off the scent. "How's Ray?"

Erin's head jerked back. "What?"

"He seems nice and funny."

"So?"

"Well, since he's the job foreman at your house, you'll be spending a lot of time with him."

"Not if I can help it."

Well, well, well. A little too sharp a response as far as Becky was concerned.

She decided to hone those interrogation skills of hers with a bit more digging. "You have to agree that Ray's not hard on the eyes."

"He's . . . and in . . . I don't—"

Interesting. "You're stuttering, sis."

Erin scrunched the rag in her hands, twirling it until Becky thought it might rip in half. "I am not."

"Do you have something to add to all the stammering?"

"He's in his twenties," Erin blurted out.

Becky had wondered if Erin and Ray were playing nice. Now she guessed Erin wanted a different kind of game with Ray and was fighting the feeling every inch of the way.

"And you're thirty-four, not dead."

Erin twisted the cloth into several knots. "How did we get off the subject of Adam?"

By a subtle bait and switch. One Becky thought had worked quite well until right that second. "There's no reason to talk about Adam."

Erin's hands stilled. "Is there something you're not telling me?"

Only about a hundred little details, including a few sexy ones involving Adam, a maid's cart, and handheld shower massager. Becky decided to keep those nuggets to herself.

"Look, Erin, I know this house is important to you. We're talking about your livelihood and your money."

"Not just me. You'll be living here, too."

There was a reminder Becky did not need. Unemployed and bunking with her big sis to save money. Yeah, not exactly where she thought her life would be at this point.

Erin pressed her lips together and made a little clicking sound with her tongue. The one that made Becky want to run out the front door.

"What's going through that artistic head of yours?"

"The fact you bought a new lipstick."

Well, crap. A woman should be allowed to buy the perfect shade of "Toasted Twilight" without convening a family meeting for permission. "So what? I needed a new lipstick." As a lie, Becky thought that one worked as well as any other.

"Right," Erin drawled out the word. "Because none of the forty-two tubes you own contain the perfect shade of pink."

"Have you tried to find a good pink lately? They all look orange."

Never mind the fact Erin didn't bother with makeup. Tall, just a few inches under six feet, with straight, shoulder-length, caramel brown hair, and green eyes the color of spring leaves. Erin knew how to flirt, how to fit in. How to survive.

Somehow Erin had turned out normal despite everything abnormal in their lives. They had come screaming into the world in a battered West Virginia farmhouse to parents who believed in strict adherence to the Bible phrase "They shall take up serpents; and if they drink any deadly thing, it shall not hurt them."

When the elder McHughs decided their religious rights were at risk, they traded the farmhouse for a compound in Idaho. Along the way came a host of mindless followers and the founding of what could only be described as a cult. That's what the media called it. What the disenchanted followers who broke away termed it.

Along the line the McHugh children got left behind. Emotionally abandoned, but dragged out whenever the authorities got too close and a public relations stunt was needed. Turned out Roger and Alma McHugh made awful parents but the perfect fringe group leaders.

They caused a furor whenever they spoke about their wacko, sometimes dangerous, beliefs. Between vocal followers, equally vocal dissenters in the legitimate religious world, and the constant attention from media outlets and law enforcement, the girls got pushed aside. Never anonymous but always ignored. That was the McHugh family legacy despite their parents' preaching to the contrary.

"What's the excuse for changing your outfit three times this morning?" Erin asked.

"Remind me to put a lock on my bedroom door," Becky muttered, as she walked over to study the huge mirror hanging above the fireplace and burn off some of the restless energy building inside of her. Getting away from Erin's nosy prying was another benefit.

"Now you're pacing. Keep that up and I'll get motion sickness."

Becky almost tripped in mid-pace. "Do you have a point?"

"Something's going on. Something more than my buying a historic house and needing help with the negotiations concerning the rehab."

Becky knew if her stomach failed to settle soon, the

"something" else happening would be her breakfast all over the floor. "I don't know what you mean."

"I didn't go to law school, but I do have eyes, Becky. You're a mess."

"Keep this up, and you can live in a shoe for all I care."

"I'll be living here, thanks. And, I'm one step closer to getting that settled." The clang of the doorbell sounded as if on cue.

"How did you do that?"

"I looked out the window."

"Who is it?" Becky tried to peek out the window but the overhang of the porch out front blocked her view.

"Adam."

"*What?*"

"Did I forget to tell you he called this morning while you were in the shower?" Erin swung her leg back and forth. "Sorry."

"You're evil."

"Yes, I am. I plan to stay that way until you fill me in on your history with this handsome lawyer stud."

"Nothing to tell." Nothing she wanted to tell.

"Right. That's why your cheeks are flushed."

Becky turned to stare at the bright red spots on her face. The big mirror emphasized the blush. And Adam.

In the reflection she could see him walk into the room. See Erin greet him. They chatted and joked, completely at ease with each other.

Flat-front khakis and a red crewneck sweater with white tee sticking out from underneath. Yeah, no question the relaxed weekend look flattered Adam's lean runner's body. Only the mussed hair and a crooked smile hinted at the bad boy lurking under all that comfortable, conservative clothing.

His cheeks, rosy from the nip in the air, helped hide his

wild side, too. Nothing else about the guy said understated. No, he stalked like an untamed panther circling its prey. That made her the gazelle. After yesterday's round with him, she didn't know if she had the strength to move up any higher on the food chain.

He turned to Erin. "Aren't you meeting Ray?"

Erin's smile fell almost as fast as her backbone stiffened. "Soon."

"He's waiting back at the office. He said something about the redesign of the porch."

Erin hissed under her breath. Becky couldn't hear her sister's comment, but the scowl combined with the amusement dancing in Adam's eyes suggested it was something pretty naughty.

"You need a new foreman." Erin grabbed up her bag and folded it under her arm. "He's impossible."

"Most people love Ray."

Becky knew Adam wanted to say "women" but changed the word. Probably to keep from getting kicked . . . or worse.

"Annoying as hell is more like it." Erin stood only an inch or two below Adam. Her rigid stance gave off that ready-to-hit-someone vibe.

Adam backed up.

Becky didn't blame him. She shuffled back about a foot to be safe and keep out of the kicking war zone as well.

Erin threw Becky an apologetic smile. "I have to get over there before Ray adds that whirlpool he keeps talking about."

Becky scanned the room for her purse. "I'll come with you."

"Actually," Adam held up a hand. For some reason both women answered the implicit command and stopped scrambling around. All of his attention centered on Becky. "You and I need to work out some details."

They did not need to work on anything other than forgetting what had already passed between them. "No thanks, I—"

He turned to Erin. "I'll drive your sister over to you at the office later."

Wrong, wrong, wrong. "No—"

"Perfect." Erin waved as she took off out of the house at a near run.

Silence fell the second Erin left the room. No ticking clocks. No noise from workers moving around. No ringing phones. Just them and silence in a rotting old house.

Never one for awkward quiet, Becky broke the standoff. "Mind telling me why you're here?"

"I'll answer your question if you answer mine."

His deep, hypnotizing voice sent her lungs plunging to her feet. "Or we could go with my plan, and you could just tell me why you're here."

"No."

"Again with the 'no' thing." She hitched one thigh up on the arm of the red chair and half-leaned, half-stood. "Is that your favorite word?"

"I usually prefer 'yes,' but we'll get to that later."

No way was she touching that comment.

"Why do you and Erin have different last names?" he asked.

Not the earth-shattering question Becky expected. But the inquiry came out of nowhere and threw her off for a second. Good thing she didn't have to lie.

"It's a married name." Becky conveniently left out the fact that she was the married one.

Was being the important word in that description. Now she was the divorced, unemployed one. Unless someone planned on stealing her shoes when she walked out of the house, she had pretty much lost every material thing she could tolerate losing.

"Look, Adam." Becky used her most reasonable and calm voice. "I need to negotiate the house rehab contract on Erin's behalf. You made it clear yesterday that you weren't ready to do that."

"Yesterday was yesterday."

The clipped tone and unreadable gaze made Becky's insides squirm. "Then I guess we understand each other."

His eyebrow inched up. "History would suggest otherwise."

The guy was an expert in cryptic comments. "I don't understand."

"That much is strikingly clear."

Yeah, he had completely lost her. Instead of continuing to go round and round in this odd circle, she tried to steer the conversation back to a suitable topic. Even though the list of those kept getting shorter.

"The rehab negotiations are not complex," she explained. She stood up and grabbed the expandable file folder filled with the contracts relating to the house off the end table.

Their personal issues and Adam's temporary lack of interpersonal skills were the *big* problems here. The same ones she intended to ignore. At least for the moment.

He cocked his head to the side and shot her a bland, flat-lipped look. "I'm happy to see you're okay, by the way."

Funny how he sounded the exact opposite of happy. And how he introduced another topic without finishing the work discussion.

She didn't remember Adam's being this difficult when they spent time together before. Of course, in her experience a guy tended to be a bit more accommodating about engaging in a bit of conversation as long as the woman was naked and the sex kept coming.

Not that she had much experience with men. Two guys in college, one in law school, a husband, and Adam. That summed up her sex life. Actually, until Adam, "boring" described her sex life.

When a woman married a guy more concerned with billable hours and how his bio read than with making the marriage work, boring was to be expected. Being a piece of some guy's public persona and little else no longer appealed to her.

Neither did Ned's insistence that they create a story to explain her past. He made the demand. The marriage ended about three seconds later. The actual divorce took longer.

"Should I not be okay for some reason?" she asked, not knowing where Adam intended to take them with this topic.

"Let's say—" he pretended to think about it. "I was concerned."

"No need. I'm fine." Tired, frustrated, lonely, and bored, but otherwise fine.

"That's a relief."

She felt the quicksand brush against her toes but waded in anyway. "Any particular reason why you asked?"

"Well, you left our hotel room so fast eight months ago I figured your ass had to be on fire." His gaze bounced down to her lower half then back up again. "No flames. No damage, so I guess not."

Chapter Five

"You went downstairs to find coffee." In the history of cool first lines to open a conversation, Adam knew those words would not register a blip. Just seemed starting with the obvious worked best.

Becky blinked a few times in reaction to his comment.

He hoped that meant she missed the tremor moving through his voice. Thinking about her previous exit, about how long he had waited for her in that stupid hotel room, ticked him off. Hell, he had skipped his morning coffee for almost a month after he got back from the conference. It was the last time he let a woman come between him and a breakfast beverage.

"What the hell are you talking about?" Becky asked with a stunned, wide-eyed look that almost came off as believable.

"Talk about your case of selective memory. Think back. Eight months ago. Any of this sound familiar?"

Sometimes a man had to stand up. Right now he felt like sitting down. No need to be uncomfortable when he learned why Becky ran out on him.

He dropped onto the couch hoping the fragile wood would not collapse beneath his weight. Hard to keep his edge if his ass hit the floor.

Tapping his fingers against his heel, he nodded at the

small wooden chair next to the fireplace. One far away from him. "Take a seat."

"I'm fine right here."

"Are you being difficult on purpose?"

"Maybe."

"What about the coffee? Still looking for that? If so, there's a deli down the block. Shouldn't take more than a few minutes to fetch it."

"Fetch?"

"Certainly less than eight months."

Becky wrapped her arms around the folder she held and clutched it tight to her chest. "Must we do this?"

"Talk?"

"Relive the past."

"That? Yeah."

She exhaled with enough strength to blow the house down. "Look, this is not a big deal. We got together. Had a little fun."

"We more or less agree on the events so far." Though he did find the word "fun" underwhelming compared to their seven days of nonstop sex.

"Good. Now can we get back to the contract?"

He admired her attempts to throw him off stride. "Are you going to sit?"

"No."

He drummed out three more taps against his shoe. "I get why we started."

"On the contract?"

"Definitely understand why we kept going for days and had to raid the maid's cart to restock the condom supply from our minibar."

"So, not the contract."

The memory of her sneaking around the hallway of the upscale hotel, half-naked in an open robe with the tie flapping behind her, made him smile. "Condoms not contracts."

"Since you insist on discussing this—"

"I do."

"You're the one who stole the condoms," she pointed out.

"And you kept watch for roaming hotel staff. You also helped me tear through the extra package, if I remember correctly." And he did. The scarlet blush high on her cheeks confirmed she did, too. "What I'm trying to figure out is what happened next."

"It's not—"

"You gonna sit down anytime soon?" Having her loom made his spine snap straight in irritation.

"No."

"Why not?"

"I don't want to." Her hands tightened until the folder crumpled under her fingers. "Deal with it."

He had been waiting for her attitude to spill out and put them on equal footing. The quiet, purse-lipped, judgmental routine left him cold. Energetic Becky was a woman he understood.

"The furniture is old but not bad." He shifted a bit, testing the cushion.

"You're mighty preoccupied with my comfort all of a sudden."

More like preoccupied with her ass. "You can hang upside down if you want. It's the battle stance that needs to go."

"Maybe I'm not ready to let my guard down around you." Even as Becky said the words, her grip on the file loosened.

"We're just having a friendly chat. Reliving old times."

"All one hundred hours of them."

One hundred and forty-one. But who was counting.

Adam started in on his mental checklist. "Was it the room service?"

Becky's arms dropped to her sides until the folder hung down from her fingertips. "Following your conversation is getting more and more difficult."

"We're still on the hotel."

"One of us is."

"I'll admit the menu was a bit limited—"

"Food?"

"At the hotel."

"Are you honestly talking about what we ate together eight months ago?" She threw the folder on the table and sat down on it.

"You're right. The meals were fine. Must be something else."

"Are you almost done?"

"The hotel, maybe? I don't think I can be held responsible for that one, since the conference picked the hotel."

"I guess this means you're not done." She leaned forward and balanced her weight on her palms. A few more inches and she would be on his lap. If he managed that, then ten seconds later she would be out of those pants.

"We used the bed and you never complained. The shower, the window seat—"

She held up a palm to stop his explanation. "Yeah, I get your point."

"In fact, twice on the window seat."

Tension moved through Becky's body until everything including her shoulders stiffened. "The hotel was fine."

"That leaves the sex. Unless you're the world's greatest fake . . ." He let the comment sit there a second. "You're not, are you?"

This time Becky's jaw clenched hard enough for him to hear her teeth click together. "No."

"Then we can safely rule sex out as the cause of the problem." This time he was the one who leaned in. With his elbows resting against his knees, less than a foot of warm air separated them. "Was it the towel?"

She engaged in the rapid blinking thing again. "Huh?"

"Towel."

"You lost me, which I'm guessing was your goal."

"You wore the robe. Instead of fighting you for it, I used the towel. I'm thinking the choice came off as too bold, which is a bit odd since we'd been all over each other by then, but—"

"Adam." Her husky voice cracked.

"Temperature was good. No weird smells in the room. Neither of us had to rush back to work." He shook his head in mock surrender. "I'm out of excuses."

"Out of your mind is more like it."

The remark rolled off her tongue a bit too easily for his liking. "How about an explanation."

She shifted on the table until her knee rested against his and her feet wedged between his shoes. Her lips hovered close to his. "Okay."

Sweat broke out on the back of his neck. He could smell the soft scent of something he knew to be jasmine only because he had seen the word on a jar when she took it out of her purse when they were together. Blind with the flu he still would recognize her unique fragrance. It was imprinted on his brain after so many hours together.

The contact of her legs against his, even with two strips of material separating them, touched off something electric and primal inside him. Something tight and coiled. Something he wanted to crush into a million pieces before it spun out of control.

Her change from confused to seductive made the temperature in the room spike. Did not help his control either.

Which only proved his brain and his dick operated under two different game plans as far as Becky was concerned.

Her eyes searched his. "You sure you want to know what really happened?"

Having spent almost eight months tracking her down, he knew exactly what he wanted. This. "Definitely."

Her palms moved to his knees. She spread her fingers out until the tips stretched up his thighs. "Now may not be the best time for this."

"I'm a guy who likes a firm beginning, middle, and end." To prevent her fingers from inching further into dangerous territory, he covered the back of her hands with his palms.

"Honestly?"

"Yes."

Her shoulders fell into a dismissive shrug. "I've been busy."

No longer rigid and upright with perfect posture. Her back eased into a small curve. The seductive purr in her voice disappeared, too. She'd morphed from bedroom Bambi into lawyer mode. The transition took less time than it did for him to blink.

"For eight months."

"Really busy."

"Have a lot of eight-month projects, do you?" he said, amazed his voice stayed steady.

"Maybe I'm concerned you won't appreciate the real explanation."

"I'm open to criticism on my style. Always striving to be better. That's the kind of guy I am." Fact was, he knew his technique was just fine. A woman did not come that many times if a guy rushed the job or missed the mark.

No way would he accept that explanation. She better make up something else.

"We need to work together," she said. "There's no reason to make the situation difficult by dredging up the past."

"You mean *more* difficult."

She sighed. "For the record, performance wasn't the issue. Does that make you feel better?"

At least she admitted that much. "Good to know."

"Then let's move on."

"Not yet. What was it?"

"Simple."

He snorted. "Not a word I would ever use in conjunction with you."

"Do you want to know or not?"

He swept out his arm, signaling for her to proceed. "By all means."

"We were done."

Uh . . .

"Over. Finished." She crisscrossed her arms in front of her in a cutting motion.

As if he needed a visual demonstration.

"Done," she added.

Or a repeat of the point.

"We did what we meant to do, slept together, and finished." She dropped that bomb and then smiled. Actually smiled.

"Speak for yourself."

"I am."

"You could have clued me in on this decision instead of lying and saying you were getting coffee."

She frowned. "I thought you knew that was code."

"For what?"

"Being done."

"Never screw with a man's caffeine."

She waved him off. "We'd spent six days together. We were—"

If she said "done" one more time, he would . . . do something. He had no idea what, but something. "Seven."

Seven nights and six days. But, again, who was counting.

"Whatever. I just thought we—"

There she was, heading straight for "done" territory again. "Your thinking is what got us into trouble."

"How do you figure that?" She pulled up her legs and sat cross-legged on the table with her palms rubbing up and down on her thighs.

"Unless my memory is failing, and it isn't, we spent time exercising parts other than our intellect while we were together. We did just fine with those other parts."

Together. A pretty vanilla word for the positions they tried and passion they burned through. But if he dwelled on that, they would never get through this conversation without their clothes landing all over the floor.

"We were in Philadelphia for a continuing legal education seminar," she said, as if he needed the reminder.

"I know I learned a few things."

"You didn't attend a single workshop." She moved her foot and kicked him in the knee.

He decided to write the whack off as an accident. "Who's talking about the conference?"

He sure as hell wasn't.

"Adam, I'm serious."

Yeah, so was he. "Wanna know how I remember the week in Philadelphia?"

Her foot kicked out again, catching him square on the kneecap. "We weren't together a week."

"Want to know what I remember from the seven nights and six days we were together? Actually, doesn't matter since I plan to tell you anyway."

She picked a piece of lint off her pants. "I had a feeling you would."

"First night of the conference, I saw you at the cocktail reception. When you left for the bar, I waited a respectable amount of time before joining you. Thought we could have a private chat."

"We did."

"Which led us to my room for something other than talking, but still very private."

"I was there, you know."

"Oh, I know." He did not understand much about Becky, but this, them, what they did together, he knew all about those things. "I didn't leave the room again for days. When I did, it was to go find you and get the coffee you promised."

"You want me to give you three dollars to make up for the missed coffee? Would that help you get over this issue?"

"I'm not thirsty at the moment, but thanks."

She exhaled. "I don't get this. Why the big scene? It's not as if I'm the first woman you've ever spent time with."

"True."

"Or the last."

He read her statement as a question. "Not true."

Her eyes widened a fraction. "You expect me to believe you haven't had sex in eight months? Give me a break."

"I've had sex." The comfortable spending time together part had been missing.

After a few more blinks, she continued. "I'm sticking with the 'we were done' response."

Her foot knocked against him a third time. He wondered if she even realized the assault she had launched against his knee.

"It's not the full story," he pointed out.

The fourth kick hit him a bit harder. Less like an accident than all the others. A little more like a significant knee injury.

"Well, Adam, it's all the explanation you're getting."

As if he'd settle for that answer after eight months of waiting and four whacks to the leg. "I don't think so."

Chapter Six

Adam draped his arm along the top of the sofa and leaned back, crushing the cushions from every direction. "The way I figure it—"

"Surely we're done with this topic by now," Becky said, knowing very well Adam had yet to move on.

"No." His other arm slipped along the sofa top until he sat there, all spread out and open for anything.

She sighed in the most dramatic manner possible. "Do I at least have time to get a bottle of water?"

"No. Now listen."

"Bossy," she muttered.

"I'm going to ignore that." To drive home his relaxed state, he sprawled, taking over two-thirds of the sofa. "The explanation for your abrupt behavior is one of two things."

Nice of him to sit there all comfortable while she got stuck with a sore butt from the hard wooden table. "Guess I missed the part where someone put you in charge."

"You're forgiven."

Becky shifted her hips and dropped her feet to the floor between his wide spread legs. She intended to stop the edge of her folder from digging into her hip. When that did not work, she tilted her pelvis and dragged the file out from underneath her.

His gaze immediately zoomed in on her lower half. Not

hard to tell where his mind wandered off to. Hers followed close behind. He narrowed the space between his legs until the khaki of his pants ran against the black of hers.

"You comfortable now?" he asked in a voice even deeper and huskier than before.

"For now."

Sitting there with her knees resting on the inside of his thighs, she was singed by the heat that washed through two layers of clothing.

She could see the barely banked fires behind his eyes. Watched him fist then uncurl his fingers. He gave off an air of calm. Inside she would bet he felt the energy zapping between them just like she did.

The smell of his cologne. The wide expanse of his chest. The way his breathing sped up and his chest shuddered with each exhale. Those signs all pointed to the same thing: he wanted her. The attraction had not faded.

She waved the file in front of his face. "Hello?"

"What?" He shook his head a few times as if trying to clear haze from his eyes.

"Go ahead."

"Ahhh, okay. . . ."

She wanted to burst out laughing but held it in. Amazing how a smart guy could get sidetracked by a bit of touching. "Don't let me stop this insightful discussion. I believe you were about to tell me something about me. You being an expert and all."

"Right, right, right." Adam dropped his arms to his lap.

"Unless, of course, you're ready to skip over this and deal with the rehab project?"

He kept talking, as if she had never spoken up. "Either Philadelphia was the only one-night stand of your life—"

Becky felt heat rush to her cheeks. "Wait just a second. Are you saying I earned a low grade or something?"

"To borrow your phrase, that's not a knock against your

performance. And stop interrupting me." He hesitated as if waiting for her to agree.

When she stayed quiet, he blustered on. "Or, second option, you had gotten out of a bad relationship, did something out of character—for which I am grateful—and suffered from a twinge of embarrassment."

She clamped her lips together to keep her jaw from dropping to her waistline. Damn, was there a big flashing sign above her head or something? Guessing was one thing. Pulling the two main reasons right out of the air was a whole other matter.

"This is a fascinating discussion and all," she said in her most disinterested voice.

"You are that."

She sat the folder up on her lap and flipped the top open. Her fingers walked through the paperwork as she struggled to figure out a way to diffuse the electricity crackling through the room.

"No response to my, what did you call it . . . insightful something or other?" he asked.

"We talked about the misspelling on page—" She broke off when he sat up and shifted to the front of the sofa. To the very edge of the cushions closest to her.

And that was not the only body part in motion. Nope. His hands did some traveling, too. They did not stop until his palms rested on the outside of her knees, holding her still when she would have backed up into a safer zone.

He treated her to a light stroke, a caress that sparked life into her skin without even touching it directly. His warm stare focused on his hands and her legs.

"What are you doing?" Not one of her smartest questions, to be sure, but a valid one.

"Nothing."

Well, his nothing was touching off a certain something in her. Something she had not felt in months. Eight to be exact.

"I'm trying to work here." She shook the papers under his nose until he peeked up at her.

"Technically, so am I."

"Adam." She put enough warning behind the word to get her point across.

"Keep going. I'm listening to your concerns about the contract."

"Then what did I say?"

"You're at page three, and I'm betting you have a lot more to discuss."

The papers folded in her fist. "Your attention is wandering."

"My focus is solely on you. I promise."

"My body, maybe. Not on what I'm saying."

Those magic fingers of his stopped moving. "I heard you talk about the misspelling."

"Impressive." A man who listened. He grew more attractive by the second.

"For some reason you think there's no 't' in 'wherefore,' " he said.

"Last I checked."

She added one more skill to his already long list of attributes. The guy had a memory as long as—well, it was pretty damn long.

"Got it now. No 't'. Anything else you want to talk about?"

How about he let her in on that concentration trick? Her lungs only functioned because she made a conscious effort to pump air in and out. While she floundered trying to breathe, Adam could remember a tiny detail she threw at him in the heat of battle. Maybe that "Y" chromosome had value other than the obvious after all.

"That was only page three." Two, twenty, or something like that. She could not remember at this point.

"How many pages do we have in total?"

"Thirty-eight."

One of his eyebrows lifted. "You might want to talk faster then."

As she flipped through the pages, black lines passed and blurred until she could not see a clear word. She tried to force her eyes to focus on something other than his long fingers and how far they had inched up her outer thighs.

"Next page." She cleared her throat. "Right near the bottom there's—"

He kissed her knee.

"A . . ."

And again. This time his lips burning through her pants.

"A . . . a . . ." The rest of her sentence caught in her throat.

"A what, Becky?" His lips traveled to her other knee.

"Umm . . ." She was sure she meant to say something.

"Did you find another spelling mistake?"

"No." Her voice actually cracked like a boy hitting puberty.

"We could skip this. Run spell check instead." With his lips pressed against the fabric at the back of her knee, his suggestion rumbled through her.

When he bent over and rested his collarbone against her freshly kissed knees, his face so close to the juncture of her thighs, the papers shook in her hands. He swept those fingers to the top of her thighs and let his mouth wander up the inside of her knees.

She dropped the contracts on the floor. No need to wrinkle them while they . . . they . . .

"I'm ready for the next negotiation point." In between each of the words, he pressed a tiny kiss on her lower thighs. Each one traveling higher than the one before. "If you have another point."

Uh-huh, point. Whatever.

Unable to resist him, she ran her fingers through his soft hair. The caress brought his head closer into her lap. Seeing his head fall against her body, feeling his hands all over her, ignited a fire deep in her belly. One that roared and danced until the flames licked up inside her.

The memories of their previous days together spun through her mind. Two strangers at a legal conference, away from home, not knowing many people and liking even fewer. She had glanced down the bar, seen him leaning over a beer and studying a newspaper rather than reading law journals or networking.

Dark, handsome, and acting like something other than an annoying attorney in a hotel filled with annoying attorneys. No wonder she slept with him.

Not that sex had been the original plan.

Nothing had been working for her at the time. Her short marriage had just ended. Her life consisted of work and work and more work. Shutting out everything and everyone had worked for her growing up. Sitting on that bar stool, watching Adam shell peanuts, she decided to give something new a try as an adult.

Or that was the excuse she used when she sent him a shy smile. When she let him buy her a drink. When he escorted her to his room.

So out of character for her and against everything she believed in. She went in seeking escape. No one warned her she would feel so much. Part of her did not want to read anything into the timing or credit Adam as the source of her intense reaction. But, she could not exactly ignore the "when" and the "with whom" parts of that week.

"Becky?" He lifted his head, his blue eyes gleaming with desire.

Need shot through her. Suddenly she wanted to feel something again.

"Can we run spell check later?" She asked the question in a whisper, as if speaking in a regular voice might break the spell winding around them.

His fingers tightened on her legs for a second. "I think that can be arranged."

Before she could wow him with an irresistible, seductive line, his hands shifted to her backside. With little more than a tug she landed on his lap, her knees straddling his thighs on the antique couch. Her sex separated from his by only a few random pieces of material.

Being tall forever, always towering over everyone, she fought the giant woman mentality. The easy way he handled her filled her with a giggling happiness. In his arms she turned petite and precious. Gangly legs and stretched out limbs disappeared. Her body fit against him at the perfect height. In the perfect way.

When she leaned down and brushed her lips back and forth over his, pressing harder with each pass, his arms swept up her back. Fingers massaged her muscles, causing her to relax against his broad chest. A rush of longing pushed against her.

Then he took over.

The light kisses gave way to deep hunger. His mouth moved and coaxed, wetting her lips, before his tongue rubbed against hers. Deep, dragging kisses stole her remaining resistance, locking her fears and doubts outside her body.

Husky male moans mixed with her soft hums. Cotton scratched against cotton as they fought to get closer, to ease material aside and press skin to skin.

When he shifted, dragging his hands around to the buttons on her sweater, the sofa creaked beneath them. She tried to ignore the sound, but he broke off the kiss. Bouncing a few times, he tested the strength of the frame.

"Damn, honey. This may not hold us."

"Do you really care?" She trailed her lips over his jaw and down his neck.

"Don't care about much other than how fast I can get you out of that sexy blue sweater."

"I like how you think."

"But, your sister might mind if we bust up her house."

Erin. Yeah, easing back into a prone position with Adam was one thing. Announcing her sex life to the world—or worse, to her nosy sister—was not an option she wanted to choose at this point.

"Oh, we can't." She sat up straight and glanced around the room looking for any sturdy surface. "What about—"

"The table." With his hands locked under her thighs he hoisted her tight against his chest and shifted their bodies until her butt hit the hard coffee table.

"Owww."

"Sorry," he muttered.

It was her turn to bounce and test out the new accommodations. "This doesn't seem comfortable."

She didn't know why she bothered with the comment. Adam was too busy loosening the line of small buttons running down the center of her sweater to hear her. Fast and efficient, his fingers worked until he peeled back the edges of her cardigan and exposed her silky camisole.

"Pretty," he whispered.

He dropped to his knees in front of her. This time his body balanced between her legs. "If I'd known that all you had on was that tiny . . ."

"Yeah?" She slid her arms the rest of the way out of the cotton sweater, leaving only the frilly white undergarment.

With his gaze transfixed on her chest, his hand glided up her body, past her tight stomach, over her ribs. To her breast.

"I guarantee you would have lost the sweater hours

ago." The reverence in his voice sent a chill spinning down her spine.

"Aren't you the sweet-talker."

He kissed her breasts where they plumped up over the lace of her camisole. "You're the sweet one. You taste like honey. Smell like flowers."

Yeah, a sweet-talker. One with too many clothes on. "You need to catch up here."

She grabbed the bottom of his sweater and tugged it, along with his undershirt, up and over his head. His hands broke contact with her body only long enough to strip.

His palms returned to her breasts, kneading and cupping her through the flimsy scrap of material. Thumbs rubbed against her nipples, scratching her bare skin with the lacy edge of the camisole. When he finally peeled down the material and the lace bra beneath, revealing her bare breasts to his hot stare and warm tongue, she jumped in surprise.

His tongue flicked against her nipple. The contact, both rough and gentle, made her gasp, a rush of air surging to the back of her throat.

He pulled her against him, pressing her breasts to his chest. Skin finally touched skin, and a wave of dizziness shot through her. While he kissed her, his mouth insistent and eager, his hands pulled first the camisole then the bra over her head between kisses, off her arms and discarded them on the floor.

"Lean back," he mumbled against her lips.

She wanted to obey, but her limbs refused to respond. The signals flashing from her brain to her body went unheeded. Adam must have noticed her hazy state because he guided her back down on the wood and put her feet on the edge of the couch behind him.

In that position, there between her upraised thighs, he concentrated on sliding her belt open and easing her zipper down. She concentrated on him.

Arms out to her sides and legs spread wide, she knew she made quite a picture. A woman lost in passion and eager for more. She should help him. At least return his caresses or something. But all she could do was lift her hips as Adam stripped her black pants and baby blue thong down her legs. Somewhere, somehow, she lost her shoes, until all she wore was a simple watch.

"You are so damned beautiful." His fingers trailed their way up her inner thighs until he found her wetness. "When I close my eyes I see your hair spread out over those white hotel sheets."

"Adam . . ."

"Your body firm and ripe." Two fingers eased deep inside her.

"Yes."

"Damn, you shouldn't have run from me all those months ago."

Before she could protest or defend her actions all those months ago, his mouth traced the path started by his fingertips. Kisses placed in random patterns over her soft skin. Kisses that ended with his tongue plunging inside her.

The balls of her bare feet pressed against the couch. "Right there . . ."

"Promise me." He licked and kissed. Caressed and seduced. "Never again."

"Never." She forced the word out as her chest lifted off the table and her hands tangled in his hair.

Just as the waves of pleasure crested, he pulled back and soothed her, drawing her back from the edge. The process repeated. Each time he brought her trembling to the verge of orgasm only to deny her and build the pressure again.

The tension multiplied with each pass inside her until her body turned to liquid in his hands. Every inch of her readied and opened for his touch. She could feel him prepping her, drawing her out of the rough shell she wrapped around herself for protection.

Her wetness covered his fingers. The more he thrust, the more his thumb traced, the freer she felt.

"Come for me, baby." His request followed some naughty whisperings. Sexy, naughty whisperings.

Her body tightened, responding to his demand. Her biceps shook. Her internal muscles clamped down hard on his fingers as his tongue licked against her. This time he let her fall.

A hard knot exploded inside, sending her back arching and her ankles hugging tight around his waist. Her shoulders scraped against the rough wood while his tongue continued to lap.

With her eyes shut, she fought off the ripples until a shout ripped out of her. Her hips bucked one last time against his mouth. The tiny pulses continued even as her breathing returned to normal.

When she finally opened her eyes, her legs dangled loose against his thighs. Her toes balanced on the edge of the sofa.

Overly sensitive and more satisfied than she ever remembered being, she tried to keep his tongue from brushing against her again. As if the sensation would be too much. An unbearable pleasure bordering on pain.

Adam lifted his head. "You okay?"

"Great."

A wide smile broke across those full lips. "My turn."

"God, yes." She spread her hands to each side and grabbed on to the far ends of the table.

When he sat back on his knees, the move brought his eyes level with her sex. "Like this."

She had to raise her head to see him. "What?"

"Do you trust me?"

Such a simple question. The answer should be no, but it wasn't. With her body, she had nothing but trust in him. He had always treated her with care. A little rougher now and then, but never hurtful. She appreciated the difference. Understood the thin line he wanted to push and reached for it with him.

"Yes."

Heat flared in his eyes at her equally simple answer.

He slipped his jeans and briefs down and stood up. Looming over her, he dropped his clothes the rest of the way to the floor and grabbed a condom out of his back pocket.

"Prepared," she said with a smile.

"Nothing readied me for you, honey. Trust me."

Before she could examine his words, he knelt on the table just under her backside. His palms started at her ankles and then moved to the back of her knees. He lifted her legs into the air, her thighs separated in a deep vee.

With her calves resting against his shoulders and her sex wide open and ready for him, he fit his erection against her. The position left her vulnerable to him. To his needs. From this angle he controlled the pressure. Controlled the thrusts.

She tightened her grip on the wood and held her body steady for the increasing speed of his penetration. Long and thick, he slid inside her. In and out, deep and firm, he plunged into her. Over and over her body rippled and tugged as he pushed to the brink then pulled out again, only to repeat the process.

After only a few minutes, her body clenched for a second time. Like a fist, her muscles stiffened until her toes pointed straight into the air. As he moved, her body clasped his. Her knees pressed tight against her shoulders. Steady breaths pounded out of him as his body slid into hers.

When the frenzy swept through her a second time, she grabbed onto his forearms with all her strength. The last thing she heard was the sound of his shout as it echoed against her own.

Chapter Seven

Making love with Becky got better every damn time. No boredom. Nothing mediocre. No letdown once the fire cooled. No mad rush to the door after he was spent.

Adam realized all of that was true. He just didn't know what the hell to do about it.

Watching Becky now as she lounged in a wooden dining room chair, he felt oddly satisfied. His gaze wandered over her bare feet where they rested on the massive dining room table. Over her lean legs to the edge of his red sweater.

Nothing underneath there either. He saw her slip on his sweater right after they tested the sturdiness of that massive table. He knew what every inch of her body looked like, and everything she wore.

Standing in the doorway in his tee and briefs, he studied her. She missed it because she was studying the rehab documents.

A sense of contentment he rarely achieved moved through him. His previous legal life consisted of getting ahead and winning the game. His current one amounted to little more than getting deals done. But here, now, something felt different. As if the anxiety and internal unease coursing through him ever since he received the first death threat had disappeared.

Part of him knew the relief would dissipate as soon as

they used the last condom, but he wondered. In such a short time, his life had changed so much. His previous priorities had fallen away, leaving him with not a great deal to strive for in terms of his career.

He had broken through and developed an expertise in the tight but lucrative field of white collar defense. No more petty crimes or clients who could not pay. No, he had made it into a different league. One where tracking big-time money made for big-time cases.

The media exposure was not the point, though he received plenty of that. No, he loved the chase. The taste of it. Feel of it.

With all of that gone, nothing excited him. Except Becky, and it had been that way from the beginning. Something in her sparked against something in him.

When she ran, a sense of loss hit him. And anger. What kind of woman walked away from that feeling of rightness mixed with undeniable attraction?

"You going to stand there and stare at me all day, or get me a cup of coffee?" She asked the question without lifting her head.

Adam had to smile at her bossiness. Mostly naked, Becky still thought she made all the rules.

"Maybe I like staring at you." He did, so that wasn't a lie.

"I'd take your peeping better with some coffee."

"Good thing I have some then." He padded into the room, his bare feet tapping against the hardwood floor. "Here you go."

When she looked up, a restless excitement showed on her face. Unfortunately, the look centered on the mug in his hand and not on him.

"Perfect." Becky dropped the papers on her lap and grabbed for the cup with both hands.

"Is your sister's husband still around?"

The mouthful of coffee Becky had just swallowed came right back up again. Her feet dropped to the floor and the papers scattered everywhere.

So did the coffee.

Between the coughing and the choking, she managed to make quite a scene. One that hadn't quite ended yet.

"You have a hell of a time with beverages, don't you?" He took the mug out of her fingers with one hand and patted her back with the other. That left his toes to move the documents from the spill zone.

She sputtered a few more times. When the coughs died down, he jogged into the kitchen and retrieved a towel.

"You okay?" he asked as he cleaned up the coffee from all of the obvious places it had landed. For now, he left his sweater alone, thinking Becky wouldn't appreciate the pawing on top of all the choking.

He sank into the chair next to her. "Can you talk?"

"I'm fine." She sounded the opposite of fine.

"For a woman who wanted coffee, you sure have an odd way of showing it."

"Yeah, well, you could let me swallow before you say things like that."

"All I did was ask about Erin's husband."

Becky took the towel out of his hands and brushed the coffee drops off the front of her sweater. "Erin's not married."

"What?"

"Wrong sister."

The blood drained out of his head. "Wrong . . . what?"

"Can't actually imagine Erin married." When Becky continued to mop up the spill rather than focus on him, Adam grabbed her hand.

"Hey!" she shouted.

"You said she was married."

"Who?" Becky tried to pull away, but Adam wouldn't let go.

"Erin." He took the towel out of her hand and threw it on the table. "I asked about the different last names, and you told me she was married."

Recognition lit Becky's face.

Adam couldn't figure out exactly what it was that had just dawned on her but something had. "Becky?"

"Erin's not married."

"But you said—"

"I said marriage was the reason for the different last names. I didn't say whose marriage."

He heard every word Becky said, but none of them computed. His mind took the sentence apart and tried to rearrange it. He had searched for her, traced her movements, worked his way back into her life. He knew everything about her, including the story of her odd parents. How in the hell had he missed the part about a husband?

"You're married?" Adam didn't even try to keep the fury out of his voice.

"No."

He should have felt relief, but he didn't. "Explain."

Becky's eyebrow inched up. "I don't appreciate your tone."

"I don't appreciate being lied to."

"I never lied."

"So?"

"I was married." She exhaled. "I'm divorced."

He needed to know more. Needed to understand how he had missed such a huge chunk of her life. "When?"

"Look, Adam—"

"When!"

"Don't you dare yell at me!"

He stared at the ceiling in a grab for patience. "Becky, I am trying to figure out if I slept with a married woman."

"Not me."

His heartbeat stopped its gallop. "Then explain."

"Ned and I divorced a while ago. Before you and I ever met."

The pieces settled into place. "How long before?"

She hesitated but answered. "Right before."

"Did you go to the conference looking for a thrill?" For some reason, the idea that he was nothing more than a guy in the right place at the right time made Adam furious all over again.

"No." She focused on her lap, taking her time before responding. "I went to the conference to get away. My firm sent me. I wasn't on the make, if that's your concern."

It was. "My concern is that you'd be sitting here with some other lawyer if I hadn't sat down first."

Her mouth dropped open. "You're judging me?"

"I'm making an observation."

"You're being an ass, Adam." She shoved away from the table and walked over to the antique tea cart in the corner.

"I have a right, don't you think?"

"No one forced you to sit down with me in that bar. No one forced you to spend days with me. To sleep with me."

Days and nights, but who was counting. "I know my motivation in taking you to my room. I'm trying to figure out what yours was in agreeing to leave the bar and go with me."

Her head snapped up. "Funny how you didn't bother to ask for an explanation then."

"I wasn't thinking about anything but getting you alone. That's not exactly a secret, Becky. I didn't hide my attraction."

"While we're on the subject of motivation, what was yours? Why me? Why that night at that bar?"

Damn. He didn't want to explain the restlessness or the need for escape. His reasons made what they shared sound cheap. Made her sound like nothing more than an available body.

He dodged. "That's not the topic under discussion."

"It can be. It's about to be."

"Becky—"

"I want to know." She crossed her arms over her stomach. The move hiked his sweater right to her upper thighs. "And then you can tell me why you convinced Erin to buy this house and if that had anything to do with me."

His mind blanked on her questions. All he could see was the dark shadow between her legs. He knew what hid under there.

That quickly, his mind raced from their argument and her past to how much he wanted her. "I introduced myself because I wanted to get laid."

She bit her lower lip but stayed quiet, so he continued. "It's the same motivation I'm feeling right now."

Her gaze dipped down to his erection then back up again. "You have to be kidding."

"What part of my dick looks as if it's telling a joke?"

"We're fighting."

He noticed that she kept getting lost in the details. Time to straighten her out. "Arguing. Sex. It's all about passion."

"You want to . . . Now?"

All the time. With her, there did not seem to be a stopping point. "Yeah."

She waved her hand in the air. The jerky movements suggested she was losing control as quickly as he was. "What about my motivations and all that stuff?"

"Can wait." He stood up and assessed the room.

The tea thing had to go. He shoved the fragile-looking piece of furniture to the side and corralled her into the corner and trapped her there with one hand on either side of her head.

"Tell me you don't want me," he dared.

"I sure as hell don't understand you." Her hands settled on his waist.

"I'm thinking we get each other just fine." He treated her to a light kiss to prove his point.

"The yelling and the control thing you do? Both annoying."

He nibbled on that fragrant space right below her ear, by her jawline. "You can't resist me."

"Maybe there's a vaccination I could take." The words held a slap but her tone had turned all hot and husky.

With his forehead resting against hers he said, "Touch me."

"We've already christened my sister's dining room." Becky's words suggested she wasn't ready for another round, but her fingers slipped under the elastic of his briefs.

"The table." This time he gave her a hard kiss, one that telegraphed the desire building inside of him. "Or, the wall."

She glanced at his hands on the wall behind her. "You're going to need those if you really want this to work."

"You first." He knew what he wanted.

When heat flashed in her eyes, he knew she got the message.

His palms stayed flat against the wall as she slid down and onto her knees. Watching her like this, from above, so close to his cock, with her light brown hair falling over her shoulders and a hand closing over him, turned every muscle in his body to stone.

As soon as his briefs dropped to the floor, her wet mouth was on him. Licking then sucking, she took him deep inside. In and out. Between her lips.

His hips bucked and a familiar clenching started just below his gut. "Now, Becky."

She didn't stop. Her mouth kept working on him until he hardened to the point of bursting.

"Damn, honey. If you don't come up here, this is going to end too soon."

She gazed up at him, her lips swollen and wet. "I can finish here."

Her whisper tumbled through him. Temptation gnawed at him. But he wanted to be inside her.

"Up," he said, as he grabbed the last condom out of his T-shirt pocket.

She slid up his body, igniting every inch of skin she touched as she went. This woman was pure fire. A witch who had cast a spell over him. One from which he didn't want to break free.

When she stood again, he didn't waste any time. He pulled her sweater off and wrapped both of her long legs around his waist. The quick move knocked her off balance and put her right in his arms. Just as he wanted.

"Are you ready for me, baby?"

"Yes." She moaned the word as her head fell back and rolled against the corner where the walls came together.

"Yes?" Wetness greeted his fingers when he dipped them inside her.

He shifted his weight and pressed against her opening, his tip moving just inside. Her muscles, already swollen from previous lovemaking sessions, protested. With a gentleness and patience he did not feel, he slowed down, easing his body into hers with measured movements.

To ease the way, he pushed deep then retreated and tried again. The friction proved unbearable. After a few shallow thrusts, he plunged deep. His mind registered her shouting of his name and the pleasure in her tone.

Then he lost all control. Mindless of the wall or the tea cart he knocked over with his thigh, he kept going. When her body pulsed and her fingernails dug deep into his forearms, he let go of the last of his restraint.

Their bodies thumped against the wall. The sounds of their deep breathing and desperate groans filled the small room. With one final push, he drove his body forward and exploded inside of her.

Dark spots burst behind his eyes as her thighs clamped down against his hips. Her body let go, bucking and tightening, right after his.

It was not until his skin cooled that he realized he sat slumped on the floor with her curled on his lap. At least now they could say they had tried the table, floor, and wall of the dining room.

For some reason, he wanted more.

Chapter Eight

Becky was pretty sure she had died. A body could not survive that sort of heart-pounding excitement and loss of oxygen, and keep going.

After the fall to the floor and the roll to her side, she lay on the floor next to Adam, both of them naked except for Adam's T-shirt. Their bodies touched only where they held hands. Out of the corner of her eye, she could see broken china and scattered pieces of the tea set behind her.

And a very broken tea cart. The thing now sat in three pieces.

"Erin is going to kill me," Becky mumbled.

"She hate great sex or something?"

Becky had to laugh at that. "Not that I know of."

"Was that the problem with your husband? Bad sex?"

Adam's question, asked in a deceptively lazy tone, sobered her. Hell, he had not even bothered to open his eyes to broach such a private and important topic.

"It was okay."

This time one of Adam's eyes did pop open. "What does that mean?"

"Average."

Both of his eyes were open now. "Low average or high average?"

"You're such a guy."

"Happy you noticed, but you still didn't answer me."

She kind of wished he would ignore that part. But he did not, and she was too satiated to evade. "Ned was a workaholic. Loved his job. Thrived on success. Needed the adrenaline only legal books could provide. I was an add-on, not a necessity."

"I can't believe that."

"I lived it. Trust me, it's true."

"Wait a damn minute." Adam rolled onto his side and perched his head on his palm to stare down at her. "Your husband was Ned Carter?"

"Yeah."

"The appellate court guru?"

"Guru?" Ned couldn't find her g-spot with a diagram and Adam thought of him as a guru? Interesting.

"He's an expert at what he does. A damn genius." Adam actually sounded impressed with the guy who had dumped her the second he learned her top-notch education came from scholarships and not courtesy of family money. The same fabulous husband who tried to bury her past and pretend her parents did not exist.

This was the kind of thing that happened when a couple married in a quickie Vegas ceremony and without getting to know each other on a meaningful level. Worse, this happened because she craved a normal family life—whatever that was—and thought she had found it with a decent guy who shared similar interests.

"Ned may kick butt in the courtroom, but he sucked as a husband."

That seemed to take the air out of Adam. "How?"

"Do we have to talk about this? I find cases from the 1800s more enlightening than the details of my short marriage." She found almost every other topic of conversation in the universe more comfortable.

"I think we do." He sat up straighter. "Yeah."

She was stuck in the conversation now. No way to turn back. "Ned worked all the time. Had political aspirations. Problem was, when his team of paid public relations people and politicos looked into my background, they decided I was a huge liability."

"You have a skeleton?"

"Don't we all?"

He treated her to one very sexy smile. "What's so bad about you?"

"Not really me. My parents. They were what some might call religious freaks."

"Oh, that."

A sudden pressure thumped behind her eyes. "You know?"

"Of course."

"How? Why?"

"When I went looking for the woman who ran out with my coffee, I found the connection. Some of the news clippings contradicted each other, but I worked it out. Also figured out Erin was your sister. Missed the marriage and figured you had changed your name."

"Ned's handlers made me disappear out of any record of his life. My parents' pretending I didn't exist made that easier." The memory made her wince. She wondered if it would always make her wince.

"Why did they—"

"Care to explain why you tried to hunt me down?"

"For my coffee."

"And why you convinced Erin to buy this house?"

"I really like coffee."

"Adam, tell me."

"I wanted to know more about the woman who ran. Then I stumbled across your parents and the cult—" His sentence broke off.

"It's okay."

"I shouldn't have said that."

"It is a cult. A very unhealthy place. The stuff you read in the news about the snakes and strange happenings is only part of it."

"Do you have any relationship with them?"

"Not really." The feel of his warm palm against her stomach settled her rattling nerves. Gave her the strength to talk about a subject she never shared with anyone other than Erin. "Believe it or not, they weren't always this way. Sure, they had odd ideas and beliefs that ventured far outside of traditional church teachings, but they had some tie to reality."

"You grew up with them?"

"On and off. Once we hit the teen years, mostly off. My father's father saw to that. Insisted on taking us out of the farmhouse and putting us in boarding school. By the time my parents headed to Idaho, Erin and I were older and away most of the time. We'd been to school. Knew our parents' ways were well outside the norm."

"And now?"

"I'm out. You've probably read their rantings about their evil daughter. That's me. Between being a lawyer and getting divorced, I destroyed whatever feelings they still had for me." She covered her eyes with the heels of her hands.

"That sucks."

"Yeah, but it might be better. For some reason, they've decided to claim Erin and have started mentioning her and giving away private aspects of her life."

"That's how I found Erin."

"I figured as much." She blew out the air blocking her lungs. "But, we don't get to pick our parents."

"No, but we should be able to expect unconditional love from them."

"Is there such a thing?"

"Of course. Parental love shouldn't come with ties. They

owed it to you to put you first. Ned should have dc
as well. The whole way around you got screwed on t
thing."

He made something so complicated seem simple. Somehow he put into words the pain she felt.

The understanding and acceptance in Adam's voice broke the dam free inside of her. Encouraged her to go on.

She let her hands fall on the floor beside her head. Let the words flow without censoring them. "Growing up with the snake handling, the poison, the danger, all of it was so scary. But I survived it. Asking me to pretend my life with my parents didn't exist was too much for Ned to expect."

Adam stilled. "That was Ned's brilliant plan? Pretend you didn't have parents?"

"He wanted me to pretend I had other parents. Acceptable parents who were dead and, therefore, unavailable to the press. He wanted me to take everything I was, everything I overcame, and bury it."

"Fucking idiot."

Becky thought so too. Erin had even stronger words to describe Ned. "I don't talk about them since I refuse to let them rule any part of my life, but my parents are part of who I am. In the privacy of a marriage, Ned should have been able to accept that."

"He should have accepted you."

Adam's rush to her defense made her smile. "You don't sound shocked or repulsed by my parents."

He shrugged. "I'm a together guy."

"And so modest."

Adam touched her nose with his forefinger, then kissed her in the same spot. "And born and raised in the South. I heard all about the snake-handling churches growing up. I've read about your parents and know you aren't like them."

She fought every day not to be them. "I only hear a faint southern accent."

"Buried it while in law school."

Now there was an interesting comment. "Why?"

"You know how it is. Competitive. Many people believe being from the South proves you're stupid."

"Certainly sounds like something Ned would say."

She meant the comment as a harmless joke.

Adam took immediate insult. "I'm nothing like the jackass you married."

Now that she thought about it . . . "Actually, you are."

"How can you say that?" Adam sat up and loomed over her, trying his damnedest to intimidate her.

She refused to be brushed aside. "You worked your way up to partner in record time. You won praise for your work in the courtroom. Your name is all over the *Bar Journal*. You're quoted in the paper. You're well known."

"Being successful doesn't make me an unfeeling ass."

"I didn't say that, but achieving the kind of success you did, and so quickly, comes with a price."

"Enlighten me, Miss Know-It-All."

What started as a joke had morphed into something very different. Something with a sharp edge.

"Like Ned, you sacrificed everything for your job. Look at you, no steady relationship. Picking up women in bars—"

"That was you!"

"And, as you said, I know why I was there." She hesitated. Hated to break the tenuous understanding they had reached. But she had to know. "Why were you in that hotel bar, Adam?"

"A man can't get a drink without having an ulterior motive?"

She refused to drop the topic. Not when Adam was so hell-bent on resisting. "Let me try it another way. Why the big change from legal star to corporate grunt?"

"Grunt?"

"Why did you give up the limelight and the prestige?"

Sitting did not work. She needed to be on her feet. She stood up and slipped his sweater over her shoulders. Something about wearing clothing made her feel more in charge and less vulnerable.

Now that she had started down this road, she kept traveling. "My guess is that you burned out. Or, you hit a snag in that fast-rising career and ran."

"You don't know shit." Adam jumped to his feet and searched around the floor.

"What are you looking for?"

"My underwear. Since you're wearing my sweater, I have to find something else to put on."

He pushed the broken tea cart aside and dragged out his briefs. After giving them a shake or two, he stepped into them. He yanked with such force, she was surprised the briefs didn't end up on his head.

"I'll have you know I left my job because I had to," he said between clenched teeth.

"I knew it." She nodded her head in victory. "For the sake of your mental health, right? Your drive burned your body right out."

"Wrong, wrong, and leave my body out of this."

"Then what was it? What derailed the illustrious career of Adam Thomas? What could possibly have wrestled you away from your precious desk and your precious courtroom?" She asked her questions in a booming theatrical voice.

"A death threat."

He did not yell. Did not use force. Just stated the fact in a tone equal parts soft and menacing.

And her bravado puddled on the floor at her feet. "What threat?"

"A money laundering case turned into a series of threats against my life, my assistant's life, and . . ."

She dreaded what came next. "And?"

"My brother's life."

"Whit?" She reached out to him, but he batted her hands away. "Adam, I'm so sorry."

"I could take whatever they threw at me. But, Whit? That was too much." Adam started pacing, watching each step and dodging pieces of broken glass and china as his bare feet hit the hardwood floor.

"Couldn't the police do something?"

Adam rubbed the back of his neck. "They shadowed Whit to offer protection, but the threats kept coming. Photos of Whit doing mundane things delivered to my mailbox in plain white envelopes. The goal was to ensure that I'd know he was being followed and at their mercy. Then photos came of Whit and his wife, Hannah."

Becky covered her mouth with her fist. "Oh my God."

"I couldn't protect them."

"So you left the practice? I don't know your brother. What was his reaction?"

Adam glanced at her then back to the floor. "He doesn't know."

"What?" She dropped her hand. "How is that even possible?"

"The FBI stepped in. I didn't want to scare Hannah or worry Whit. This solution was easier."

"Giving up everything you worked for? Adam, that's insane."

"So, I guess I'm less like Ned and more like a quitter now, huh?"

Adam had that part wrong. Dead wrong. In her book, he was not anything like Ned. Sure, when she initially made the comment, she thought Adam's work ethic mirrored Ned's. Now she knew Adam towered above Ned in all things, including ethics.

Adam's problem was too much loyalty. Too much caring. Not too little.

"I didn't say that," Becky insisted.

"You didn't really have to. The judgment is pretty obvious in your voice."

"Then you're not paying attention."

Adam's face went blank. "Let me ask you something."

She steeled her spine, knowing he was about to deliver a blow. She could see it flashing in his eyes and in his stiff stance. An offensive strike.

"Go ahead." She said it, but did not mean it.

"Don't you think it's a bit hypocritical of you to judge me, when you're the one who lost her job due to improper conduct?"

There it was. More of her past. The part she refused to own because it was all lies.

"I didn't do anything wrong."

"That's not what I heard," Adam said in a smug tone.

Dizziness threatened to knock her over. "How did you hear anything?"

"I told you. I checked you out."

"Right." All of her muscles failed her. Her hands dropped to her sides and her butt fell into the nearest chair.

"I'm not the only one who enjoyed some success. You did pretty well. Until your boss's wife found out you were screwing her husband, of course."

Becky's insides felt as if someone had scraped them out and left them hollow. "That never happened."

"The way I figure it, I was part of your pattern. You lost your husband, then went out looking for fun. There I was. You hitched your legal wagon to a bigger star, but then went too far and had to regroup. Looking for some fun again, who do you track down? Me."

All of his perceptions and assumptions were wrong. Nothing Adam said had any basis in fact. Her emotions wavered between fury and disappointment. Both did battle inside her.

Anger won.

Becky launched herself against his chest. All of her weight landed with a thud against him. Beating her fists on his muscles and calling him every name she could think of, she didn't care if he even could feel her, she just wanted to hurt him.

"Becky! Stop."

She continued to clobber him. It was either hit him or cry all over him. She never wept and certainly didn't intend to start now.

Adam tried to calm her, to wrap his arms around her. She shoved him away. "No. Don't touch me."

"Becky, listen—"

"No." She smoothed the sweater down to make sure every bare part of her stayed covered. "You have everything wrong. I didn't sleep with my boss. I found out he was playing with the firm's escrow account. Something for which he would have been disbarred. Rather than take the risk, he discredited me. Got another associate, one almost as desperate as Ned, to back up the story. Convinced the wife it was better to have people think he fooled around than have him get caught with a hand in the till, lose his job, and her lose her source of funding."

Adam reached for her again. "Listen to me."

She slapped his hand away. "I don't know why you bothered to check on me, but whatever you found wasn't true. I was a damn good attorney."

"You haven't caught a break."

"I don't expect breaks."

A look, one almost of sadness, filled his eyes. "What was I to you?"

She refused to be swayed. The wound was too fresh. "A distraction."

Letting out all of that frustration felt good. Freeing. All those pent-up denials and all that disappointment flooded out of her. Adam presented her with the perfect excuse to lose control. To vent. To spew all the nastiness that had built up inside of her.

And she intended to keep up the steady stream of rants as long as she could. She feared stopping. Feared letting the sadness drift back in. To do so would invite pain.

Loving Adam sucked.

The idea settled in her brain with enough force to crack her skull wide open. Adam made her feel cherished and special, alive and powerful. For the first time, she had found someone who accepted her for her.

That's what she thought until two seconds ago when he made her feel dirty and stupid.

"Okay." He blew out a long breath. "We've gotten off course."

Just in time. If Adam had not turned on her, she might be in his arms right now. She might have let herself believe. She knew from experience that road did not lead anywhere good for her. Ever.

"I think we're finally right where we should be." She lifted his sweater over her head.

"What are you—"

And threw it at him.

Adam did not try to catch it. The material slid off his chest and fell to the floor.

Standing naked and proud, she stared him down. "I wouldn't dream of taking your clothes. Of taking anything from you."

"We need to talk about this."

"No, we don't. We are done. Finished."

"I didn't—"

"Hope this ending is clear enough for you."

Chapter Nine

Done. This time Becky had said the words.

Adam decided he liked it better when she made him guess.

He slipped on his pants and shoes and gathered up all of the documents scattered on the floor. He would get the rest of the mess later.

Upstairs he could hear water running and a good deal of stomping around. At one point he even heard Becky yelling into her cell phone. He wondered what poor bastard was unlucky enough to be on the receiving end of that.

By the time she pounded down the stairs an hour later wearing her professional outfit, everything was in place. Not even a hair dared to land in the wrong position on her head.

She saw him sitting on the living room coffee table, documents stacked on his lap, and stopped dead. "You're still here?"

"We have to finish the contracts."

"I thought your answer to everything was a big, fat 'no,' or have you changed your mind?"

He had. Just not on the topic she thought.

Before Becky, he could not feel anything. Did not care about anything. Then she walked into his life and turned it upside down, leaving a lingering memory that would not fade. Hell, he had never tracked down a woman in his life. The woman who had never known true love, had never had one person except her sister love her for her, refused to leave his head.

Whatever they had together amounted to more than great sex. Great sex did not drive a man to his knees or make him reorder his priorities.

He was falling for her. The truth was he had fallen for her months ago. Those feelings simmered and grew until he saw her again. Then they exploded in his face.

"I owe it to your sister to see this through. So do you." Playing on Becky's loyalty was not his most attractive moment, but desperation pushed him. He could not let her walk out on him again.

"All of a sudden you care about Erin?"

"I care about doing my job."

Becky dropped her purse on the floor with a thud and entered the room. "Of course. I should have known. Work."

She sat down hard on the couch. As far away from him as possible. Good thing the sofa was short or she would have been in the next room.

He handed the documents to her. "Where were we?"

"I don't remember." Her tone was as cold as the look in her eyes.

"I do."

She stared at the documents. "Go ahead then."

"My job loss was supposed to be temporary."

Becky did not lift her head, but she stopped pretending to read. Her eyes focused on the top of the page.

"The idea was to let the people issuing the threats think they'd won and then go after them on the sly. That's happening now. That's what the FBI is doing as we speak."

Becky looked up this time.

"But, I don't know if I can go back." He wiped his hands on his pants. His nerves of steel abandoned him. For the first time in his life he had a speech to make and a wave of nervousness flipping through his stomach threatened to stop him.

"Why?"

"The idea of putting people I care about in danger is intolerable."

"Makes sense, but—"

He needed to get it out. Could not let her sidetrack him with another subject. "It was easier to stay unattached. To not let someone else into my risk zone. See, it never occurred to me Whit would become a target. Or Hannah."

"You want to protect them."

"To protect *everyone* I care about. Everyone I love and am starting to love." He exhaled long and hard. "For a man who took calculated risks in front of juries, I don't have any experience with the same in my personal life."

Her eyes narrowed in confusion. "Meaning?"

He shifted to the side until he sat in front of her. When he slipped his fingers through hers, she did not grab hold, but she did not back away either.

"When you walked out eight months ago, you took a piece of me with you. I never expected it. Never asked for it."

"Adam—" She choked a little, so he pressed on before she could tell him to go to hell.

"I hunted you down because I didn't want whatever we had to end. For the first time in my life, I found something, someone, who gave me a bigger high than practicing law. You filled the void left when I walked away from the courtroom. I didn't need the adrenaline or the success. All I wanted was to spend time getting to know you."

"I didn't know."

"I could tell by the way you ran like hell."

"You weren't the only scared one."

There it was—a reason for him to press on. "Finding out about you was easy enough, except for the Ned part. Who your parents were never bothered me. If anything, seeing who they were and knowing who you had become made me even more impressed with you."

She caressed his cheek. "Oh, Adam."

"When I heard about your job . . ." He stopped, not sure where to go from here.

"It's not true, Adam."

He grabbed her hand before it dropped from his face. "I know. I believe you."

"You didn't an hour ago."

"I was mad. Lashed out. I'm sorry for that."

She shot him a lopsided grin. "It's okay."

"It's not. But, know that I never doubted your integrity. I know you're telling me the truth." He did with a rock hard certainty that hit him out of nowhere. "At first it was easier to believe the rumors and decide you were a certain type of woman than to believe you walked out because you weren't interested."

She scooted to the edge of the couch and looked into his eyes in a way that even a clueless moron like him could see included caring and maybe even the seeds of love. The knowledge filled him with a satisfaction that had him smiling.

But he needed to hear the truth.

As if sensing his concern, Becky filled in the gaps. "I was restless and lonely when I walked into that bar eight months ago. I didn't go looking for a fling. An escape is more like it. Then we . . . you . . ."

"You can say it."

"So bossy." She rolled her eyes. "Let me tell it my way."

"Sorry."

"The feelings inside me. The sense of rightness and comfort that hit me while we were together. I panicked."

He didn't understand this part. "Damn it, why? Why run?"

"You were an extended one-night stand. I didn't know if this was the kind of thing you did. All I knew was a bit about your reputation. That you loved the law like Ned loved the law. I couldn't handle one more person who put me second."

"Your parents."

"Second to their perverted view of religion." She squeezed his fingers. "I wanted to be first. To mean something."

"You did." Adam needed her to believe, so he tried again. "You do."

"When Erin told me she had been dealing with you, well, I had to see. I thought if we met again, I'd see it was a short-term fizzle and be able to move on."

"Sounds a lot like my plan. Once I found out Erin was looking for a home and a studio, the rest was easy." Expensive but easy. "I let Erin lead me to you. All I had to do was add a few not-so-proper terms to the agreement and let her lawyer sister come to the rescue."

She chuckled. "I thought if we met up again we might laugh about what happened at the conference, get a drink, and become friends."

"I don't think of you as a friend."

That killed her laughter. "You don't?"

He held up a hand. "For people who make their living communicating, we're doing a piss-poor job."

"I thought I was doing okay."

He moved to sit next to her on the uncomfortable sofa. One arm wrapped around her shoulders and the other held on to her fingers on her thigh. "Let's try this again."

"Okay." She smiled up at him with a warmness that pushed out the lingering cold inside him.

"If you hadn't left the hotel that day, I would have told you I wanted to see you again. Wanted to figure out what we had and could have."

"Why, Adam, I do think you're a romantic."

"Then wait until you hear this part." He swallowed a bucket of pride and went for broke. "Sometime during the last eight months I would have made an admission. Would have told you that I fell for you during those initial days in the hotel. That I wanted to keep falling for you."

Her eyes grew shiny. "Falling as in . . . ?"

The happiness inside him turned to laughter. "Are you trying to get me to say something?"

"I'm not getting any younger while we're sitting here."

The word no longer felt wrong or odd on his tongue. "Love."

"After only a few days?"

"Shocked the hell out of me too." He shook his head. "Look, I don't pretend to understand it. All I know is that being with you now, I don't see how I could be without you again."

For a second Becky just sat there in a perfect lawyer pose.

Then she whooped and jumped into his lap. With her arms wrapped around his neck, she rained kisses all over his face. "I should let you talk more often."

He kissed her right back. "I guess this means I'm not alone."

She pulled back and shot him one of her seductive smiles. "That depends."

"Care to tell me on what?"

"On how smart you are."

"Want to see my law school transcripts?"

"Definitely not." She tipped her head to the side. "Work."

"You lost me."

"You have to go back to the work you love. I'm sure Whit wants you to be happy. I want you happy."

She whipped him in so many directions that Adam did not know what to think or say. "I can't risk it."

She placed a finger over his lips. "When you're ready, we'll talk to Whit. Then you'll go back to the job you love."

"All I want to get back to is you."

"Good answer. Now, don't go thinking my life is all about Adam or something." Her cocky swagger grew serious. "But loving you means wanting what you want and what's best for you."

"Loving, huh?"

"Looks as if it's going that way." She said it. She felt it. After only a few days, they had an unbreakable bond.

"Good to know I'm not alone." He kissed her then. He could not hold back one more second. She offered him everything. Gave him permission to stop feeling guilty.

She hugged him close. "Anything else you want, Mr. Super Lawyer?"

"Well, one thing . . ."

She frowned but had trouble holding down the corners of her mouth. A smile kept trying to come out. "Tell me."

"Let's try out that big bathtub upstairs."

She threw back her head and laughed. "I offer you anything, and you ask for a bath?"

"You naked in a tub with me." He winked at her. "Got it?"

"I think we're communicating just fine."

"And it's going to stay that way."

"Count on it."

MAN AT THE DOOR

Chapter One

"I need to move in."

Ray Hammond dropped his morning bombshell without missing a step. He walked into the historic house in the middle of Washington, D.C., holding a moving box in his arms. Kept right on going through the living room and into the kitchen.

Erin McHugh was not the sort of woman to run after a man, but Ray had her jogging to keep up. "Move where?"

"Here." He called the answer over his shoulder as he slid the box onto the counter next to the sink. The move lifted his baseball shirt up just far enough to flash a thin sliver of taut, muscled back.

Erin looked everywhere but at the peek of skin. "As in my house?"

"Where else?"

"You do have a house of your own you can live in."

"It's a condo." He rummaged around in the box.

"So?"

"I'm losing too much time driving back and forth. It makes more sense for me to be here and work at night."

"Are you asking me or telling me?"

This time he turned around and faced her. No matter how many times she saw him head-on, the impact did not lessen. The light brown hair hanging over his forehead. Those dark brown eyes sparkling with mischief. The wide, sexy shoulders. The slim waist. The boyish smile. All of it knocked her on her drooling butt.

"If you want the house renovated in time for the wedding, I need to stay here." His eyes narrowed. "We talked about this."

"You mentioned something about travel time."

"So what's the problem?"

A lack of self-control and a case of fading common sense. "We didn't decide on anything."

"You want to vote on my temporary living arrangements?"

"I just think you should ask me. Not assume."

"So, this is a semantics issue." He picked up her bagel and took a big bite.

"More like a courtesy issue." She watched the bagel get smaller and smaller. "And, help yourself."

"Thanks."

"I was being sarcastic."

"Believe it or not, I could tell."

Even though she had every right to stand there and make her point, she debated slinking back out of the kitchen. Something about Ray's self-assurance and larger-than-life presence always managed to suck the air out of her lungs. But skulking did not suit her style either.

The point of settling down and buying the old house, fixing it up, and building a new life, was to put a stop to all of the hiding and running. She needed a quiet life outside the media spotlight. Her career as an artist provided that solitude.

Until Ray stepped into her life and stomped all over her sense of calm.

Ray abandoned whatever he brought in the box and her mostly eaten bagel. Walking nice and slow—and no man on

Earth possessed a more potent strut than Ray Hammond—he closed in on her before she could slip out the door.

With her back pressed against the wall and his palms balanced on either side of her head, he leaned in close. "May I please move in with you, Ms. McHugh?"

No. No. No. "You're crowding me."

"That's the idea."

"What happened to being courteous?"

"I'm asking your permission all nice just as you requested."

She swallowed a big ball of lust and pointed to the sink on the other side of the room. "You could do it from over there."

"I could, but you know what?" His lips hovered right over her ear, close enough to send puffs of air against her skin. "I prefer being close to you."

His woodsy smell, a mixture of the outdoors and musky masculine soap, wound around her head and dove deep in her senses. "We shouldn't—"

"Talk?"

The dizziness that hit her the second his skin brushed against hers refused to go away. Ray had affected her this way almost from the start. Despite the different backgrounds. Despite his love of the limelight. Despite the seven-year age difference between them. Despite it all, she wanted him with a white hot energy that made her stupid.

So she kept her distance. Except for now when the space between them equaled less than zero.

Big mistake.

"Erin, are you daydreaming?"

He pulled back just far enough for her to see the gold flecks in his dark brown eyes. Being close in height, her five-eleven to his six-foot-one, she did not have to look up or down. She saw him more or less straight on, which only highlighted his potency.

The low-riding jeans and shirt skimming his hips suggested a carefree easiness in his skin. So did the lazy, come-play-in-my-bedroom look lingering in his eyes.

Erin chalked up his appeal to his being a bit rough around the edges and very open about his sexual needs. The sort of comfortable she associated with a parade of women marching through his bedroom. In other words, trouble.

"This is my house."

"And this is my job." His hands stayed balanced against the wall while his eyes conducted a quick search down her body.

The suggestive glances had started weeks before when their relationship morphed from bickering to flirting. A gentle brush against her shoulder here. An occasional touch of his legs or hands against hers there. Sitting close as they reviewed house plans. More and more hours at the house with her.

Either Ray was making a move or her fantasies had torn from her dreams and started haunting her waking hours. The options sounded good on an emotional level. Not on an intellectual one.

"Unless you want Aubrey to fall through the stairs in her wedding dress, you need to let me do things my way," he said with a focused attention that made Erin squirm under her skin.

Instead of showing a reaction to his closeness, of reaching out and grabbing him around the waist like she wanted to, she plastered her palms against her khaki pants and dug her fingernails into her thighs.

"The house is not that bad."

"Have you seen the inspection reports? There's a crap-load of work to get done."

She cut him off before he gave her a list. "We've made significant progress."

"Which means the house now is structurally sound. But

if Cole weren't in such a huge rush to race Aubrey down the aisle and slam a ring on her finger, I'd suggest we postpone the ceremony for a few weeks to get the details done."

Erin tried to imagine Cole's reaction if Ray suggested a postponement. The guy had practically frothed at the mouth when Aubrey insisted on an actual ceremony rather than a quickie exchange of vows in Las Vegas. Cole and Aubrey met in this very house six months earlier. Cole proposed after four.

"Cole would kill you."

"He threatened to do more than that." Ray shook his head in a mixture of awe and confusion. "The guy fell in love and lost his fu—"

"Yes?"

"Mind." Ray let out a half-cough, half-swear and all fake sound. "Lost his mind."

"Uh-huh."

Erin had to smile at Ray's stumble. She knew he watched his language around her. But between Cole and Aubrey's wedding plans, and Adam's dropping to one knee and proposing to Becky two weeks ago after being together only a few months, one would think all of the men at their company, T.C. Limited, had gotten stuck in the tush with Cupid's arrow. Erin half-expected Ray to pack his bags and head to wherever the single men hung out to escape wedding chatter.

The thought of Ray's leaving, of not seeing him every single day like she had for months, sobered her. "Could you back up a little?"

"I'm fine right here."

The man was more than fine, but his proximity made her mind wander well off task and straight to him. "I'm betting you don't move in at every house construction job you have."

"Some."

"Oh, come on."

His eyebrow lifted until it disappeared underneath the sweep of his bangs. "Want to see my pay sheets?"

That seemed like a bit much to ask. "Of course not."

"When the amount of time left to finish the job is short, I make compromises. If one of those is sleeping somewhere other than in my own bed, so be it."

"That doesn't seem fair."

"I make it work."

She had no one to blame for the potential delay but herself. "I know I've been pretty firm about not having strangers in my house—"

"Understandable."

"—but maybe we could hire on more people."

"Not necessary. I can do the job."

She guessed he could do just about anything and make it seem easy. Ray turned out to be one of the most capable people she had ever met. From plumbing to electricity to basic construction to car repair, the guy excelled at it all. That combined with his raw sex appeal and ability to hold a conversation on just about every topic, meant Ray bordered on irresistible. Which made writing him off as just another attractive young guy even harder.

"Besides, Whit and Cole are pitching in." Ray shot her one of his playful smiles. "Hell, even Adam promised to throw off the lawyer suit and help out."

"Adam knows how to use a hammer?" Erin tried to picture her future brother-in-law using his hands on anything but her sister and could not do it.

"He does when Cole is standing behind him barking out orders."

"It's just that the house has to be done in three weeks no matter what." Erin knew Ray understood all of this, but she laid it out anyway just to be clear. "I want everything perfect for Aubrey's wedding."

"Cole and Aubrey."

"What?"

"The wedding's for both of them." Ray's smile filled his face with a warmth that sent her stomach tumbling down to her shoes. "And the house will be ready."

"I believe you."

"Good." He leaned in closer until less than five inches separated his lips from hers. "Because I've never been anything but honest with you."

"They met here." She blurted out the comment when his gaze moved from her eyes to her lips.

He moved back an inch. "I know."

"Started falling for each other right in this room."

His dark gaze met hers again. "I know that too."

"They've spent a lot of time in the house. It means a great deal to them."

And with that, she officially moved into babbling.

Erin tried to stop the verbal spill but the words kept rushing out. The more she tried to slow down, the faster she bumbled along. Talking about romance and thinking about Ray's sleeping one floor away kept the nonsense words flowing.

"That's not news either." His smile grew wider until his perfect white teeth peeked out. "See, I was around when Cole and Aubrey got together. Saw the whole thing."

"Really?"

"Well, not the good parts."

"Aubrey will be relieved to know that."

"My point is, I know how important this job is and take it seriously. That's why I'm moving in."

"You're still not asking."

"You're the one with the deadline." Ray shifted his head, letting his bangs slide off to the side. "But the wedding isn't the only reason this house needs to get done."

"The wedding is the important thing."

"There's also the part where this is your house and your future place of business."

She shrugged as if that part was unimportant, even though the opposite was true. "Uh-huh."

"Your sanctuary."

She had never told him about her life, her needs, or her desire for privacy. Still, from the beginning, he seemed to sense her need to be in this house. To not have a constant stream of workmen walking through the place.

"You need the house completed," he said in a husky tone that dipped even lower than usual.

"True."

Ray's dark gaze searched her face then locked on her mouth.

This time there was no mistaking his intent. His elbows bent bringing his body close to hers. Against hers.

His voice dropped to a harsh whisper. "So, will you open up and make room for me?"

In the universe of suggestive comments, that one ranked right up there. Erin thought about laughing the moment off, shoving him off her, and playing the whole thing as a joke. Problem was, nothing about the moment seemed funny.

"This is for work only."

"What else would there be between us?"

"I'm serious." One of them had to be.

"You're the boss." He nodded in the least convincing show of agreement ever. "Your rules."

Right. "Then you should back up."

"You sure?"

She had no idea. "Yes. This has to stay professional."

"This?"

"Us." She tried to wave her hand between them but ended up knocking her fist against his firm chest and yanked it back.

"Why is that again?"

Yeah, why? "Because . . . because . . ."

"That's what I thought." He lifted his hands and backed

away until there was almost enough space for another person to stand between them. "You win."

"Good." Not good but necessary. "I'm happy we understand each other."

"We do. You set the pace, and I'll follow."

"I said rules not pace."

"You have your words. I have mine." He leaned back against the kitchen table. "I am a patient man, Erin."

The curveball had her shaking her head. "What does that have to do with rehabbing the house?"

"Not a damn thing."

"Then—"

"That's what I'm trying to tell you." He crossed one ankle over the other and rested his weight back on his palms.

Confident. Calm. His relaxed stance said it all.

"You lost me."

"As far as I'm concerned our relationship has very little to do with construction at this point."

Her head started spinning again. "Well, sure. We're also friends."

"I don't need more friends."

"What does that mean?"

She liked him. Really liked him. They should never be lovers. In the range of bad ideas, that one ranked way up there. But, she wanted them to be more than civil acquaintances.

"Until you decide what you want and when you want it, I'll be right here." He rapped his fist against the table in a knock.

"In the kitchen?"

"In your house."

"If you think that's necessary."

"Sleeping downstairs in the small room next to the bathroom."

Just hearing the words sent a tremor skipping down her spine. "Fine."

"Waiting."

For her. He did not need to add more. She knew exactly what he meant. They had been circling each other, toying with the idea of sex without ever talking about the possibility . . . or about what would happen after, during the awkward, post-sex period.

They knew all the same people. He would move on. She would get back to work. Being together in a group after being together in bed would be strained. His endless rounds with women would start over again. And she did not want to be a part of any of that.

"We've gotten off topic," she said in what was one of the biggest understatements of all time.

"Not as far as I'm concerned."

"We should put up the molding in the parlor today."

One of his eyebrows pushed up. "It's not like you to hide from a challenge, but if you want to keep running around in circles, I'll play along."

"I didn't—"

"For now." He slid off the table to stand in front of her one more time.

A smart woman would have moved away from the wall when she had the chance. Maybe—for protection—picked up a frying pan, or whatever protected a smart woman from a twenty-seven-year-old guy who dripped with frank sex appeal.

She just stood there plastered to the wall. Ready for another round. "Thank you."

"You should know something."

He did not touch her. Did not have to. His mere presence made her heart dance around in her chest.

"What?"

He leaned down and whispered against her ear a second time. "My bedroom door will always be unlocked for you."

Chapter Two

"You look like a man with something on his mind." Whit Thomas delivered the comment without ever sparing a glance at Ray.

"A guy gets married and starts thinking he knows everything," Ray muttered under his breath.

"Damn straight."

"Your radar is off. Nothing's wrong."

Covered in dust and tired from hours spent repairing the floor, Ray plunked his butt down on the coffee table. He sat there in the middle of Erin's living room and peeled off his work gloves.

"Doesn't sound that way," Whit said.

"You're a voice expert now?"

"I don't remember your being this defensive when you signed on as job foreman with our company."

Ray wiped his hands on the T-shirt under his flannel shirt. "I didn't know any better then."

"Do you now?"

Ray's head shot up. The fact that Whit still had not bothered to make eye contact with him ruined the delivery of Ray's otherwise perfect kiss-my-ass scowl. "I could kick that ladder out from under you."

Whit's hands froze in the air. "You get one shot, then you better run like hell and keep on running."

"Unless you plan to use the car, I'm not worried about getting caught, old man."

Whit belted out a sharp laugh. "This old man can still outrun you."

Ray did not doubt it. Whit might be an architect, but he was no desk jockey. The guy worked harder than almost anyone on the T.C. Limited crew.

"Now that we've gotten that out of the way. What's up?" Whit shifted away from the crown molding repair and rested his elbow on the top of the ladder to face Ray down. "I can hear you thinking from over here."

Ray knew trying to divert Whit's attention qualified as a waste of time. "Women."

"Ah." Whit nodded in a basic male understanding of the absolute unpredictability of the opposite sex. "Figured a female might be the root of the problem."

"They suck."

Whit waited a few seconds before commenting. "Never heard a guy complain about that before."

"What?"

"Maybe your women aren't, you know, doing it right or something. You could teach—"

That was more than enough of that conversation. "Damn, Whit."

"I'm trying to help."

"Suck, as in speak a different language and worry every little detail to death."

"Oh, that kind of suck." This time Whit hummed as he considered the global ramifications of trying to understand women. "Yeah. Who would have guessed that such soft, adorable creatures could cause so much trouble?"

Whit's wife owned a construction company. Hannah was tall, blond, beautiful, and downright lethal. Ray had heard the woman yell at workmen twice her size, then seen her turn around and plant a porn-worthy kiss on Whit. An amazing woman. Not at all soft and sometimes scary.

"Bored with married life already, old man?"

Whit shot his friend a satisfied grin. "Do I look bored to you?"

"More like stupid-ass in love." Ray slapped his gloves against his jeans and watched the resulting dust cloud. "There's a lot of that going on around here."

"You should try it."

"Pass."

Whit climbed down and sat on the floor next to the ladder with an arm balanced over his knee. "Which woman is making you chase your tail?"

"None."

Whit scoffed. "Give me a break. You've stopped going out. You've all but moved in here and taken up the life of a monk."

Since the celibate part was not far off, Ray ignored it. "I officially start bunking here tomorrow."

"You work round the clock."

"So?"

"You used to have a social life. Months ago you went out with those twins. Then there was that brunette with the huge—"

"Your point?"

"What happened to the guy with all the hot date stories?"

"Ray's telling a hot date story? Perfect timing." Adam came down the stairs wearing his now regular stupid grin. "Count me in."

"I don't have any stories."

Whit nodded in the direction of his brother's untucked shirt. "Guess you're here to give Becky a wake-up call."

"It's one of the benefits of being an engaged man."

"I heard Becky banned you from the house. Put a big 'keep out' sign over the bed." Whit smiled at the thought.

The reminder slapped the amusement right off Adam's face. "She said we couldn't live together before marriage, which is the damn dumbest idea I have ever heard from a woman."

"But funny," Whit said.

"Is it a religious thing?" Ray knew Becky and Erin's family history and figured the idea tied back to their unconventional upbringing.

"More of a torture-the-future-spouse thing," Adam said in his most tortured voice.

"Poor Adam isn't getting any."

Ray knew otherwise. "From the stupid grin, I'd say he's doing fine."

"Becky has some strange ideas," Adam explained.

"Just what I want to hear, since she's about to become our company lawyer." Whit wore a pained expression. "Are you sure you want to go back to criminal defense work and pass your business work to her?"

"It was your suggestion." Adam's smile returned full force. "And since she's not forbidding me from sleeping with her here, I'm not going to take the risk and piss her off."

"She probably just forgot to tell you to quit coming around," Whit said.

"Don't you have a wife waiting for you somewhere?" Adam shot back.

"I do, but Ray needs my help."

Adam glanced around the room. "With what? Looks good in here so far."

"Wrong problem. The one on the table deals with women and how they suck—"

Adam chuckled. "How's that a problem?"

"Wrong kind of suck," Whit explained. "Suck as in women trouble."

"Oh, that." Adam nodded in silent agreement. "Remember those days well."

Ray had hoped the brothers' jabs would keep their attention off him. Apparently this was not his lucky day. "I do not need help with women."

"He's grumbling," Whit said.

"And sulking," Adam added.

"I am not." Ray said while trying not to sound sulky.

Adam slid into the nearby chair. "Definitely women trouble."

"Not women." Ray justified his answer as being a half-truth.

The real answer was woman. Singular.

Erin.

Before she walked into his life, he was a sane person. Dated, had fun, got his work done, and led a normal guy life. Now he spent every damn day thinking about her. Worrying about her. Wanting to lure her into bed, even though Becky lived under the same roof, and Adam came in and out every few hours.

Ray tried subtlety. She balked. He tried cornering her. She spouted crap about their being friends. Now he had a case of involuntary celibacy topped off by a total disinterest in any woman but Erin.

And he knew the feeling ran both ways. That was the damnedest part. Erin wanted him and ignored her feelings without any trouble.

Women sucked.

The bad kind of suck.

"Come to think of it, I haven't heard about any of your dates in weeks." Adam stared up at the ceiling as if he was actually calculating the days. "Not about the twins. No woman talk at all. Why's that?"

Because he had not gone on a date. Had not wanted one. Ray blamed Erin for that too. "I like my privacy."

"This is serious," Adam said.

"Sounds pretty clear to me. He's hunting and she, whoever she is, is hiding."

Ray entertained second thoughts about knocking the ladder over and onto Whit's head. "You're off base."

"Uh-huh." Whit rubbed his hands together. "So, how can we help?"

"By getting back to work. Cole will be pissed, and Erin is already nuts about the possibility of our not meeting our construction deadline." Ray knew the reminder would not throw them off the scent, but he tried anyway.

This time Whit clapped. "That's it."

Adam played along. "The woman?"

Ray tried again. "There is no woman."

"Who is she?" Adam ignored Ray and asked Whit.

Ray nodded in the general direction of the trim in a desperate attempt to stop the train wreck he saw coming. "That molding is not going to hang itself."

"Forget the wall." Whit aimed a finger directly at Ray's head. "I got it."

Ray swore under his breath. "Are you taking medicine to get rid of it?"

"Erin," Whit said.

Ray ran out of curse words.

Adam's mouth dropped open the second before he started smiling at Ray. "As in my future sister-in-law and your boss, Erin?"

Leave it to Whit to get to the truth too fast and Adam to take off running in the wrong direction.

"Erin is not my boss. You are, you dumb-ass."

Adam screwed up his lips in a frown. Probably trying to look offended, but the way his lips kept turning up in a smile blew his fake indignation. "Now that's a nice way to talk to your superior."

"That's what we get for giving the guy a piece of the company," Whit said.

"I'm not his boss?" Adam asked as if he was serious about the question.

"No."

"Well, damn."

Ray watched the Thomas brother volleys with growing dread. He had worked with them long enough to know that when the conversation circled back around, they would grab on to his feelings for Erin, whatever they were, with even more tenacity.

"Definitely Erin." Whit thrummed his fingers against the metal ladder.

"That would explain why Ray looks like he wants to vomit," Adam said.

"Hey," Ray said, outraged at Adam on Erin's behalf.

Adam snorted. "That's not what I meant. There's nothing wrong with Erin."

Except how she kept him in a state of semi-arousal with no end to the torture in sight, Ray thought. "Damn straight."

"The green cast to your skin is because we figured out your secret," Adam said.

"Technically, I figured it out," Whit pointed out.

"But I'm at the house all the time now. I would have seen him sneaking out of Erin's room or something." Adam fell right into arguing mode.

Ray just wanted the brothers to stop talking. Erin lived in the house. Last he checked, she could hear just fine. And this was not a conversation he wanted to share with her.

Adam shot Ray a smug look. "This is the real reason you're moving in. This isn't about the job."

"Sounds more like a booty call to me," Whit said.

The term hit Ray wrong. "It is not."

Adam sobered. "Better not be. Erin is going to be my sister. I will not allow anyone to take advantage of her."

Ray's temper exploded with a bang inside of him. He was trying to watch his language around Erin, so he reined in his comments to avoid letting loose with a string of profanity. "Shut up before I make you do some real work."

Whit nodded and could not seem to stop. "I would bet my life on the woman problem being Erin."

The steady beats from Whit's tapping drummed through Ray's ears and right into his brain. "It is not Erin."

"He's got it bad for her," Whit said, clearly warming to the topic.

"How the hell did I miss this?"

Ray ignored Adam and repeated his mantra, louder this time. "It's not Erin."

"What's not Erin?" asked the Erin in question as she walked down the stairs.

Whit chuckled. "Now, this is getting interesting."

Chapter Three

Erin had pulled her caramel-colored hair back in a ponytail. Her paint-stained blue jeans hugged her hips and thighs, highlighting every inch of her long legs and nearly six-foot frame.

She spent a lot of their time together pointing out their seven-year age difference. To Ray, the years did not matter. She was hotter than most women ten years her junior, in part because she had a depth and grace other women he had dated lacked.

Adam treated her to an awkward wave. "Hey, Erin."

"Good morning, gentlemen." She glanced around at each of them, sparing only the quickest peek for Ray. "Anyone going to answer me?"

Ray made sure the answer to that one was *no*. "Adam, here, was just whining about having to do hard work."

"Nothing unusual there," Whit agreed in backup.

"Why are you even here? I thought my sister banned you from the house until you guys had your turn to get married."

Adam's cheeks flushed red. "Becky did not—"

"Apparently Becky missed some important details." Whit cleared his throat. "She should have included her bedroom in the forbidden zone 'cause Adam—"

Erin held up both hands. "I don't want to know."

Seeing Adam speechless was a rare occasion, and Ray enjoyed it. But with Erin standing there fresh from her morning shower, her skin all pink and shiny, in a slim, faded Georgetown University T-shirt that drove him wild wondering what she had on underneath, laughing was out of the question. Hell, breathing strained his lungs to the breaking point.

"Since I am being defamed," Adam bellowed in his best lawyer voice. "I'm going to the office."

Whit jumped to his feet. "Sounds like your usual attempt at avoiding labor."

"That's what I was thinking." Ray agreed fast, happy to have someone else take his place on the hot seat.

"That makes three of us." Erin wound her arm around Adam's neck and pulled him close. "At least he's a cute suit-wearing robot."

"The term you're looking for is lawyer." Adam gave Erin a peck on the check before giving way to a smile.

Ray almost missed the conversation. Words muffled and blurred. All he saw was Erin's hands on Adam. The exchange of smiles and intimacy.

Sure, Adam was engaged to Becky. And, sure, Erin and Adam treated each other as siblings. Despite those truths, seeing Erin hug Adam and, worse, seeing him hug her back, sent heat rolling through Ray's body. Not the good kind either. The need-to-punch-someone kind.

He knew the jealousy was misplaced and stupid, but if Erin wanted to play around with anyone, touch a man in any way, the man should be him. Ray had few rules in life. Lately that was one of them.

"Someone in this company needs to work, so I'll be heading to the office." Adam pulled Erin close for a brotherly kiss. One he planted right on her lips.

Ray felt the contact right down to his spine. He clamped his back teeth together to keep from shouting for them to break it up.

Just when Ray thought he could unload one of his friends, Erin got chatty with Adam again. "Not going to help with the construction today?"

Whit groaned. "Does he ever?"

"A man should stick to his strengths."

"A desk?" Erin gave Adam's shoulders one last squeeze before letting go.

"I'm going to be the bigger man and ignore that." Adam winked at his future sister-in-law. "When it comes to the house, I leave you in Ray's capable hands."

"Thanks," Ray said.

"I'm here for you, bud." Adam lowered his voice as he smacked Ray on the back. "But I will expect details."

Ray did not bother to soften his tone. "Go to hell."

"Something wrong?" Erin asked.

Ray went with the safe answer rather than the true one. "You can't hire good help these days."

"Tell me about it." Whit kept his head down and his hands on the ladder as he climbed back up to work on the intricate molding above the door frame.

"So," Erin stole a quick peek at Whit's back before taking a step closer to Ray. "Did you bring your stuff?"

"Stuff?"

"Your clothes and . . ." She cleared her throat. "Whatever you need to stay here."

Interesting how she never made direct eye contact with him as she spoke. How she kept rubbing her palms on her jeans. Ray took both as good signs.

"Does this mean you're warming to the idea?" Damn, he hoped that was the case.

"You said it was necessary."

If only to give him a shot at getting past the awkward flirting stage with her. "Absolutely."

At the creak of the metal ladder, Ray looked up and

caught a glimpse of Whit's turned head and raised eyebrow behind Erin's back. Both of which he ignored.

"So, while you're here, do you expect . . ."

When she did not elaborate, Ray prodded. "Erin?"

"Food."

Food? Wrong kind of nourishment as far as Ray was concerned.

"If you're volunteering to feed me, I won't turn you down. No bachelor in his right mind would."

"What else would I be talking about?"

"Yeah, what else could there be." Ray mumbled the comment, then watched Whit's shoulders shake in response with what he assumed to be laughter.

"Excuse me?" Erin asked.

"Nothing." Ray slapped his hands together more to break the tension running through his veins than anything else. "I need to get back to work."

"Oh, sure." Erin took a giant step back and slammed her heel against a toolbox. She would have taken a big tumble, but Ray caught her in mid-fall.

"Whoa." With his arms wrapped around her and her fingers stretched over his chest, his mind wandered to something and it was not food.

For the fifth time that morning he wondered if staking out a bedroom in Erin's house was such a great idea. He needed to pick up the pace to make Cole and Aubrey's deadline. Staying here was the reasonable thing to do. But his motivation was anything but rational. More like the act of a desperate and horny male.

She slid her palms down his chest until they rested on the top edge of his belt. Right next to the very spot he longed for her to touch. At this point, all pride was gone. She could touch him with Whit in the room for all he cared.

"Okay." She dropped her hands. "Well, I need to get back to work."

Ray was a little slower to let go. When she backed up, his hands refused to release her upper arms.

"New project?"

"Finishing one, but I can help out around here later."

"Uh, Ray?" Whit asked in a sing-songy voice filled with laughter.

"Huh?"

Whit hitched his chin at Erin's back. "I need your help over here."

That reminder helped to get Ray's hands moving. He wanted to hold on but settled for letting her go.

"I'll be in the other room." She gave Whit a little wave as she left.

Ray watched her walk away, those slim hips swaying. A renewed commitment to break through her anti-Ray shield rumbled inside him. He had to have her. And soon.

"Real smooth there, buddy." Whit rolled his eyes. "And to think you used to be so good with women."

"Still am."

"Not from where I sit, and she's not much better. You two act like you're in high school."

"You do not know what you're talking about." Ray said it, but he knew the exact opposite to be true.

Something about Erin robbed him of his good lines and usual charm. He turned into a bumbling idiot. All thumbs and no style. Luring women to bed had ranked as one of his skills until he met Erin. He could not even lure her into a car to go pick up building supplies.

"You know what the problem is, don't you?" Whit asked.

"That I invited you over today instead of a trained monkey?"

"You've got it bad for her."

Ray rushed to deny the charge. "I don't—"

"Admit it."

"You're—"

The ladder wobbled as Whit turned around and sat on the top ledge. "It *is* Erin, our Erin, isn't it?"

Ray felt the sigh move up from deep down in his chest. "Yeah."

"Thought so." Whit made a few indistinguishable sounds before continuing. "You just interested or at the lost-your-mind stage?"

Definitely the latter. "Somewhere in between."

"What are you going to do about it?"

Ray plunked back down on the table. "I have no fucking idea."

"She's skittish."

"No kidding."

"Her childhood messed her up." Whit tapped the handle end of his knife against his open palm. "From what Adam says, screwed with Becky, too. Erin is rock solid on the inside but not as outwardly tough as Becky."

Ray knew about odd childhoods. He also knew people could overcome them and move on. "They are adults now. Isn't it time to let all of that go?"

"Easy to say. Hard to do."

"I guess."

"The real question is whether you want to go along for the ride as she figures it all out."

"No idea."

Whit's tapping stopped. "Try again."

"What?"

"You've got it bad for her." Whit started that know-it-all nodding again. "Deep down, lose control and never get it back, bad for her."

The man was right.

Damn him.

"It sucks." The really bad kind.

Whit grinned. "You, my friend, are screwed."

Chapter Four

The next afternoon, Erin channeled all of her energy into not slamming the phone down. One more call from a reporter, and she would do something violent. Or reconsider scream therapy.

After months of quiet, the vultures had found her again. Not that locating her was all that difficult, since her parents had announced her whereabouts live on national television. Or so she was told. She stuck with a newspaper and even then only to the parts not guaranteed to drive her nuts, which meant the food and arts sections.

"Problem?" Ray stepped into the sunroom doorway with a drywall trough still in hand.

Seeing him took the edge off her anger. He looked far too tasty for comfort. The way the faded jeans balanced on his hips, anchored by a wide, brown leather belt. Today's work uniform consisted of a short-sleeve shirt stretched over a long-sleeve shirt was a style favored by the twenty-ish crowd. It fit his relaxed demeanor too.

"Everything is fine," she said in a voice still drawn stiff with anger.

"I'm assuming that wasn't Becky or any other person on the planet you happen to like."

"No."

"Want to give me a hint?"

She tried to wave him off. "It doesn't matter. I'm fine."

"Doesn't sound like it."

She could not survive another verbal wrestling session with Ray. Not now. To deal with him she had to be very focused. No mental wandering. No surprises. Ready at all times to bob when he weaved.

"I'm going to go—"

"Hold on a sec." He held up a hand to delay her planned speedy exit. "Tell me what's wrong."

"Not important."

"Let me decide."

His bossiness brought her defenses to the up and ready position. "Frankly, Ray, it's none of your business."

"You know what?" He set his tray down on the table just inside the doorway with a loud clank. "A month ago that would have worked."

"What?"

"The superior act. The attitude."

"How dare—"

"Now I know better."

"I don't have any idea what you're talking about." But she did. So, this time she tried to move around him and avoid the confrontation rather than engage in it.

He stepped into the doorway and blocked her path before she could stage her escape. "We're not done."

"Move."

"I'm fine right here."

His frame filled the entire entry. Unless she wanted to go through him or out a window, she was stuck. "This is my house."

"So?"

Her usual tricks never worked on Ray. He was immune to threats, veiled or not, and female fury. His refusal to back down appealed to her on one level. Showed his determination and personal strength. Ticked her off on every other level.

At that moment, she would have settled for his being a bit more intimidated and a lot less sure of himself. "I don't appreciate the way you hover and try to order me around."

He held up his hands and turned them upside down to show his palms. "I'm not touching you."

"You know what I mean."

Despite their comparable heights, he managed to loom over her. Look down at her in a way that made her feel petite and vulnerable. Not in a physically at-risk way. More like he was demonstrating that he could see right through her and any block she tried to throw in his path.

"You better get used to me. As of this morning, I live here."

There was a reminder she did not need. As if she had thought of anything else for the last twenty-four hours. "I can take back my permission."

He laughed at her. "Push all you want. Take on that bitch goddess role you love so much. I'm not going anywhere."

The insult refused to compute in her head. "Name-calling?"

"No."

"You just called me a bitch."

"No, I didn't."

"I heard you."

"I called you difficult, and you are."

"That is not true." But he was not the first one to make the charge, so she feared the complaint was right on target. The two decent men she had dated recently had broken it off with charges of her being closed and guarded.

"We can fight about that issue later."

From the beginning, he had orchestrated every little thing between them. Their fights would not be on that list.

"We can talk about it now," she insisted.

"I'd rather talk about the call. Someone upset you. Who?"

She glanced around the room. Light streamed through the windows on each wall of the small area. It highlighted the dark streaks in his straight hair. The space was big enough for a large piano and a few chairs. She had moved the baby grand out to make space for more seating and a small refreshment bar. With its view of the English garden in the backyard and the airy feel of the towering glass she considered the room the perfect place to relax. Not that she felt particularly calm at the moment.

Quite the opposite. Her nerve endings jumped. Her hands clenched and unclenched at her sides to keep from, at various times, either shoving Ray on his smart ass or grabbing him close for that kiss his eyes kept promising.

"Erin, tell me."

His eyes grew soft, almost loving, as his hand moved to her cheek. With a touch so gentle and warm it left her breathless, he cupped her cheek. The sudden change in his demeanor from frustrated to caring zapped the building heat out of the room and replaced it with something else. Something tender and sweet.

The wall she had erected between them crumbled a bit at the base. "Ray."

"Who was on the phone?"

She gave up the fight. "A reporter."

"About?"

"Nothing—"

"Your parents, right?"

She never told him the story. Did not really have to. He just seemed to know the truth. Picked up bits and pieces by being near her and through whatever Adam told him. Once played bodyguard when a reporter tried to confront her in a bookstore and never asked for an explanation.

He deserved to know. Living here, he would hear the phone. Be confronted by interested reporters. "There was this article."

"I know."

"It said . . ." She tried to understand what he just said. "How?"

"Adam warned me. I checked it out."

Adam. Right. He would know because of Becky.

With their backs against the wall and their questionable religious practices under a microscope, her parents did what they always did. Rambled on about family and how Becky had lost her way, turned to evil, and was punished with a divorce. Becky pretended the jabs did not hurt. Erin knew how much they pained her sister.

Being the daughter that Roger and Alma McHugh, renowned cult leaders, claimed was no fairy tale either. She spent her life trying to live down their odd legacy. They spent their time using Erin's life as an example of their legitimacy.

The press, the questions, the strange looks, the guys who asked her out so they could turn around and sell the story to a tabloid. She lived through it all. Hated every minute of it. Despised the lack of privacy and ability to just live her life.

"They told everyone where I live." She leaned into his hand and let those feelings balled up inside her spill out. "I cannot figure out how they even found me. We don't talk. Never visit."

"More than likely some reporter tracked you down then fed the information to them to get a reaction or angle for a story.

"I moved to D.C. to be close to Becky and to find some anonymity. And they blew it for me." Without thought, she rested her balled fists against Ray's flat stomach. "They ruin everything."

"We don't get to pick our parents."

"And how fair is that?" She twisted his cotton shirt in her fingers. "I used to try, you know. Time would pass, and then I'd go back. Attempt to reason with them or get them to ease up on Becky."

"Get them to love you?"

She looked up into his dark eyes, so knowing and non-judgmental. "That makes me sound pathetic."

"It makes you human." He folded her tight against his shoulder and tucked her head under his chin. "And, believe it or not, wanting to reconnect with them makes you normal."

"I would rather be abnormal."

His rich laugh rumbled against her chest. The closeness, the warmth, the amazing comfort of his arms, made her want to stay there all afternoon.

"You turned into the woman you are. Thrived despite all you have been through and had to endure. Those things mean more than whatever some slob prints in the paper."

She peeked up at him. "When did you get so smart?"

"Birth."

His joke made her laugh. "And how do you know so much about the limelight?"

"You don't read the paper much, do you?"

She lifted her head. "Meaning?"

"Nothing." His gaze searched her face. "You want me to answer the phone from now on?"

"I can pick up a receiver."

"I meant to shield you from the calls."

"I'm a grown-up." She talked faster when he started to butt in. "Besides, that would only cause more interest."

"Because a guy would be answering your phone?"

"Exactly."

"So what?"

He understood so much, but he would never comprehend this. You had to live through the unrelenting pressure to get it. The simple question made sense to people who led normal lives. She did not fall into that category.

"I'm not looking to be a newspaper headline for anything other than my art."

"I see."

His attitude change from empathetic to cool threw her off. Even the warmth behind his hold ebbed; he turned icy and distant.

"What's wrong with you? You act as if you're an under-cover journalist or something." She laughed off the joke.

The possibility floated through her mind, then swam on out. No way would Ray play her. Even if he got by her, he would have had to hatch the plan long before she met Whit, Adam, and Cole, and somehow have conned them too. Not possible.

"You're kidding." His monotone voice did not sound amused.

"What?"

He dropped his hands from around her waist. "You're reasoning it out, aren't you? I can see you turning it over in your mind. Wondering if I'm an inside man."

The sun beating down on the glassed-in room did nothing to ward off the chill. Without his touch, she rubbed her arms to keep the blood flowing. "That's not true."

"You, my dear, have trust issues."

She battled those insecurities every single day, but he was not supposed to notice. At the very least, he could have had the courtesy to keep the realization to himself.

"Do you blame me?"

"When it comes to not trusting me, Erin, yes, I do."

His response stopped the comeback in her throat. Hard to follow-up on a commonsense put-down.

So, she said the only thing she could. "I'm sorry."

He folded his arms across his broad chest. Even smiled. "For?"

Not quite the response she expected. "Uh . . ."

"See, that's the problem."

His determination not to cut her a break made her feel jumpy. "I apologized."

"It doesn't count if you have no idea why you bothered to do so in the first place."

"Oh, and you're the expert. You wrote the international manual on forgiveness on something." She grabbed on to the back of the nearest chair. Contemplated smashing it over his head.

"At least I took the time to read the manual. There was a chapter on being genuine, in case you didn't know."

Quick and smiling. That qualified as a deadly combination coming from Ray. The sort to run through her defenses, leaving her control in a pile on the floor.

"There is nothing fake about me," she said.

Ray's gaze did a quick dip to her breasts.

Not a surprise. Give a man an opening like that and a little gawking was bound to happen.

Not that she planned to cut him any slack. "You're impossible."

"Honest." He leaned against the door frame. "One might even say *genuine*."

"Try annoying."

"While you work on your apology, I'm going to go unpack and settle in."

"Fine."

"You sound thrilled."

Concerned. Hot. Bothered. And, yeah, even thrilled to some degree. "I'll do a backflip later."

He glanced around the small room. "I wouldn't do it in here. You might go right through a window."

"That would be my luck."

"Luck is overrated."

She felt the same way. "More honesty?"

"Let's just say I believe in going after what you want instead of sitting around and waiting for it to drop in your lap."

Chapter Five

From shoulders to thighs, Ray threw his weight behind the sanding project on the fireplace mantel. His legs grew numb from kneeling against the hardwood floor. After nearly an hour of pounding his muscles into the ground, his biceps burned and his back begged for mercy.

Despite the cool morning breeze, his body produced enough heat to generate electricity for an entire city block. He had stripped off his sweatshirt to wipe the sweat rolling down his face. Even in his T-shirt, he had heat pounding off his skin and soaking through the cotton.

But he had no plans to stop.

Back and forth he scraped the block against the intricate carvings and brushed away layers of cheap paint. Mindless work but fulfilling in that he could see the progress. Watch the bad decorating choices of the past give way to the natural wood and Erin's vision for the room.

Erin. The one and only reason behind his unspent energy. He needed to exhaust his body or, thanks to her, he was facing another sleepless night. Last night, his first evening under the same roof with her, had been as pleasant as being set on fire.

The clanking of the pipes as she took her shower. Hearing the floor creak above his head as she walked around. Imagining her undressing, wrapped in a towel or naked.

Pure fucking torture.

All he asked for was a few hours to pound his body into oblivion without having to see, think of, or smell her. The sort of rub-your-knuckles raw hard labor that wiped a guy's mind clear.

"How's it going?" the woman problem in question asked, as she entered the room.

"I thought you had a gallery meeting." He made the comment without looking up from the fireplace.

Talking to her proved hard enough. Looking at her amounted to overkill.

"Did. It's over."

"Good." Yeah, fantastic. Now she would be home, walking around looking like she did and smelling so good.

"Ended early."

"That's—" He glanced over at her and nearly fell on his stupid face.

Gone were the jeans. She wore this . . . dress. A sexy little navy number that hugged every curvy inch of her. It dove into a vee in the front, wrapped around her, and tied on the side.

Never in his life had he wanted a present this much.

"Nice outfit."

She looked down as if the clothes had gotten there without her help. "It's not my thing."

"It should be."

He stood up in slow motion. Any faster and he would trip over his feet or smack his head on the fireplace mantel or do some other half-assed thing.

"You're making great progress in here."

On the room, yeah.

On everything else, not so much.

"You mean the fireplace." He figured they needed clarification.

"Uh, yeah."

Once again he emphasized one thing and she focused on another. "Got up early. I've been at it for hours."

"Did you have trouble sleeping?" She walked over to stand next to him.

All he saw was a pair of shapely legs headed his way. High heels. Lots of bare leg.

The torture continued.

"You could say that," he said, rather than risk saying anything else.

"Was the street noise too loud?"

"Didn't hear a thing outside my window."

"Good." She skimmed her fingertips across the top of the mantel as if caressing the wood. "You have everything else you need to be comfortable?"

She sure did know how to ask a loaded question. "No."

"No?"

If she wanted to know, then he would give her a real answer. "No."

She narrowed her eyes. "You forgot your toothbrush?"

"Have all my bathroom supplies, but thanks."

"Sheets and towels?" She balanced her portfolio on the fireplace ledge and crossed her arms over her stomach.

The move provided him with a peek at perfect cleavage and seared yet another sexy visual image on his brain. He guessed sleep would elude him again tonight. No surprise there.

"Everything was all clean and right where you said they would be. Again, thanks."

"Clothes?" Her tone switched from confused to frustrated.

She should try being him. "Done."

"If you expect me to fluff your pillows, you're out of luck."

He thought of something more along the lines of seeing her sprawled across his sheets. "Nope."

"I'm not a maid."

"I know exactly what you are."

"And what is that?"

He hesitated. He hated to start a fight with any woman who looked this good.

"Well?" she asked.

"Scared."

From the way her back snapped straight, he knew he touched an open sore. "What?"

"Of me."

"Because you're *so* scary." She topped off her snort with a dramatic eye roll. "Get real."

"You talk tough—"

"Because I am tough." She flexed her arm as if she wanted to haul off and demonstrate.

"Except with me."

"You've been inhaling too many paint fumes."

Interesting how her snide comments did not quite rise to the level of a denial. "You act as if we're friends."

"We aren't?"

"You know there's so much more happening between us." He stayed still. Probably could not move if he tried. "Your eyes beg me to kiss you but your mouth says something else."

"That you're insane?"

More tough talk. But she stayed in the same place too. Right next to the fireplace, hanging on to the mantel with a hold-on-for-your-life grip that washed the color out of her knuckles.

The room crackled with energy. Something invisible but potent zapped back and forth between them.

Rather than push her, he waited to see how she would react to the truth. "You want me."

And he wanted her right back.

"Your ego is outrageous," she said.

"Maybe."

"Oh, that's not up for debate."

"Then tell me I'm wrong. Tell me you don't want me."

Erin tried to open her mouth but it would not budge. The words sat right there, lodged in the back of her throat, but refused to break free no matter how many times she exhaled.

"We work together." A little off subject, but she thought the argument worked.

"You have to find a better excuse. That one is wearing thin."

So, not a great comeback. She tried another. "How about the fact we're friends and know all the same people."

"Uh-huh. And?"

She held out her hands and turned them around as she tried to act out her thoughts. "It would be complicated."

"You're kidding."

"What?"

"That's not really the best argument you've got, is it?"

She had an entire list. The same one she read off in her head anytime he did that thing where he hovered too close and scattered her otherwise good sense.

"There's the age difference."

He rolled his eyes. "I was worried you would go five minutes without mentioning that one."

"It's significant."

"Only in your head."

"I am seven years older than you." Her age had never bothered her before, but when compared to his, it meant something. Highlighted their differences and opened them up to further scrutiny, which was something she could not tolerate.

"So you've said." He yawned.

"I'm thirty-four."

"Using my advanced math skills, that would make me twenty-seven. Again, so?"

"When I turned twenty-one and was out drinking and partying, you were fourteen. Fourteen! A kid."

"Unless you're thinking we'll date in some sort of time machine, life thirteen years ago is not relevant to anything happening right now."

"The press would love to take this information and run with it. Can't you see it? The older maiden daughter of religious wackos shacks up with a young stud."

There. She'd said it. Maybe she was scared. Hell, she had a right to be. She had been tracked down, exposed, questioned by police, yelled at by relatives of her parents' followers, and called to testify before a congressional committee. Not the average stuff for a reclusive artist.

"Stud?"

"You know what I mean."

"If you say so, but, for the third time, who cares?" he asked, clearly unimpressed with everything she had gone through.

"I do!"

"Your parents are cult leaders, and you think newspaper reporters will get hung up on my age?"

Okay, when he said it like that . . . "I can't take the chance."

"You can."

"We're not arguing about this."

"Agreed." Before she could take a breath of relief, he opened his arms wide. "Kiss me."

When did they move off her why-they-needed-to-stay-two-rooms-apart-at-all-times list? "What?"

"The only excuse that matters, the only reason for our staying apart, is the one you're not saying."

"Which is?"

"Your not being interested."

"Well, sure. It's obvious."

His grin grew wide enough to flash all of his teeth. "Yeah, honey, it is."

Honey? "I don't think—"

"And that's a good start." With one step she stood between his arms and well within kissing range. "Kiss me."

"This is ridiculous."

And dangerous.

And forbidden.

And far too tempting.

His next step pressed his thighs against hers. "Prove me wrong."

That was the one thing she could not do. Kissing him would lead to more kissing and potentially hours between the sheets and then . . . disaster.

She tried one more time. "We should stay professional."

"Come on, Erin. We passed that point months ago." His arms skimmed up her back and down and settled around her waist. "We are far into the sniffing stage now."

"Next thing you know, you'll pee on me to mark your spot."

"Not into that. Sorry." His face crowded closer until she could feel his warm breath on her cheek.

"This isn't—" The shake of her head put her mouth right where it should never be. One more inch and her lips would brush over his.

"Worth arguing about? I agree."

"Isn't there a twenty-year-old chick out there somewhere?"

"Don't care if there is since I only want you."

The admission sent a lightness soaring through her chest. "Ray."

"Kiss me." The roughness of his voice morphed into pleading.

The change broke through her resolve. Before she could

whip out her mental list and run through it one more time, she gave in. Her eyes eased shut as her mouth hovered over his, just a breath away.

"I hope we don't regret this," she whispered.

"The only regret is how long it took to get here."

With that he took over. Lowered his mouth, slanting his lips across hers in a slow pass. Once, twice, he brushed against her open mouth. Gentle but focused, he reeled her in until her head tipped back and her knees buckled.

Then he took full advantage.

The kisses switched from seductive to sexy. Hot mouths. Wet lips. His tongue licking against hers. The touch moved from testing to tasting.

She had known being with him would steal her strength, but her guesses paled in comparison to the real thing. To the feel of being thrown into the middle of a tornado with no chance of regaining control. Need whipped around inside her, draining away the last of her resistance. Rather than fight, she grabbed his shoulders and rode along.

His fingers dove into her hair. His other hand pressed the small of her back tight against the bulge in his pants. He wanted her as much as she wanted him. Try as she did to ignore it, his erection told the truth.

The man kissed even better than he looked.

And he looked spectacular.

When he lifted his head, his lips were puffed from her kisses. His eyes sparkled with a need she had never seen before. Desire lingered there, making him appear less commanding than usual and more vulnerable.

She half-expected him to throw her on the couch and strip her naked. The idea spelled trouble. Still, she had no plans to fight off the attraction. His kiss wiped away her fears, at least temporarily, along with her bones. She turned to mush in his arms.

Her breasts felt achy. Her lower body heated to a burning

fire. When his mouth turned to her neck, her mouth yearned for more attention.

"Erin?"

"Yes." And she meant *yes*.

"Admit it."

"What?"

The nibbling kisses stopped. He tucked his forehead in the space between her cheek and shoulder. "You are killing me, woman."

"I don't—"

"Understand. Yeah, that continues to be the problem." He pulled back when she thought he would dive in.

"What are you talking about?"

He fit his hand tight against her hips. "I've been honest with you. I want you. Only you."

The ice water roared through her brain before racing like a river through every other part of her body. With only a few words, he had extinguished her desire. "So what's the problem?"

"You."

She glanced down at the small space between their bodies.

"Are you blind?"

"No." He blew out a long, agonized breath. "And that's the problem. It would be easier if I felt this way alone."

Her hands slid away from his neck to rest on his biceps. It was either that or strangle him. "I don't like games."

"Me either." He shut his eyes for a second before he moved back and stopped touching her. "So, come to your senses quickly."

"I thought I made my needs pretty clear a second ago."

"Are you ready to say the words?"

Her mind blocked out all reasoning. She wanted to feel, not think. "I still don't get what you want."

"Figure it out soon because I'm not sure how much more of this I can take." He broke all contact.

The physical separation stabbed through her. He wanted them together. She agreed. Now he wanted something else. Kissing and touching no longer satisfied him. And she had no idea how to fix that.

"I guess this is some new dating ritual used by twenty-somethings."

"The cold shower has been used by males throughout time to temper this problem." He glanced down at his erection.

She could not help but follow his stare. "I hope you don't need whatever it is you say is missing from your room to resolve that problem."

"The only thing missing from my bed is you."

She paced away from him in search of some air. He said seductive things like that, she fell for them, and then they ended up fighting. They needed another way to talk to each other.

"Let's calm down," she said, in as rational a voice as possible while the nerves in her stomach played basketball.

"I have to get back to work."

Screw rational. "The fireplace can wait."

"To stay on schedule we need this room to be done today." He grabbed his sanding pad and squatted by the fireplace.

"You've got hours to work on that."

"Only till four."

Seven to four might be a full day for other men. It qualified as a half day for Ray. "You usually work until late."

"Can't tonight."

"Why?"

"I have to go out."

Her breath whooshed out of her lungs so fast that she was surprised he could not hear the sucking sound. "You have a date?"

The idea repulsed her. Him with another woman. Kissing, hugging, or more.

"I'll be back late."

Shock gave way to rage strong enough to knock her over. She held on to the mantel to keep from falling to the floor. The attraction, the confusion—it all exploded inside her.

"Then why were you kissing me?" Before she could grab on to her control, her voice rose to a squeal. "Was I just the appetizer for this evening's woman?"

"No."

His nonchalance set her mind running in the opposite direction. How dare he stay calm while the air in the room turned into a solid.

"No?" She towered over him. Thought seriously about jumping on top of him and pounding him into her newly buffed floors.

"Ask me," he said in a soft voice.

"What?"

He glanced up. His voice never wavered, but his locked jaw and flat dark eyes suggested he felt her wrath and held in a little of his own.

"Ask me where I'm going tonight and with whom."

"I don't care." Oh, but she did. Down to her toenails did.

"Sooner or later you are going to stop fighting and just ask for what you want."

"All I want is to stuff you in the fireplace."

"That anger inside you, that backbone of steel you have on the outside, it hides something."

"We are not analyzing me right now."

"Maybe we should be." He sighed. "Figure out what you want and ask for it. Until you do, I'll focus on the house."

Chapter Six

Erin clunked the coffee mugs down on the kitchen table with a bit more force than intended. Adam caught his cup before it bounced into his lap. "Rough day?"

This was Ray's fault. He wore down her defenses. Got her to the point where she no longer knew up from down. And just when she decided to lower the guard, to give Ray a chance, what did the young stud do?

Turned. Her. Down.

"Let's just say I'm ready for it to be over."

Becky snuck a peek across the table at her husband-to-be before resting her hand over Erin's shaking one. "Where's Ray?"

Ray. Now there was a subject she wanted to avoid. "Upstairs."

"He's not known around the office as a guy who skips a meal. Dinner is a big one for him." Adam winced when Becky stepped on his foot under the table. "What was that for?"

"Did he already eat?" Becky asked.

"Who knows," Erin mumbled as she threw—not placed, but chucked with a bit of force behind it—the dinner dishes into the old white sink and let them clatter and crash.

Oh, she knew. She had heard every single step the guy took for the last eight hours since breaking off their kiss.

Thumping and swearing as he finished the fireplace. Stomping around. Showering. Showering again.

She kept her distance but no matter where she went in the house, she felt him. Actually smelled his scent when she inhaled. Closed her eyes and shivered at the memory of his breath against her bare shoulder.

The more she pushed him away and pulled a mental security blanket tight around her, the more he wormed his way into her brain. Time passed and their dance continued. Truth was she looked forward to the flirtatious sparring. Despite her protests, she enjoyed his company, was flattered by his advances. Depended on his being there. Waiting for her.

And now he was off to date someone else.

She heard a scrape of a chair against the floor. Felt a firm, confident presence standing right over her shoulder.

"You okay?" Adam asked in an uncharacteristically understated tone.

"Of course." She spun around with a smile plastered on her face. "Do you guys want dessert?"

"Sis?" Becky did not try to hide her concern. She frowned hard enough to create lines across her forehead.

Erin decided not to clue her sister in on that fact. "What?"

"Ray."

"He's upstairs."

Adam laid a hand on Erin's arm. "Everything okay?"

"Sure." She waited for her face to crack from the force of the smile.

"Erin, come on. We grew up together. You always stunk at lying. Nothing has changed."

"I resent that."

"I've known you for a much shorter time than that, but you'd never be a witness in one of my cases. Not credible with that lying face." Adam squeezed her elbow. "Fess up. What's going on?"

"Nothing."

Becky tapped her mug against the table. "Erin, stop it."

"He's getting ready for his date." When her voice came out overly shiny and happy, Erin tried to tone down the fake happiness. "That's all."

"Date?" Adam asked.

"Ray's dating?" Becky asked at the same time.

"Isn't that who you asked me about?"

"Since when is Ray dating?" Becky directed her question to Adam. "You told me he stopped seeing anyone right after he met . . . I mean, started working here."

"Absolutely."

"Are you sure?" Becky telegraphed a you-are-not-sleeping-with-me-tonight undertone.

Adam picked up on the sexual threat without any hints. "Don't take this out on me. I know I'm right about this."

"Guys." Erin tried to break up the fight before she was not the only one in the room throwing dishes. "This is not a big deal."

"It is," Becky insisted.

"Ray is going out. He's young and single." Erin almost choked on the words. "He's free to come and go as he pleases."

"And you don't care?" Adam said the words slow, leaving a significant space between each one.

Except for the fact she was ten seconds from chewing through her arm in frustration, no. "Of course not. He's a guy isn't he? Is it really so strange he would want to go out?"

"Lately?" Adam screwed his lips together. "Uh, yeah."

"Well, he deserves an evening off." Forget that all of a sudden she wanted him to spend his evenings only with her.

"I'm going to go check on him." Adam kissed both women on the cheek and then sprinted from the room.

"The big chicken." Becky shook her head at Adam's retreat, then turned her full attention to her sister. "Spill it."

"What?"

"Don't be an idiot."

"I try not to be." Erin grabbed her cup of coffee. Gave her hands something to do so she would not fidget.

"He wants you. You want him. You're living together. I can't figure out what the problem is here."

"Whoa." Erin held up a finger to emphasize her point. "We're not living together. We live in the same house."

"Didn't I just say that?"

"There's a difference."

"Funny how the living issue is the only part of the comment you denied." Becky's smile reeked of smugness.

"The inaccuracy of the rest was obvious."

"Look, I'm the one with the law degree and the right to twist words into nonsensical sentences, not you. Give it up and get back to the real subject."

"Dessert?"

"Depending how you look at it, yeah." Becky dragged her finger around the rim of her mug. "Ray. Talk. Now."

When Becky moved into lawyer mode, Erin always lost. Rather than fight the inevitable, she started talking. "We're grown-ups."

"Which makes the sex so much more fun."

"We haven't had sex."

"That's a shame."

Erin thought the same thing. "He has a date. He stopped work early, which he never does."

"The toad."

Exactly. "Has been primping ever since."

Becky's scowl returned. "I may strangle Ray when he comes down here. Might even use his tool belt."

"What did I do now?" Ray walked into the kitchen with Adam close at his heels.

Not that Erin even saw Adam. No, she was too busy taking in Ray's classy black tux. Combed hair. Long, lean fingers with perfectly trimmed nails.

One hundred eighty pounds of perfect hot male.

"You look nice." Anger still laced through Becky's voice. Despite how good Ray looked, and he did look good, Becky was not ready to forgive him for leaving the house tonight.

"It's for the charity event."

Becky's jaw dropped and her deep frown disappeared. "Oh, *that* date."

"Yep." Adam grinned like a simpleton. "Told you."

Erin had no idea what the heck was going on.

She could have asked. Should have. If she had not been so busy trying not to stare and drool at Ray, she actually might have. As it was, all she wanted to do was get back to the kiss they had shared this morning.

The man wore jeans and a T-shirt better than any man ever in the history of time. Now she knew his dressing skills extended to tuxedos. There was nothing he could not do. Nothing he could not wear.

Erin despised the woman who would hang on his arm this evening. Whoever the bitch was. Not her usual thought process or style to wish another human harm, but this was a special case.

"Erin?" Ray's eyebrow lifted along with his question.

"You do look very . . . uh . . ."

Nice did not really cut it. Spectacular was closer, but with their audience and the sting from their last meeting, compliments did not exactly roll off her tongue.

"Passable?" Ray smiled, which just made him look hotter.

"Yes. We'll go with that."

Adam barked out a laugh that turned to a grunt when Becky kicked his shin. "We're going to have a talk later about your sudden propensity for violence."

"Count on it."

Ray ignored the couple's bickering and stepped closer to Erin. "Help me?"

She hoped he was asking her to strip the suit off of him, because that is exactly what she wanted to do. "With?"

"My tie."

Oh.

"It's crooked." He tapped a finger on the material to prove his point.

Fixing his wardrobe meant getting close. Like, right on top of him close. She glanced over his broad shoulders to their audience. Adam now occupied a chair, and Becky sat on his lap. Gave her the perfect view of Ray's back.

"Erin? I need to get going," Ray said.

Apparently his blond airhead liked her men on time. Or that's the portrait Erin painted in her head. A vapid, thoroughly unlikable chick who was really a man under all that makeup. Yeah, that visual image worked much better.

"Can't be late," he said.

Not exactly a phrase guaranteed to get her moving. "Uh-huh."

And what was with the amusement dancing around in those dark eyes of his?

She fought off the urge to poke them. Instead, she sent orders from her brain to her shaking hands to drop the mug and fix the tie. His cologne enveloped her the minute she moved between his open arms. She stared straight at his neck to avoid being lured in any further. He belonged to someone else tonight. The dude in the blond wig.

"Ask." That was it. One word said in Ray's usual husky whisper.

She did not pretend to misunderstand. "It's none of my business."

"Ask anyway."

All motion and noise in the room stopped. Not so much as a pinky finger moved. If Becky and Adam were breathing, they did not show it. Even their chests stayed perfectly still.

Erin ignored it all and focused on Ray. "You seem determined to tell me."

"Only if you ask."

"I told you I'm not fond of games." She fiddled with his tie, not really caring how it looked, and fighting off the urge to pull the end tight.

"Yet you continue to play them."

She lowered her hands to her sides. "All done. Your tie is straight."

Ray blew out a long, loud breath. "I told you once I was a patient man."

She peeked at Becky and Adam and noticed how they did not even pretend to do anything but listen in. "This isn't the time."

"It's running out."

The comment pulled her attention back to Ray. Only to Ray. Forget everyone else. She only cared what he had to say.

"What does that mean?"

"Twenty-seven might seem young to you, but I'm old enough to know when to give up." He lowered his head until their noses were close enough to touch. "You might want to remember that. I won't wait for you forever. Get your act together now."

"Wow," Adam said, with more than a touch of admiration in his voice.

Instead of elbowing Adam that time, Becky agreed. "You said it."

Erin was not quite as impressed. Terrified and confused, yes. "I don't like threats any more than I like games."

"I've given you time," Ray said, oblivious to her anger.

"I'm not the one who broke it off this morning."

"Now that's interesting," Adam mumbled.

"But you held back." Ray shook his head. "It's all or nothing."

The gauntlet lay at her feet. So final. "You're getting ahead of yourself, aren't you? When did we—"

"I'll be home early." Ray bent his head and stole a quick, hard kiss from Erin. "You can decide whether or not you want to wait up for me."

Before she could shove him off or deepen the kiss, he was gone. He did not run. Just turned and walked his usual slow, sure walk right out of the room.

Her stunned gaze moved from Ray's retreating back to Adam and Becky's smiling faces. "Don't you two have somewhere better to be? Preferably somewhere that's not here?"

"Blame your sister. I've tried to get her to move in with me and leave you alone."

"Not gonna happen until I have a wedding ring on my finger."

"We'll talk about that later too." Adam flashed Erin the smile he usually reserved for winning a case. "Well, Erin, what's your decision going to be about Ray's ultimatum?"

"I know what I'd choose," Becky said.

She made it sound so easy. Erin wondered if it was.

Chapter Seven

Ray kicked off his shoes and shot them across the room. He probably could have smashed them through a window if he had lifted his leg a little higher. Sexual frustration did that to a guy. Made him homicidal.

And the day had started out so well. He finally kissed Erin just as he had been dying to do for months. Moved them from kissing to caressing and almost to the bedroom. Gave her a decision to make. Saw a spark of jealousy.

But all of that brought him to the edge. Erin had to be the one to push them over. She pulled back instead.

He spent the entire evening thinking about her. Wondering what she was doing back at the house. Hoping she would be there in his bed waiting for him when he arrived home.

What happened when he walked in? Nothing.

At least the charity event had gone as planned. Five months of preparations with him promising to tag along, a vow he desperately wanted to break after his morning with Erin.

He danced. Chatted. Played the role of the perfect escort. The charity got some press and raised piles of money. The newspapers took some photos, all of which he ducked. Erin hated publicity. He was not about to give her another reason to run from him.

He had accomplished all the non-Erin tasks on his list for

the day. All that, and he was home pacing around his room by eleven.

Only a woman could cause that sort of self-denial.

The old Ray would have hung around the party, enjoyed a few drinks, checked out the other patrons. The new Ray pined for Erin like a pathetic kid who had crashed his first car.

Women sucked.

He shrugged out of his jacket and let the tie fall loose against his crisp white shirt. Maybe the third cold shower of the day would wipe the memory of her mouth clean from his mind. God knew the first two did not do a damn thing to soften the part of him that insisted on staying hard around her.

He had gotten two buttons undone on his shirt before he heard the faint knock at the door. At first, he ignored the sound, thinking his mind was playing tricks. Seemed a guy could crave something so hard as to make it happen in his mind.

The second time, the knock turned to a bang. No mistaking that sound. He had a visitor, but the only visitor he wanted would not come to his door without an emergency.

"It's open."

The door swung in and Erin poked her head around the corner. "Hi."

He saw her wide eyes roam down his chest.

That's all it took to take his body from relaxed to ready. "You can come the whole way in."

"Thanks." But she did not move.

Worse, the door still blocked her body from his view.

"This is your house," he said, because he really did not know what else to say.

"But it's your room."

"You have a standing invitation." He made the comment and then waited for her to bolt. As usual.

"Which is why I'm here."

His body flushed with heat. "What?"

She nibbled on her lip. "You are alone, aren't you?"

He hoped not for long. "Of course."

"You didn't bring her back?"

"There's no one here but me, Erin."

"Good."

More like ill. The corners of her mouth bleached white. The rest of her looked a tad colorless as well. "Are you okay?"

"Honestly?"

"Always."

"I'm nervous."

Of all the answers she could have given, that one did not give him any hint as to the reason for her visit. "Because of me?"

She gave him a small smile. "Because of what I'm about to do."

Every nerve ending in his body clicked on. Her. Here. At night. Every fantasy he had started this way. And ended with clothes on the floor and him inside her.

A few more words from her and his arousal would give way to a full-scale erection. One he would never be able to hide in his slim black tux pants.

"Do it."

"What?" Her grip on the door tightened.

"Whatever it is that has you blinking in panic."

"You."

He swallowed. It was either that or lose the ability to speak. "I'm willing to beg for it."

"No need." Her head disappeared for a split second before she stepped out from behind the door.

"Holy shi—"

His eyes wandered over her near-naked five-foot-eleven form. Those toned legs went on forever. Tiny black panties with pink stitching on them that sat high on her perfect thighs. A matching bra that pushed up her breasts to overflow then continued halfway down her torso until it unveiled a thin strip of firm stomach.

Erin smiled. "You can say the word."

"Shit, woman. You are stunning." He shook his head to kick-start his brain. "I mean, I knew that. It's just that you—"

"You're rambling."

"I'm trying not to pass out."

"That's flattering."

"Come over here and I'll do more than that."

"What a line." Her wide grin ruined her eye roll.

He had other things on his mind, including how to get that sexy lingerie off of her as fast as possible. "I lost my ability to do smooth the second you walked in the room."

"I bet you still know how to go nice and slow."

His stomach lifted then slammed back down again. "Hell, I hope so."

"This tux does not look too comfortable."

"It does feel tight all of a sudden."

Her fingers went to his buttons. "But you look so handsome."

Screw that. "Help me out of it."

Her husky chuckle blew across his exposed chest as she slipped the buttons loose to his waist. "Poor baby."

Every dream of her came to life. For so long, he had closed his eyes and seen her right there, in his bedroom, undressing him.

This time he would not stop her. No matter what she said. If she refused to budge off the ledge, he would let her sit there and would pleasure her until her resistance dropped and she gave herself to him, mind and body.

But first he had to clear away any misunderstanding. He had faults. Being unfaithful was not of them.

"Anything you want to ask me?"

She flattened her hands against his stomach. "I have a few questions."

"Ask."

Her gaze burned into him. "Is she your girlfriend?"

"I don't have a girlfriend."

"You mean it's not serious with her?"

Finally. "I mean I have not dated another woman, serious or otherwise, since I met you."

"Why?" Uncertainty battled with triumph in her eyes.

"Because I didn't want to."

"Then," she lowered her gaze to his chest. "Why didn't you call off the date tonight?"

He tipped her chin back up. He needed her to watch him. To see the truth. "Couldn't. I promised months ago that I'd go."

"Does she know about me?"

"Yes." Every last detail.

"She doesn't care that you're here with me instead of her?"

"No." He buried his nose in her hair and let his lips press against the rim of her ear to calm the anxiety he felt building under her muscles. "It's not like that."

"Oh."

He pulled back just far enough to see her eyes. "Just ask."

She hesitated then shook her head. "Right now the only thing I care about is us."

"Erin—" His explanation died in his throat when she started tugging his shirt out of his pants.

"No more talk."

"None?"

She passed her hand over his erection. "Not about your date."

"It wasn't a date."

"I." She kissed his chin.

"Don't." Her lips moved to his neck.

"Care." And her hands unfastened his pants.

"Damn, woman." He leaned his forehead against hers. "I've waited forever for this."

"Wait no more." She slid his shirt off his shoulders before caressing his chest with her palms.

With every press of her skin against his, the fire inside him flared. Touching her in his dreams paled in comparison to real life. Her skin was more pink, softer, than he imagined.

And her body. Damn, she was tall and fit and slim except in those places where a woman should be round. The way her breasts plumped over the edge of her bra begged for him to taste her. So, he did.

His tongue swept across the top of her bra before dipping underneath the band to her distended nipple. It was not enough. He needed to see her. He peeled down the lacy fabric, revealing full, round breasts.

"Beautiful."

"With you."

"Always."

He lowered his head, taking as much of her in his mouth as possible. The smooth globes fit his hands. Her nipple slid between his teeth. He treated one breast then the other to gentle caresses and increasingly urgent kisses.

She did some exploring of her own. Her hands moved from his hair to his shoulders and finally back to the top of his pants. She cupped him. Rubbed him. Pushed him right to the edge of his mental limit.

"Bed." She said the word then pulled away before he could grab on to her.

There was no way he was going to fight this moment. He wanted her to take the lead. Needed to see what she would do and if she could ask for everything her body needed.

She balanced on the very edge of the bed with her legs spread wide and her back straight. The position put every inch of her impressive body on display.

"Come here."

She did not need to ask twice. He stepped between her legs, his erection level with her gaze. Without a word, she peeled his pants and underwear down his legs, skimming her palms along the path as she went. Everywhere she touched, every patch of skin she brushed, came alive under her hands until he stood before her in nothing more than an unbuttoned shirt.

Pure joy raced through him when she drew her fingertips back up his calves, to his knees and finally to rest on his erection. With one hand wrapped around him and the other clasping his thigh, she bent down.

From a boring charity event to her hot mouth in less than an hour.

His dreams were never this good.

She took him inside, holding him in her mouth, guiding him deeper until he thought he would explode. Her hands traveled to his lower back before she pulled him closer.

Seeing her like that, below him, loving him, made him want to be gentle, despite the screaming from his cells to take her now. "Baby."

She moaned, never letting up on the pressure and sweet suction.

He tried to watch her but his neck muscles gave out and his head dropped back. "Damn it, Erin. That feels so good."

Too good. A few more minutes under a combination of her hands and her bold touch and he would lose it right there in her palm.

"Lie back." His words came out as a sharp gasp.

If she noticed, she ignored it. Her mouth continued its sensual torture, spinning his insides until everything snapped tight and a band of red flashed in front of his face.

Another two minutes and this would be over. The idea of spilling into her mouth appealed to him on a very primal level, but he wanted this first time together to be for both of them.

"Erin?"

"Mmmmmm."

He had to give her shoulders a gentle push to break free.

Leaning back on her hands, she looked up and scowled as if he was ruining all her fun. "What are you—"

"My turn."

A satisfied smile spread across her lips. "No arguments here."

He dropped to his knees between her legs. "I am dying to see what you have under all this pretty underwear."

"Just me."

"Perfect."

Since time no longer worked in his favor, he did not waste any. His hands slid between her thighs and the bed. His tongue licked a trail up the inside of her legs, stopping to kiss the inside of her knees. The fleshy part of her upper thigh.

Heat radiated out of her as her stomach drew taut with her labored breathing. Both his hands slipped in her underwear. One of his thumbs pushed deep into her wet center. Sliding between her lips, he found the spot he wanted and heard her suck in a huge gulp of air.

"Holy shit." She flopped back on the bed with her arms spread wide and the most sensual smile on her face.

"Why, Ms. McHugh, did you just swear?"

"Keep using your mouth and you'll hear even more than that."

The suggestion echoed inside him. Bounced off every edge before settling in his mind. That was his plan anyway. Hearing her ask for what she wanted made the idea all the more sweet.

Nice and slow, he pulled the panties down her thighs, over her knees, and off her legs. He unwrapped his precious gift. The one he had been praying for every single night.

With the panties on the floor and her bra pulled down,

every inch of her body was exposed to his mouth and hands. "God, yes."

For a brief second she closed her legs and let them fall to the side. Her hands moved down her bare body to cover his.

"Shy, baby?"

"Not with you."

"Then open for me."

When her thighs fell open again, a huge wave of relief crashed through him. He said a quick prayer of thanks before scrambling to the side and picking a condom out of his nightstand drawer.

With his control waning, he wanted protection nearby. Once he had a taste of her, he would have to be inside her. He just knew.

Without using his hands, he dragged his tongue through her wetness. He saw the ripple move through her, felt it vibrate against his lips. The smell of water and the sea pulsed through him. Now that he knew her unique scent, it would never leave his head.

His tongue delved deep while his fingers circled around and inside of her. With every sweep he learned more about what excited her and what touches stole her breath. How her body liked to be caressed. Which spot, when he touched, forced her hips off the bed and which patterns across her clit made her moan in delight.

He kept touching and sucking and kissing until she grabbed the sheets in her fists and started tugging. "Ray."

"Tell me, baby."

She ripped at the bedding as he rotated between using his fingers and his mouth on her. Her body clenched around his finger. Her neck stretched as her head dug into the pillow to expose miles of creamy neck.

He never let up. He learned all about her, kept pushing her control to its limits, until she unleashed the tightening inside her and let the orgasm rip through.

As she pitched and her head rolled, the vibrations trembled on his tongue. Her lower body bucked as her wetness coated his fingertips.

The sight of her in release stunned him. So free. So damn beautiful it almost hurt to watch her.

"I'm so happy I asked," she said a few seconds later, in a voice as breathless as if she had run a mile at a sprint.

"You know we're not done, right?"

She lifted her head and stared down her bare body at him. "Just resting."

"Not on my account."

With one hand holding the condom, he shimmied up the bed to balance his body on his elbows over her. Only the band of her bra and the flaps of his shirt where it lay open on his chest separated them.

"Hi there." She stretched those lean arms over her head and shot him a satisfied grin. Almost looked as if she could yawn and then drift slowly off to sleep.

Wrong choice. "You look mighty happy."

She wrapped her arms around his neck and pulled him down for a deep kiss. "I have you to thank for that."

"Then you should do it properly."

She scraped her fingernails across his shoulders. "Any suggestions?"

"They all involve my being inside of you."

"Really?" She raised her knees and trapped his hips between them. "No one is stopping you."

Thank God. Blood pounded in his dick. He tried to breathe deeply through his nose, to draw in enough breath to cool the fire in his veins, to keep from slamming into her with all the finesse of a sixteen-year-old boy on his first time. She deserved some finesse. A little skill. Not a quick mating.

But when she linked her ankles behind his back, he lost all control. Ripping the packet open with his teeth, he grabbed the condom and slid it on before time ran out on him. No way would he last more than a few minutes without making love to her.

"Let me." Her palm slid around his erection.

The touch sent his adrenaline racing. "Do it."

She pressed his tip against her, sliding him back and forth in her wet slit, dipping deeper with each pass. The tissues inside her were plumped from his earlier attention. She was wet and full and ready for him.

The shaking started in his legs and moved higher. The need to be inside her grabbed his body and would not let go. With his hands covering hers, he guided his body deep inside. Inch by excruciating inch he lowered his body until he filled her.

When her mouth dropped open on a moan, he swooped down and kissed her. Treated her to a shattering kiss meant to telegraph all of his feelings for her. With their bodies locked he could feel every little shudder. Every tremble. Every hitch to her breathing.

The ability to be gentle abandoned him. His body screamed for a raw mating. One meant to burn his impression on her and stake a claim.

He switched to his knees and tunneled his hands up under her backside so he could lift her hips higher. Position her for the fullest penetration. From his angle, he had full reign over her body.

She belonged to him.

And he refused to let her go.

Fingernails dug into his shoulders as her lips brushed against his ear. "Yes, Ray. Yes . . ."

He pulled out, moving slow enough to make her squirm. When he plunged back in, the pace increased. His hips flexed as he pushed in, then retreated. The friction of his cock against her wet inside, the soft creak of the bed against the floor, the heated smell of her excitement, it all backed up on him until his last edge of calm disappeared.

Steady and sure, he pressed inside her, retreated, and then plunged again. With each pass, her internal muscles grabbed on to him, refusing to let go. He pressed deeper, harder, until her body shook and her head slammed back into the pillow.

On the verge of orgasm, he refused to go first. He wanted her to find satisfaction before he found his own. Wanted her to know blinding pleasure.

This was all for her.

He slid his finger over her clit, circled, and pressed until her body grew stock-still; her eyes flew open. "Ray."

"Now, baby."

His mouth pressed against hers in a deep, loving kiss. His fingers caressed and excited. His hips ground against hers. With one last long push, her body exploded. When her orgasm crashed through her, she groaned. Her shoulders shook as her breath escaped in tiny pants. Her fingers clenched and unclenched against his biceps.

The tightening of her thighs against his hips sent an unconscious signal to his brain. His body twitched and jumped. He ground his hips against her as the tightening inside him unwound and released. His body bucked and shuddered as he came. The force knocked his knees out from under him until he collapsed on top of her.

"That was incredible," she said a few seconds later.

"I'll move in a second." He mumbled the promise into the pillow next to her head.

She squeezed him in a bear hug. "You're fine right here."

He finally found the strength to lift up and look down at her. From her wide smile to her shiny eyes, all he saw was happiness. "You looked pleased with yourself."

"With both of us."

That was exactly what he wanted to hear.

Chapter Eight

Erin held on to the edge of the kitchen table for balance as she straddled Ray's lap the next morning. "Where are Adam and Becky?"

"Who cares?" Ray nibbled on her neck as his hands trailed up and under the white tux shirt she wore. "This looks fabulous on you, by the way."

"Evening wear is my thing."

"Even better when it's off. Doesn't matter anyway since, in my head, you're not wearing anything."

She lifted her hair to give him greater access. "You're stamina is amazing. No one would ever know we slept all of ten minutes last night."

"That, my dear, is the benefit of sleeping with a younger man." His mouth moved to hers.

As morning kisses went, this one was a doozy. Firm and sexy with just a touch of tongue and the right amount of pressure.

"One of the benefits. I can think of others."

"Tell me."

"I'm not feeding that ego. You're already impossible."

"I knew I could turn you to the dark side."

Ray could turn a nun to the dark side. Between his innate sexuality and charm, a woman did not stand a chance.

"Really, though, we should move this to my room," she suggested.

"Why?"

When he tried to unbutton her shirt, she slapped his hands away. "What would you do if they walked in and saw us?"

"Who?"

She rolled her eyes. "The Army. Who do you think?"

"Marines?"

"Adam and Becky."

"Oh, them. I'd tell them to get the hell out."

"Ray."

"Sorry." He threw her an unrepentant smile. "To get the heck out."

"That's better." She wound her arms around his neck. "Guess you have lots of work to do today."

"Not if we can convince Cole and Aubrey to get married in the middle of the street instead of inside the house."

"That should be easy."

"The sidewalk?" He shifted his weight until her hips came in direct contact with his erection.

Not his most subtle moment. "Very rational and not at all motivated by your self-interest."

"My only interest is you."

"Ah, you say the nicest things."

"I am much better with actions." He wiggled his eyebrows before reaching for those shirt buttons a second time.

She put her hand over his. "Stop."

"Why?"

"Anyone could walk in."

He shrugged. "This is your house."

She almost told him it was his home as well, but she stopped before making that sort of commitment. One night of sex did not mean they had a long-lasting relationship.

The mere idea of bonding to someone, of joining her life with Ray's, even if he did want that, scared the crap out of her.

Sex was one thing.

Love and a happily ever after was another.

"Becky lives here too. That means Adam is always skulking about."

"Damn that Adam."

Since Ray said it with a smile, she ignored the profanity that time. "And it's a construction zone."

He sighed as if he was taking on the stress of sexually frustrated males everywhere. "Fine."

"You poor thing."

"Remember this moment." He kissed her. "You owe me."

"Seems to me Adam owes you." She unwrapped her body from Ray's. The move was the right thing to do. The safe, smart thing. But leaving him sitting there left an empty hole in her stomach.

Especially with him sitting there in nothing but a pair of unfastened jeans. She hated to waste a near-naked opportunity.

"I'm not kissing him," Ray said.

She held on to his hand for as long as possible before letting it drop and turning to the counter to reload on coffee. "That's a good choice."

"I'm going to check it out."

She did a double take. "I hate to even ask what you're talking about."

"Recon."

"See, I knew I'd be sorry." She took a sip of coffee.

"If our roommates aren't here, you better get ready."

"For what?" As if she didn't know.

"Another round. In fact," he pointed at the mug. "Pound that caffeine just in case."

The thought of making love with him again made her

knees give out. She sat down hard in the chair to keep from falling on the floor.

"I'm starting to think you're superhuman."

"We've tried nighttime sex." He trapped her in the chair and leaned down for a lingering kiss. "Now we're going to try daytime sex."

Who could argue with that kind of logic?

Erin chuckled as she flipped open the newspaper to look at the movie ads. Heading out in public with Ray, snuggling next to him in a seat while things exploded onscreen, sounded fabulous. She scanned the pages looking for just the right show.

She saw something much worse.

With the newspaper trapped in her hand, she stalked into the living room. She did not care if there were nails or land mines on the floor. She wanted a piece of Ray. Preferably on the end of a stick.

Seeing Becky and Adam on the couch, laughing over something Ray had said, did nothing to abate her fury. If anything, his lazy comfort ignited a bomb that exploded in her head and threatened to spew out over everything else.

"Nice outfit, sis."

"Very." Adam coughed when Becky slammed her elbow into his gut. "What the hell was that for?"

"She's my sister."

"A guy can appreciate a good pair of legs."

"Look somewhere else," Ray said with a harsh edge to his voice.

As far as Erin was concerned, she held the rights to being angry. "Leave them out of it."

"Yeah, Ray." Adam smiled. "But, I do have a question. Is clothing optional in the house now?"

"Adam," Becky warned.

"Hell, I'm not complaining. I just want to know before I try to talk you out of those sweats."

"As you can see, they are, unfortunately, still in the house." Ray had zipped up but his shirt remained off.

By the way Becky kept sneaking peeks, it was pretty clear she noticed Ray's bare chest.

Despite the banter and good fun, all Erin saw was red. Anger clouded her vision and flushed her body with heat.

"What is this?" She crumpled the newspaper in her fist and threw it at him.

"What are you doing?" Ray said with an innocent look that made Erin want to punch him.

"Uh-oh." Adam stretched his arms along the back of the sofa.

"We should go," Becky said.

"No damn way."

"Adam's right. Stay. We should all hear Ray's explanation for his supposed non-date last night," Erin said.

Ray's eyes narrowed. "What the hell was in that coffee?"

"I bought it. Every lie you told. Hell, you didn't even have to work for it. I gave in and persued you." And that fact hurt the most.

"Did Erin just swear?" Adam asked.

Ray threw his hands up in the air. "I have no idea what you're yelling about."

"You and your date. There is a photo of the two of you together in the paper." She choked out the words and closed her eyes on the memory of the picture.

Ray with his arm around some stunning blonde, laughing and joking. A woman who looked about Erin's own age.

The guy chased older women. She was just stupid enough to get caught in his trap.

"What is this?" Ray scooped up the crinkled newspaper and read it. "Oh, shit."

"Yeah, you got caught."

"Doing what?" Adam asked before turning to Becky. "And do not elbow me. You want to know too."

"You told me the woman did not matter. Look at you!" The screech bounced around in Erin's head. When she noticed all three of them staring at her, she knew it came out shrill in the room as well.

"You okay there, sis?"

"I'm furious." Erin shoved against Ray's shoulder. "At you. How dare you sleep with me when you're dating someone else."

"I'm not." He sounded furious.

That made two of them. "It sure as hell looks like it. For heaven's sake, Ray. I'm not blind or stupid."

"That's more than I've heard her swear in a month," Adam muttered under his breath.

"In a year," Becky agreed.

"Give me that." Erin ripped the paper out of Ray's hand and shoved it in front of Becky. "Does that look like a woman who doesn't matter?"

Adam and Becky studied the photo. Then studied each other. Then looked at Ray.

Not exactly the response Erin expected. "Well? Look at her. Look at the way they're looking at each other."

She wanted fireworks. Hoped Becky would jump to her defense. Thought Adam would at least question Ray.

Nothing.

Ray stared at Becky. "Tell her."

Becky blushed. "Uh, Erin, do you really not know who this is?"

"The woman he *isn't* dating," Erin said in her most sarcastic voice.

"She doesn't know." Adam glanced at Ray when he made the comment.

"Because she never bothered to ask." Ray had not moved from his spot on the hardwood floor. His hands stayed fisted at his sides. His jaw clenched.

Adam turned the newspaper over in his hands. "Erin, hon. This isn't what you think."

Becky sucked in air through her teeth. The resulting whistle was not one of happiness. "I should have said something sooner."

Why weren't they mad? the fact her own sister did not rush to her defense put Erin on edge. "You guys know her?"

Adam nodded. "About her. Everyone does."

"Tell her." Ray's flat voice rang in Erin's ears.

"Enough of this. Forget them. Ray, you clearly want me to know something. Say it." Erin sank into the chair next to the sofa and waited for whatever bombshell was about to land.

"I'd be more inclined to do that if you stopped screaming at me."

"If you want to hear me yell, keep stalling."

Ray's only movement was to rest his hands on his hips. "She's my mother."

"What?" Erin squealed this time around.

Becky and Adam nodded.

Erin grabbed the paper back and studied the photo. No way was that woman a mother of a twenty-seven-year-old guy. "She looks my age."

"She'll be thrilled to know you think so." Ray did not give up his position on the other side of the coffee table.

"How is this possible?"

"She had me right after she turned nineteen." Ray's voice held no emotion.

The information would not compute in Erin's head. Why the secrecy? Why not just tell the truth?

And how could a woman who looked like that, so young and in love, be his mom?

"In your defense, she does look thirty-something," Adam said with a slight tilt of his shoulders.

"In person, too." Becky agreed with a nod.

"You've *met* her." Erin's fury extended to her sister for not spilling the information sooner. Becky knew details, private details, about Ray and had not shared them.

"At the office. I was moving stuff in. She was taking Ray to lunch."

"Why didn't you tell me?" Erin asked.

"I figured you must have asked. Ray told you to ask."

Like she was some sort of trained pet or something. "Well, I didn't."

"Do you watch the news?" Adam winced as he asked the question.

"She doesn't need to. She fills in the details, right or wrong, all by herself," Ray blurted out.

The harsh edge to his tone made Erin flinch. "I guess she's famous."

How bad could this get? Beautiful. A celebrity. The pieces rumbled around in her head.

"We need to go." Becky stood up and pulled Adam along with her.

"Why?" Adam asked, clearly not wanting to miss a minute of the conversation.

"Because I said so. Now."

Before they got to the stairs, Ray started explaining. "My mother is in the paper a lot."

"Oh." Erin felt her anger puddle on the floor at her feet.

"My father is a congressman. I have his last name."

Representative Hammond. The memories clicked in Erin's mind. When the committee called her in to testify about her parents and the allegations of interstate fraud, Representative Hammond sat up there on the dais. He never said a thing, but she remembered him. Could see the face of every single one of them if she closed her eyes and concentrated for two seconds.

"I know him. Well, I met him."

Ray nodded. "I know."

"When I had to testify."

"He was in the room."

She tried to think through the headache pounding against her brain. "Why didn't you tell me who you were?"

"You know who I am."

The man she knew was not a rich congressman's son. He was a self-made, work-with-his-hands guy. "You know what I mean."

"Since you seemed so damned determined to push me away and come up with one lame excuse after another to keep me there, I did not want to feed you any ammunition."

"I would not have judged you based on your parents. Frankly, your dad did not offend me anyhow." She learned that lesson long ago. From personal experience, she knew the sins of the parents often did not transfer to the children.

"When it comes to questions about people's personal lives, my dad stays quiet."

"That's admirable."

Ray's shoulders tensed. "It's necessary, since my parents aren't married."

"You really thought I'd care about the fact you have divorced parents?"

His shoulders sagged as he slid into the seat Adam had abandoned. "Not divorced. Never married."

She could see how the public might frown on that lifestyle choice by a congressman. "Some people don't believe in marriage."

"Well, my dad did. Up until a few years ago, he was married."

None of the phrases made any sense. "So your parents are or aren't married?"

"Not to each other."

"That means . . ."

"You are not the only one with a family who likes to hog the spotlight." He rubbed his hands over his face. "My mom was the mistress. I am the product."

The news banged against her with the force of a hundred-pound weight. "You've always known?"

"Try being the open secret of Washington, D.C."

She tried to process the information overload. "Are they married now?"

"My mom has no interest. I think she's grown fond of the attention and freedom her lifestyle provides."

"You were her date to the charity event." She waited for him to nod in agreement. "I still don't understand why you didn't just tell me."

He tapped his fingertips together. "I wanted you to care enough to ask."

Since sitting down he had refused to give her full eye contact. He fidgeted. Shifted in his seat. Acted as if he did not want to look at her.

"I'm sorry." She whispered the sincere apology. With the anger gone, she lacked the strength to say it any louder.

"I told you once I'd never lie to you."

"Don't all men say those sorts of things?"

He stopped moving around and glanced at her with an unreadable expression. "I can only speak for me."

She had offended him. The hit struck his ego and honor, and he was not reacting well.

"Now what?" she asked.

"You have to decide if you can stand to be linked to the bastard son of a longtime congressman and his always visible mistress."

More press. More exposure. The thought made bile rush up the back of her throat. "Don't call yourself that."

"It's a word."

"I don't know what to say to you." She didn't. She needed time to think and to reason it all out.

"I'm sure you'll think of something."

"With a little time."

He shook his head. "And I'm sure whatever you say will piss me off."

Chapter Nine

Cole passed a second round of beers to Whit and Adam as he sat down next to them on the house's front porch. "What are we doing?"

"Watching Ray implode," Whit said between swigs.

"Better than talking about wedding details," Cole mumbled.

Whit tipped his beer in a salute. "I warned you."

"You forgot to mention that Aubrey would lose her fucking mind. Man, I swear her head spun around the other day just because of some stupid problem with flower color."

"What exactly is the problem?" Adam waited until a truck passed before asking the question.

"Something about them being the wrong shade of purple."

Adam swore under his breath. "I meant with Ray."

Whit chuckled. "I'll give you one guess."

"Ahhh." Cole nodded. "Must be Erin."

Ray broke another piece of rotten wood from the fence outlining the yard and threw it on the pile next to him. "We are not mentioning her name."

Cole looked around at his friends before asking, "Today?"

"Ever," Ray stepped back.

"Does she know that?" Adam asked.

"Who cares," Ray said.

Cole's eyes widened. "This is serious. Do we know what happened?"

"Becky said something about Ray giving Erin an ultimatum."

Cole shook his head in male sympathy. "I'm thinking she picked the wrong choice."

Ray threw more wood on the stack. The physical labor and the crashing of the pieces as they hit against each other helped burn off some of his anger. Also drowned out the street noise and the old lady chatter of the men lying around on the porch.

"Any of you sissy girls want to pick up a crowbar and help me out over here?" Ray asked.

"No," Adam said. "There's just nothing as satisfying as watching another guy work."

"And I'm already married," Whit said. "Seems to me Cole should chip in and help since the cleanup is for his wedding."

Cole didn't miss a beat. "I'd rather hear about Erin and this ultimatum."

The word grated on his nerves. Chicks gave ultimatums. He *reasoned* with Erin. Explained that his parents' choices were not his choices. That the fact reporters liked to follow him around did not matter.

The conversation went okay until he mentioned something about her need to "get over it" and move on from the past her parents had handed her. Yeah, that did not go over very well.

A week had passed with almost zero conversation and absolutely no contact between them. In his mind, it was her job to come to him. She jumped to conclusions and insisted he lied. She doubted his honesty and blamed him for things he had never done. She owed him.

Big-time.

"I did not give her an ultimatum. I told Erin she had to make a choice." Ray walked over and stole Adam's beer.

"That's mine."

Ray took a long swig, hoping to drink away all memory of Erin for one day. "Get another, lawyer boy."

"Is it too late to fire him?"

Whit handed a replacement beer to Adam. "'Fraid so."

Cole leaned against the post on the front corner of the porch. "Maybe I'm unclear on the definition of the word *ultimatum*. Doesn't it have something to do with making a choice?"

Ray did not even hear him. He had used beer the last three nights to drown out all sounds of Erin. But even getting drunk did not get the job done. Staying away from the house was not possible due to his rehab deadline. Nothing worked to ease the ache he felt in the dead center of his chest.

"I'm sick of guarding every word I say with her. You'd think after we . . ."

Adam perked up. "Sounds like we finally got to the good part."

"Gentlemen. Let's use some tact." Cole said. "Go ahead, Ray. You were talking about after you two did the deed."

"Damn, Cole. You said my phrase lacked tact. Erin is my future sister-in-law. How about we exercise a little decorum?" Adam suggested.

Ray snorted.

Adam's eyes widened. "Or not."

Ray paced the yard in front of the other men. "Being with a woman is supposed to make your life easier."

"Who the hell told you that?" The look of horror on Whit's face said it all. Life with women never got easier.

"Are we still just talking about sex?" Adam asked.

Ray ignored the comments and downed the rest of his beer.

"Let the man finish." Whit reached for another bottle and handed it to Ray.

"You meet the right girl, try to do the right thing, settle down." Ray dropped to his butt on the small patch of grass. "No one tells you that being in love makes thing worse."

"Whoa," Cole held up the hand not holding his beer. "Love?"

"You love her?" This time Adam yelled the question over the roar of a passing truck.

"Hell, man. That changes everything." Cole and Adam grunted in agreement with Whit's comment.

Ray's gaze traveled from one friend to the other. They all wore sympathetic frowns. "How?"

"Wanting her and loving her are two very different beasts," Whit explained.

"Well, sure."

"Dude, you're screwed," Adam said in his least lawyerly tone.

Ray knew they were right. During the last few weeks he had slipped from liking Erin and wanting her in bed to loving her and never wanting to be without her. In between, she had accused him of lying and had forgotten him the second after they shared the sheets.

Ray fell back in the grass. "Women suck."

Cole glanced at Whit. "Isn't that a good thing?"

"This is the bad kind of suck," Whit said.

Yeah, Ray thought. The worst kind.

"What are they doing out there?" Aubrey asked, while eyeing how she looked in her strapless wedding gown in the mirror.

"If you don't stop moving around, I'm going to stab you," Becky mumbled over the pins in her mouth.

Erin sipped her wine. "You better listen to her, Aubrey. She's the only one of us who sews."

"I'm serious. What's happening out there?" Aubrey tried to spin around for a better look. "Anything good?"

Hannah sat on the second floor bedroom windowsill and watched the men hang out in the yard. "If I had to guess, I'd say drinking and complaining about the women in their lives."

"Not women. Woman. Erin," Becky said.

"What did I do?"

"If Adam's reports to Whit were correct, you slept with Ray and then, while wearing his shirt around the house, accused him of screwing around on you." Hannah ended the report with a smile.

"You're lucky you're blonde, pretty, and stronger than a bull." Erin shook her head at her friend's odd combination of compelling characteristics.

Instead of getting angry, Hannah laughed. "Whit's wedding vows sounded a lot like that."

"Well, you and Ray better make up before the party tomorrow night." Becky stood up and brushed off her black dress pants. "We have all sorts of good business news to celebrate, and I'm tired of seeing Ray drag his butt around like a wounded hound dog."

"It's a very nice butt." Hannah raised her glass to the room.

"You are a married woman." Erin wanted to avoid talk about Ray or his butt or any other part of his perfect anatomy.

"Not a dead one."

"He's too young."

Hannah screwed up her lips in a frown. "Ain't no such thing."

"And Ray's never struck me as immature," Aubrey said.

"I mean in terms of his age." Erin pressed her point, hoping to find a receptive audience. "He's twenty-seven."

"That's legal, you know." Becky went around to everyone's seat and Aubrey's outstretched hands to pour another round of wine. "I learned these things in law school."

"His mother and father aren't as famous as my parents, but close. Can you imagine living with that sort of publicity? Well, I can. No thanks."

"Our parents." Becky set her glass on the nightstand with a clink. "And his parents don't preach drivel or try to pretend their kids don't exist."

Becky's sharp attack struck a nerve. Erin knew that no matter how hard life seemed for her, Becky had always had it harder with their parents. "I'm sorry."

Becky plunked down on the ottoman in front of Erin and rested a hand on her knee. "It just seems to me if one of you has a right to complain about getting stuck with a partner who is loaded down with baggage, it's him."

"Does he even care about your parents?" Aubrey asked.

"No."

"So, why do you care about his?" Hannah asked the question, but Aubrey and Becky's stares, each woman focused, as if they had stopped breathing in anticipation of what she might say, suggested they all wanted an answer.

The ball of anxiety rolling around in Erin's chest fell. "You guys think I'm being stupid."

Becky scooted up the ottoman and put an arm around her sister's shoulders. "No, babe. Just cautious."

Something in Hannah's eyes softened. "We all have that self-protective gene. It's a good thing. But sometimes the real issue is about being scared."

Erin had to chuckle at that one. "I can't imagine you ever being afraid of anything."

Hannah did not join in Erin's amusement. "When I thought I lost Whit, I was a wreck."

"What did you do?"

"Got bold. Fought for him. Made a move that let him know I was as interested as he was."

"She used handcuffs." Aubrey lifted her glass in a toast. "Let's hear it for Hannah."

The news shocked Erin. "What?"

Hannah sat down on the ottoman. "It's a long story. The point is, you have to make up your mind about whether or not you want Ray."

"Then?"

"Go after him."

Chapter Ten

Ray stood in the living room doorway and tugged on the collar of his oxford shirt. He had been to enough parties to be comfortable working a room and engaging in mindless chatter. Since most of the folks there were employees and friends of their company, and since the room was the living room of the house he had been working on for months and living in for almost two weeks, the party did not faze him.

Erin did.

She played host, showing off her mostly remodeled house and otherwise pretending not to be an introvert. This was the second time he had seen her wear a dress, and he could not handle it any better this time around. The fact that this one was cherry red and hugged her upper body like skin did not help.

She had her hair pulled back off her face in a style that made her seem more carefree. Younger. And those spiky black heels. Damn. Those things highlighted her long, lean legs in a way that should be illegal. Remembering what she could do with them in bed nearly blew the back of his head off.

The room had been cleaned and buffed to perfection. A makeshift bar sat in one corner. People mingled and admired. The moment should have been a satisfying one for him.

Then why did he have to fight off the urge to vomit every six or seven seconds?

Whit walked up behind him and slapped him on the shoulder. "How are you doing?"

"Been better."

"I know you'd rather not be here."

Not as if Ray had a choice. "It's a good night for T.C. Limited."

"Sending Adam off into private practice with a bit of a bang seemed appropriate."

"Just wish you had waited until the house was ready."

Whit downed a glass of something that looked like ice water. "Hey, I rented a room at a hotel. Erin was the one who insisted we switch to here."

"Figures."

"Besides, this is a good dry run for Cole and Aubrey's wedding."

Ray half-listened but spent most of his time staring. Erin breezed in and out saying hello to everyone, as if nothing in her life had changed in the last few weeks. For her, maybe life did chug on in the same way.

For him, it sucked. Every time he saw her or entered a room and smelled her, the area under his heart ached. Since she was headed right for him now, he waited for his heart to burst.

She stopped and treated both men to a big smile. "How are we doing?"

"The house is still standing." Ray was grateful, since in one of his drunken stupors he had contemplated taking it down piece by piece with his bare hands. The thought had scared him sober.

"There's some positive thinking." Whit shook his glass,

letting the ice cubes crash against each other. "I'll go re-fill this for you."

Erin watched Whit go, then turned back. "That was subtle."

"Typical Thomas brothers' behavior."

Erin scanned the room, nodding to a guest here and saluting someone there. "The house looks great."

"It's getting there."

"That's all thanks to you. I appreciate it."

Yeah, that's what he wanted. Her gratitude. "It's my job."

She stopped socializing and focused on him. "You've gone above and beyond on this project."

One more word of idle chitchat and what was left of his brain would dissolve into a puddle. And standing this close to her without having the right to touch her . . .

"I better go check on Whit," he said, to keep from saying all the things he wanted to say to her.

"Now who's running?"

"Excuse me?"

She clicked her fingernails on her glass. "I asked for some time. You're acting like I walked away."

"Felt like it to me."

She waved to someone across the room. "Because you've tried so hard to stay connected over the last week."

No anger. Her tone stayed light, almost cheery. As if the moment called for flirting instead of a serious talk.

"What are you saying?" he asked because he really did not know.

"A wise man once told me if you want something, ask for it."

That did not sound like a final kiss-off. "Erin?"

"Oh, I see someone I need to talk to. I'll be back." With a bounce in her step, she took off for the fireplace.

Ray glanced over her intended path and at the only

woman in the room not associated with T.C. Limited. Sleek hair. Bright-colored suit. Eyes of a predator.

He grabbed Erin's elbow before she could get too far. "Stop."

"Is something wrong?"

Everything. "That's a television reporter."

He was outraged on Erin's behalf. It was one thing for the pests to call and bother her. Coming to the house and sneaking into a private party ventured way over the line.

Erin nodded with a big smile. "I know."

"I can get rid of her."

"I invited her."

He had to be dreaming this. None of it made any sense. "Why would you do that?"

"She's been hounding me for a special interest story."

"And you told her to go to hell."

She wore one of those secret woman smiles. "The first few times."

She hated reporters. Hated the spotlight. Up until a few seconds ago, he would have said she hated him.

"What changed your mind?"

"Honestly?"

"Of course."

"You." She forced her glass into his hands. "Hold this."

"Erin." When a few people glanced his way, he realized his call came out louder than he expected. Now that he had their attention, running after Erin would not work.

He needed to play it cool. With a few nods and hellos to the people mingling in the living room, he made his way over to Erin. Not that she noticed. No. She was too busy chatting it up with the enemy.

Just as he stepped next to Erin and prepared to issue a threat or two to the reporter, she took the glass back.

"It's speech time." She nudged him in the side and nodded in Whit's direction.

The last thing Ray wanted was to hear anyone, even Whit, drone on about any subject. His plan consisted of escorting the reporter out the front door and cornering Erin for an explanation. He might even throw in a lecture about how you did not give a guy hope and then back to the party without another word.

"Erin—"

"Shhh. Whit's about to talk."

"I don't care."

She elbowed him again. "Just listen."

Ray felt the last bits of his sanity slip away. He had walked into the party tonight determined to stay cool and not show any emotion. Erin had him running around in circles.

"Thank you all for coming," Whit said to the crowd.

The mumbles and laughter died down as everyone turned to watch Whit. Everyone except Hannah and Aubrey, who were looking at Ray with big, knowing smiles.

He leaned over and whispered to Erin. "Is something going on?"

"Exercise some of that patience you're always talking about."

His head snapped back at her response. He was ready to crawl out of his skin, and she wanted him just to sit there?

Whit started. "We wanted to gather you all together to celebrate some of the changes that soon will take place at T.C. Becky will come up here in a few minutes to say hello to those of you who don't already know her, though I can't imagine how she would have gone unnoticed around the office lately."

The crowd laughed and chuckled.

"Then Adam will come up here and tell us all how much we'll miss him when he's no longer coming into the office on a full-time basis."

More laughter. A few of the men raised their glasses to that one.

Ray appreciated Whit's comments on one level. If he were not ready to drag Erin into the kitchen and sit her down until they could hash this out, he might even have enjoyed the speech. As it was, every word Whit uttered angered him, because he was losing time with Erin.

Whit grinned. "We'll get to all of that. First, though, Erin McHugh would like to make an announcement."

Ray caught the end of the sentence. "Erin?"

"Hold my glass again, will you?"

"But—"

She winked at him. "Patience."

Erin stepped to the middle of the room. She did not know how she was going to say anything, since she felt like she had swallowed her tongue. All the fake smiles and stupid conversation had worn her down.

She had listened to Hannah's suggestion and decided that Ray needed a big gesture. Erin now wondered why she did not choose the same tactic she had used on him last time: seduction with sexy lingerie.

"Whit was nice enough to allow me to use a few minutes of your time for my announcement." Her gaze traveled between the reporter's interested expression and Ray's confused one. "For those who don't know, I'm Erin McHugh."

"Go Erin!" Cole shouted his encouragement.

Cole and Aubrey, Whit and Hannah, Adam and Becky. That's what she wanted. Love and acceptance. A lifetime and a forever.

Her gaze went back to Ray. She could look into those dark eyes every day for the rest of her life and never regret it. He belonged to her. Had from the day they met.

Age, family, experience, none of that mattered. Without even trying, she had found the man she wanted to spend her days loving. And as terrified as she was to take this step, she was more afraid of losing him.

"All of you also know Ray Hammond." She gestured to him.

"Cheers to Ray!" Someone who sounded like Adam, and probably was, shouted from the audience over the laughter and cheers.

She turned all of her attention to Ray. "Here, in front of your friends and coworkers, I want to tell you something."

She watched his dark eyes clear and a smile tug on the corner of his mouth. His budding happiness gave her all the encouragement she needed.

"I love you."

The mumbling and surprise of the audience gave way to silence.

She swallowed the last of her fear and took the plunge. If the outcome was having Ray, nothing else mattered.

"Forever," she added, through a throat clogged with unused tears.

Ray shoved the wineglass in the reporter's hand. "Take this."

"Ray?"

He stepped in front of her, blocking her view of most of the crowd. "It's about fu—"

This time she almost let him say it. Only the presence of the reporter stopped her.

"Ray!"

"Time." He grabbed her up in his arms and lifted her right off the floor. "It's about time."

Cheers and clapping filled the room. All she saw was Ray. His eyes glistened. His hands clenched her close against him.

"I do love you," she whispered against his lips when he finally put her back on her feet.

"Speech, speech!"

Erin did not know who started the chant, but she would bet money Adam was involved.

Ray held up a hand to quiet the crowd. "I have a thousand things to say, but they are all private and are all meant for Erin's ears only."

A few "ah"s could be heard in the charged room.

"But, I can say one thing to all of you." He faced her again. "I love this woman. And now I'm going to kiss her senseless while you watch."

Cheers rang out as he lowered his mouth and treated her to a long, lingering kiss. One filled with promise and commitment. One that had her falling off her shoes.

He finally broke the kiss and rested his forehead against hers. "I can't believe you did this."

"For you."

Ray shook his head. "But, the press and publicity?"

"I want everyone to know how I feel."

His smile vanished. "I thought I had lost you."

She slid her hands up his arms and around his neck. "You should have known better."

"Why?"

She did not fight the smile. "Once I had you in my house, I was never letting you go."

"You better always feel that way." The laughter returned to his voice.

"Damn straight."

He broke out laughing and did not stop until *she* gave him one of those knock-me-senseless kisses.

The tension is electric in
THE BAD BOYS GUIDE
TO THE GALAXY,
the newest story from Karen Kelley,
out this month from Brava . . .

"Where's your dress . . ." He waved a finger around—"thingy . . . robe, whatchamacallit?" He finally pointed toward her.

She raised an eyebrow. He didn't seem to notice the clean floor. Disappointment filled her. She'd hoped for more. Silly, she knew. After all, he was an earthman, and she shouldn't care what he thought.

"My robe was getting dirty along the hem, so I removed it."

Her gaze traveled slowly over him, noting the bulge below his waist. It was quite large. Odd. She mentally shook her head.

"Your clothes are quite dirty. Once again, I've proven that I'm superior in my way of thinking," she told him.

"You're naked."

She glanced down. "You're very observant," she said, using his earlier words. "Did you know there's a slight breeze outside? It made my nipples tingle and felt quite pleasant. Not that I would be tempted to stay on Earth because of a breeze."

"You . . . you . . . can't . . ."

She frowned. "There's something wrong with your speech. Are you ill? If you'd like, I can retrieve my diagnostic tool and examine you." He was sweating. Not good. She only hoped she didn't catch what he had.

"You can't go around without clothes," he sputtered. "And I'm not sick."

"Then what are you?"

"Horny!" He marched to the other room, returning in a few minutes with her robe. "You can't go around naked."

"Why not?" She slipped her arms into the robe and belted it.

"It causes a certain reaction inside men."

"What kind of a reaction?"

What an interesting topic. She wanted to know more. Maybe they would be able to have a scientific conversation. Kia had only talked about battles, and Mala had talked about exploration of other planets, but Sam was actually speaking about something to do with the body. It was a very stimulating discussion.

He ran a hand through his hair. "I'm going to kill Nick," he grumbled. "No one said anything about having to explain the birds and bees."

"And what's so important about these birds and bees?"

He drew in a deep breath. "When a man sees a naked woman, it causes certain reactions inside him."

"Like the bulge in your pants? It wasn't there before."

"Ah, Lord."

"Did my nakedness do that?"

"You're very beautiful."

"But I'm not supposed to think so."

"No, we're not talking about that right now."

She was so confused. Sam wasn't making sense. "Then please explain what we are talking about."

"Sex," he blurted. "When a man sees a beautiful and very sexy naked woman, it causes him to think about having sex with her."

He looked relieved to finally have said so much. She

thought about his words for a moment. A companion unit did not have these reactions unless buttons were pushed, and even then, their response would be generic. This was very unusual. But also exciting that her nakedness would make him want to copulate. She felt quite powerful.

And she was also horny now that she knew what the word meant. She untied her robe and opened it. "Then we will join."

He made a strangled sound and coughed again and jerked her robe closed. "No, it's not done like that. Dammit, I'm not a companion unit to perform whenever you decide you need sex."

"But don't you want sex?"

"There are emotions that need to be involved. I'm not one of those guys who jump on top of a woman, gets his jollies, and then goes his own way."

"You want me on top?" She'd never been on top, but she thought she could manage.

He firmly tied her robe, then raised her chin until her gaze met his.

"When I make love with a woman, I want her to know damn well who she's with, and there won't be anything clinical about it." He lowered his mouth to hers.

He was touching her again. She should remind him that it was forbidden to touch a healer. But there was something about his lips against hers, the way he brushed his tongue over them, then delved inside that made her body ache, made her want to lean in closer, made her want to have sex other than just to relieve herself of stress.

Sometimes it's okay to do something
JUST FOR HER.
Turn the page for a peek
at Katherine O'Neal's latest,
in stores this month from Brava.

"You won't find what you're looking for, I'm afraid."

He jerked around into the moonlight streaming through the window from which he'd entered.

And as he did, she saw him more clearly—a tall figure, clad all in black, the fitted material clinging to a body that was muscular and sleek. A specifically fashioned mask, also black, concealed the top of his face . . . hiding his nose and cheeks . . . sweeping over his head to cover his hair . . . the only feature visible a clean-shaven jaw and the faint gleam of dark eyes through the slits of his disguise. He stood poised and alert, his hands at his sides, ready to pounce. The effect was both masculine and feline, calling to mind images of the jungle cat to which he'd been so aptly compared.

All at once, he darted for the open window. But she was closer. Instinctively, she stepped in front of it, blocking his path, reaching behind her to pull it closed.

He stopped in his tracks.

"I have a gun," she told him, her voice shaky.

She could see his head swivel as he quickly surveyed the room, looking for another escape. Two doors. One, behind him, led to the hallway, but it was closed. The other, the one connecting to her bedroom was closer and open. He stared at it, then back at her. No doubt wondering if she would really shoot him if he made a dash for it.

Astonishingly, despite her advantage, she sensed no fear in him. His presence sparked and sizzled in the room, sucking the air from it so she could barely breathe. A raw, stalking presence, wholly male, predatory and sexual in nature, making her suddenly aware that she stood before him in nothing but a lace and chiffon nightgown. She could feel the vulnerability of her soft female flesh, of the swells and hollows of her body, in a way that made her feel it was *he* who held the upper hand.

For a moment—an eternity—he didn't move. He just stood there, his gaze locked on her. She could feel the heat of that gaze as though his hand was passing itself over her. She tried again to swallow. Heightened by the danger, it seemed to her that every pore of her skin radiated and throbbed with her awareness of him.

And then, like lightning—so suddenly, she had no time to react—he lunged across the room and wrenched the pistol from her hand.

For a moment, he just stood there, the weapon aimed at her. Her hand aching, Jules could feel the frightened rasp of her breath. Her imagination running wild again, she pictured him pulling the trigger, heard in her mind the roar of the gun's retort.

The silence was deafening. Her nerves were raw.

But then—quickly, efficiently—he flipped open the barrel, let the bullets drop to the floor, and tossed the pistol aside. Jules felt a momentary relief. But it was short-lived. Unthreatened now, he skirted around her and started for the window from which he'd come.

In desperation, she sprang to block his exit, flinging herself back against the window, her arms spread wide to prevent his escape.

"Please, don't go."

He stopped at once, his instincts honed. She imagined him grabbing her and hauling her aside.

Instead, with a stealthy grace, he veered to his left and started for the open door that led to her bedroom and the terrace beyond. Realizing his intention, she ran after him.

"Wait!" she cried.

He wheeled on her threateningly, his hand raised. "Stand back," he warned, speaking in Italian—a deep, whispery, dangerous growl.

Switching quickly to Italian, she told him, "I just want to speak with you. That's why I lured you here."

"*Lured* me?" He glanced about warily as if expecting a contingent of police to burst into the room.

"There's no one here," she rushed to assure him. "I don't want you captured. I just—"

He wasn't listening. She could feel his urgency to get away. He crossed the room, rounding the bed on his way to the French doors, the terrace, and freedom beyond.

Fueled by despair, Jules shot after him and grabbed him by the arm. Beneath the black sweater, it felt like iron.

He jerked free with a strength that sent her tumbling back. "I don't want to hurt you, but I will."

Jules was past caring. All she knew was that she couldn't let him walk out the door, and out of her life.

She grabbed onto him once again. This time he shoved her back onto the bed. "Don't you care what happens to you?" he snarled.

"No," she confessed. "I have nothing to lose."

"You're mad," he rasped.

"Am I?" She stood slowly, careful not to cause alarm. "Perhaps. All I know is that fate has brought you to me."

"Fate?"

"Destiny has sent you to me, Panther. You can't run away now."

"Can't I?"

He turned to leave, but she gasped out, quickly, "I have a proposition for you."

That stopped him. Slowly, he asked, "Now, what kind of proposition could a woman like you have for a man like me?"

Her eyes roamed the feral black-cloaked phantom before her. Unbidden, the first line of Byron's "Don Juan" sprang to her lips: "I want a hero."

"You want *what*?"

She took a breath and spat out the words.

"I want you to kill my husband."

And keep an eye out for Donna Kauffman's
THE BLACK SHEEP AND
THE ENGLISH ROSE,
coming next month from Brava . . .

"I only ask for one thing."

She arched a brow and decided to give him the benefit of the doubt. "Which is?"

"Until the sapphire is in our hands, we operate as a team. No secret maneuvers, no hidden agendas."

Her whole life was a hidden agenda. Well, half of it anyway. "And when we have the necklace? Then what?"

"See? I like how you think. When, not if."

"Which doesn't answer my question."

"I don't have an answer for that. Yet."

She laughed. "Oh, great. I'm supposed to sign on to help you recover a priceless artifact, in the hopes that when we retrieve it, you'll just let me have it out of the kindness of your heart? Why would I sign on for that deal?"

He turned more fully and stepped into her personal space. She should have backed up. She should have made it clear he wouldn't be taking any liberties with her, regardless of Prague. Or Bogota. Or what they'd just done on her bed. Hell, she should have never involved herself with him in the first place. But it was far too late for that regret now.

"Because I found you tied to your own hotel bed and I let you go. Because you need me." He toyed with the end of a tendril of her hair. "Just as much, I'm afraid, as I need you."

"What are you afraid of?" she asked, hating the breathy catch in her voice, but incapable of stifling it.

"Oh, any number of things. More bad clams, for one."

"Touché," she said, refusing to apologize again. "So why are you willing to risk that? Or any number of other exit strategies I might come up with this time around? You're quite good at your job, however you choose to label it these days. Why is it you really want my help? And don't tell me it's because you need me to get close to our quarry. You could just as easily pay someone to do that. Someone who he isn't already on the alert about and whose charms he's not immune to."

"Maybe I want to keep my enemies close. At least those that I can."

"Ah. Now we're getting somewhere. You think that by working together, you can reduce the chance that I'll come out with the win this time. I can't believe you just handed that over to me, and still expect me to agree to this arrangement."

"I said maybe. I also said there were myriad reasons why I think this is the best plan of action. For both of us. I never said it was great or foolproof. Just the best option we happen to have at this time."

"Why should I trust you? Why should I trust that you'll keep to this no secret maneuvers, no hidden agenda deal? More to the point, why would you think I would? No matter what I stand here and promise you?"

"Have you ever lied to me?"

She started to laugh, incredulous, given their history, then stopped, paused, and thought about the question. She looked at him, almost as surprised by the actual answer as she'd been by the question itself. "No. No, I don't suppose, when it comes down to it, that I have." Not outright, anyway. But then, they'd been careful not to pose too many questions of one another, either.

"Exactly."

"But—"

"Yes, I know we've played to win, and we've done whatever was necessary to come out on top. No pun intended," he added, the flash of humor crinkling the corners of his eyes despite the dead seriousness of his tone. "But we've never pretended otherwise. And we've never pretended to be anything other than what we are."

"Honor among thieves, you mean."

"In a manner of speaking, yes."

"I still don't think this is wise. Our agendas—and we have them, no matter that you'd like to spin that differently—are at cross purposes."

"We'll sort out who gets what after we succeed in—"

"Who gets what?" she broke in. "There is only one thing we both want."

"That's where you're wrong."

She opened her mouth, then closed it again. "Wrong, how? Are you saying there are two priceless artifacts in the offing here? Or that you can somehow divide the one without destroying its value?"

He moved closer still, and her breath caught in her throat. He traced his fingertips down the side of her cheek, then cupped her face with both hands, tilting her head back as he kept his gaze directly on hers. "I'm saying there are other things I want. Things that have nothing to do with gemstones, rare or otherwise."

She couldn't breathe, couldn't so much as swallow. She definitely couldn't look away. He was mesmerizing at all times, but none more so than right that very second. She wanted to ask him what he meant, and blamed her sudden lack of oxygen for her inability to do so. When, in fact, it was absolute cowardice that prevented her from speaking. She didn't want him to put into words what he wanted.

Because then she might be forced to reconcile herself to the fact that she could want other things, too.

"Do we have a deal?" he asked, his gaze dropping briefly to her mouth as he tipped her face closer to his.

Every shred of common sense, every flicker of rational thought she possessed screamed at her to turn him down flat. To walk away, run if necessary, and never look back. But she did neither of those things, and was already damning herself even as she nodded. Barely more than a dip of her chin. But that was all it took. Her deal with the devil had been made.

"Good. Then let's seal it, shall we?"

She didn't have to respond this time. His mouth was already on hers.